THE LAWYER'S LEGACY

THE LAWYER'S LEGACY

A prequel to The Witchfinder's Well

JONATHAN POSNER

Winter & Drew Publishing

Contents

JONATHAN POSNER

Before becoming a full-time author in 2021, Jonathan worked for many years as a marketing and advertising executive. He now lives in the South West UK, and when he is not writing, he enjoys walking, theatre and presenting a regular show on a local community radio station.

He is fascinated by Tudor history, and after writing a trilogy of novels that address the question 'what might happen if you time-travelled back to the 1560s?' he has now started to broaden out within the Tudor world and characters he has created. This has started with *The Lawyer's Legacy*, and he plans to explore more stories and adventures for his characters.

He has also written three full-length musicals, a one-act play and a book of short stories.

For more information, visit his author website at https://jonathanposnerauthor.com.

Jonathan is published by Winter & Drew Publishing

ACKNOWLEDGEMENTS

I would like to thank all those who helped make this book happen.

Jane Rayner, Maggie Saunders and Angie Chadwick of my Devon Novelists critique group, whose constructive comments helped smooth out many of the rough edges in early drafts; Sinead Kelly for her thorough editing and encouragement (as always), and to Caroline Holmes for proofing.

I would also like to thank the following who read the book in beta, and were kind enough to give me their honest feedback and support: Shirley De Vivo, Luke Morton, Mike Cunningham, Jason Mann, Vicki Masters and Alison Ridout.

I

CHAPTER ONE

A forest in Devon, England. Late April 1535

The attackers dropped out of the trees like predatory hawks.

Their sudden appearance on the forest path made the young girl's horse rear up neighing and nearly unseat her. There were three of them; roughly dressed men armed with knives. As the girl fought to control her beast, one made a grab at her leg.

"Help me!" she yelled at the two men who were riding with her, as she kicked out with her heel. "Protect me! As is your duty!"

But neither of them made any move to intervene.

The attacker managed to secure his grip on her calf and started to pull. The girl squeezed her legs against the side-saddle, and for a moment she thought she could resist. "Do it now!" she screamed at her companions, "for the sake of Christ!"

But again, neither made any move.

She looked down at the man who was holding her. He had a shaved head that was covered in scars, suggesting he had fought many battles. "You!" she snarled. "Let me go or you will regret this! Do you know who I am?"

"I believe I do," the scar-headed man replied with a sly grin. "Mistress Ophelia Williams, youngest daughter of Sir Francis Williams of Salisbury." He tightened his grip. "And those fine clothes on that privileged back of yours will fetch us a pretty sum."

"You know me?" she stared down at him. "Then this was planned?" She looked round and caught the eye of one of her travelling companions. "I say again, help me!"

But it was her attacker who answered. "He will not," he said. "Will you, Nick?"

Ophelia gasped. Nick was on the side of these attackers? He was not going to protect her?

The man Nick looked down rather than continue to meet the girl's accusing gaze. Her eyes narrowed. "And you, Edmund?" she said to the other man.

"Him too," said the one holding her leg.

"By Heavens!" she shouted at Nick and Edmund. "My father will hear of your treachery! He charged you to keep me safe!"

"Then he should have taken more care with his choice," said Scarhead. He gave a sharp pull on her leg. Taken by surprise, she found herself unseated. With a scream that was of anger as much as fear, she fell to the earth. She landed on her back with all the breath knocked out of her.

Immediately Scarhead flipped her over onto her front. She felt a series of small tugs on the stitching of her bodice, as if he was cutting it with his knife. Then he ripped it open, before pulling her roughly to her feet. Both her hands were grasped and pulled out wide. She glanced left and right. Her wrists were each being held by the other two attackers, making her stand on the sunlit forest path as if she were Christ upon the cross.

Nick and Edmund were still sitting on their horses. Unmoving. Watching.

The first attacker then advanced on her from the front, holding up his knife. "What are you going to do to me?" she breathed, staring wide-eyed at the blade.

"First I will take what I can sell," he answered. "We will start by having this rich clothing." He moved in close and put the blade up to her throat, while his companions untied the lacing on each of her sleeves and pulled them away.

Scarhead then tugged the gown down to her ankles, followed by the kirtle. Moving the knife away from her throat, he said, "Step out."

"These are but my travelling clothes," she said. "Worth very little."

"They are worth much to me," he said. "As well as the other, no doubt finer clothes in yonder cases." He indicated the bags on Ophelia's horse, as well as those carried by Nick and Edmund on their horses. "Step out, I say. Or must I pierce your slender neck to make you do it?" With a scowl Ophelia stepped out, dressed in nothing now but her shift. "And the shoes," he ordered. Her scowl deepened as she took them off and kicked them towards him.

He glanced at her feet. "Those fine stockings are worth a coin or two as well," he said. He bent down and grasped her foot. She tried to kick out at him, but his grip was too strong. "Do not struggle, my pretty," he said, "for I will have my way whatever you do." He tightened his grip, so much that she gave a small yelp. "See?" he said, looking up at her. "We can do this with pain or without. Which do you favour?" She stopped trying to kick. He reached up under her shift and untied the laces holding her stockings up. The touch of his rough hands on her leg made Ophelia want to gag, but she breathed in deeply to control it as he pulled each stocking off. He threw them onto her gown with the shoes. Then he looked up and gave a knowing smile. "Aha. Is that gold I spy through your shift?"

No! Not that! Anything but that!

She struggled against the men holding her wrists, trying to free herself; to stop him taking the fine garnet and pearl pendant she had worn day and night for three years. Scarhead reached up and grasped the collar of her shift, then wrenched it down.

"No! You shall not have it!" she snarled. "It was my mother's!" She looked across at her companions. "Nick! Edmund! You were hired by my father to protect me! For the love of God, do your duty!"

"Save your breath, young mistress," said Scarhead. "They are my men not yours, and have been since they first offered their service to your father." He turned the pendant over in his hand. "And in case you were wondering how they passed his rigorous scrutiny, you should know that they are not in truth the men that they claimed to be." As she tried to take this in, he suddenly reached round and unclasped the chain.

"Give it back!" she snapped, continuing to fight against her captors. "You have no right to that!"

"Nay, it is mine now," he said, standing back. Unable to free herself, she could only look on with impotent rage as he held the pendant up, watching it spin slowly in the bright sunlight. It was a fair size, beautifully made in gold and pearls, set with a large square-cut brown garnet which was itself surrounded by four further garnets in a pearl-edged star shape. "A fine piece indeed. Quite beautiful. This alone makes the whole venture worthwhile." He dropped it into his purse. "Right," he said, his tone becoming very business-like. "Our work here is done. This girl is to be... disposed of." He lifted his knife and said, "Understand child, I bear you no ill-will personally, but your presence now is... let us say... unnecessary."

He put his free hand on her shoulder and drew his knife back.

Ophelia suddenly shifted her weight onto one foot, then slammed the other knee up as hard as she could into his crotch.

With a thin scream Scarhead doubled up, dropping the knife. The man holding her right wrist reacted by loosening his grip. With a sharp tug she pulled it free and in desperation swung her fist round at the head of the man on her left. It was not a particularly accurate punch and had little power behind it, but the element of surprise was enough to make the man let go of her left wrist.

Now free, she picked up the knife and ran behind the

crouching Scarhead, then brought it round and up to his throat. As he straightened up, straining his head away from the knife, she reached down to his belt and pulled the pendant from his purse.

"Goodbye," she said in his ear. "Nothing personal either, but I would not stand here and be killed."

Then she ran across the path and leapt over a fallen log into the thickest part of the forest.

—o—

The dense vegetation she had entered might make it harder for her pursuers to follow on foot – and particularly Nick and Edmund on horseback – but it made it difficult for her also. Her progress was hindered by high roots, low branches and heavy foliage, so she was continually having to jump, duck and use the knife to cut her way through.

And all while barefoot in nothing more than a thin shift.

This was much more exertion than she was used to, so it was not long before she had to pause in a small clearing with her hands on her knees, fighting for breath.

Had this ambush been planned? Had Nick and Edmund led her deliberately into a trap? Ophelia panted through tightly clenched teeth. How could her father have trusted them? How could he have sent her on a journey with two such rogues? She took a few deeper breaths and shook her head. But was it not to be expected? Was her father particularly unconcerned with his youngest child's safety, compared with that of her sister and two brothers?

Once she was breathing a little easier, Ophelia took the

opportunity to re-fix her mother's pendant round her neck and tuck it back under the collar of her shift.

She allowed herself a small glance back. Had she been followed? There was no sound, other than the rustling of the tops of the trees in the spring breeze, the occasional cawing of rooks and the coo-cooing of wood pigeons. Equally, there was no sign of any movement visible between the trees and branches, although the forest was so thick, she was not sure if that meant anything.

Then she heard a new sound; a man's shout.

With a renewed burst of energy, Ophelia turned and pushed through the nearest branches – to find herself faced by a particularly thick tangle of hanging fronds. She raised the knife and was about to cut her way through when she stopped. That may be how they were tracking her; fresh cuts made with the knife would stand out as a clear sign that she had passed that way.

Not to mention how she must appear in her white shift against the dark forest.

She lowered the knife and felt for the edge of the fronds, until she was able to squeeze round them and carry on.

A short while later the thick roots and branches opened onto a clear path running through the trees. She decided to take the opportunity to move a little faster and broke into a steady run, glancing frequently over her shoulder for signs of her pursuers.

There was another shout from over to her left.

With a small cry, Ophelia turned off the path to the right and again found herself again pushing through close-packed vegetation, until it opened out into a clearing.

A further shout from behind. She glanced back as she ran across the space.

And fell headlong across the high root of an oak tree.

She landed with a forceful thud on the soft earth and lay at full stretch for a moment as she tried to gather herself. Had she broken anything? Gingerly, she felt each leg. They felt sound, apart from a tender spot on her left shin where she must have hit the root, making her wince as she touched it. She looked at her fingers. There was a small amount of blood on them.

By Heavens, she could not run forever!

Pushing herself to her feet, she looked up at the offending tree, and the white sky just visible through its many branches. She looked down at her white shift, now streaked with earth.

I wonder...

She reached for the lowest branch and pulled herself up. The next branch was not too far away, so she was able to clamber onto it. From there she was able to climb from branch to branch, until she reached one she thought was high enough.

She lay out along the branch and looked down.

'With luck they will not look up,' she thought. 'And if they do, my shift will be just one more patch of white among the branches.'

—o—

A few minutes later, the bushes at the edge of the clearing started moving like waves on the sea, then a man pushed his way out. His shaved head shone like a beacon in the sunshine.

Two further men pushed out after him, and stood beneath

the tree looking about. They glanced round as the bush moved again behind them, and two more men appeared.

Ophelia scowled. The treacherous Nick and Edmund!

These two traitors had originally arrived at Father's house a few weeks back. And had they not made themselves so very useful? Oh yes, they had offered to run errands, undertake manual tasks and even accompany Ophelia and her older sister Cressida into Salisbury as guards. So much so, that when Father asked them to accompany Ophelia to their house near Penryn, Cornwall while he went to London, no-one doubted their trustworthiness. Cressida had stayed in Salisbury; as the older sister she was the woman of the house since their mother had died. Ophelia had begged her father to take her to Cornwall, where she could be free of her sister's dominance, and be able to do as she wished. She had even offered to go ahead to make sure the house was ready for Father's arrival, and he had agreed, so long as she was accompanied by some guards – and no-one had questioned the choice of Nick and Edmund. After all they had done to build her family's trust, who would have thought that they planned all the while to rob her? And it seemed, to kill her, so as to cover their crime? Ophelia took a breath to steady herself and gripped the branch as she looked down on the men below.

"She could be anywhere by now," said the one who had held her left wrist.

"Let her go," said the other. "There are plenty of mud swamps she could sink into and I am sure there are wild beasts who would delight in feasting on her. And if she avoids those, she is hardly dressed for the cold nights."

"I want that jewel back," said Scarhead.

"You have her horse and all her clothes. Is the jewel worth so much? The rest will keep us fed for many months when we sell them." This was Nick.

There was a silence, as Scarhead must have been considering this. "She also has my knife. But mostly I would make her pay for what she did to me back there. She tried to unman me."

"By Heavens," Nick said. "She is but sixteen years, and you were about to stab her! What would you have had her do?" Scarhead did not respond. "I would we leave her, and be safe in the knowledge that she will soon be dead anyhow."

"Come," said Edmund. "Let us go back to the horses and cases before they are taken by thieves and we lose everything."

Ophelia suppressed a small chuckle at the thought that these brigands could themselves be robbed, as the men all pushed back through the bush.

Silence descended on the clearing.

—o—

Ophelia waited until the sun had moved across much of the sky and was starting to set in the west before she clambered down from her perch. She dropped to the ground and started walking away from the direction the men had gone. With luck she had waited long enough that they had left the forest completely, although perhaps she should leave it two or three days, just to be sure that they were not lying in wait for her.

She stopped and looked at the lengthening shadows. What now? Night would soon fall, and she had no real clothing or shelter. She shivered and clasped her arms around her body as the chill started to bite. It was as Nick had said; she would soon be dead of cold.

Or from the bite of a wild beast.

What must it be like, to be dead? Would Jesus welcome her with open arms? She hoped so, but it was not certain. She had originally tried to be a good child, but since her mother had died and Cressida had taken on the management of the houses in her mother's place, Ophelia always seemed to be in the way, getting under the feet of the rest of the family, causing them to shout at her in annoyance and sometimes if she was being particularly what Cressida called 'wilful', her father would lock her in her chamber. So she had become even more disobedient, slipping out of the window and climbing down the ivy-clad walls to freedom, then running into the town alone, to be brought back by the constable like a stray dog. Then her father would lock her again in her chamber, shouting that she was dishonouring the family name. This seemed to matter much more to him than her safety.

So, if her father and sister found her to be so wilful and disobedient, how could Jesus accept her into His Kingdom when she died alone in this forest?

Would they even know she was gone? Sir Francis was not due back from London for a few days, and Cressida would assume her little sister had arrived safely in Penryn. If she even thought of Ophelia at all; she was so busy being the responsible adult, running the house in Salisbury and looking to their father's every whim. And their brothers were no longer there now. Thomas was in Oxford, while Jasper was on some business or other in the North; business no-one would explain to her, for all she would ask.

What of the servants in Penryn? Would they miss her when she did not arrive? Ophelia shook her head again. They were not even expecting her. It would have been a surprise when she turned up, so they would hardly raise a concern when she did not appear.

Would she be much missed when she was dead? Ophelia shook her head. Unlikely. Cressida and her father would probably rejoice that she was no longer causing them annoyance.

No, she was all alone, with only her wits to keep her alive.

A distant howl made her jump, then whimper in fear. A wolf? Was that how this would end?

Not if she could help it.

With a deep breath, Ophelia grasped the knife, lifted her chin and set off towards the setting sun.

—o—

The little cottage sat alone in a small clearing.

Ophelia approached it cautiously. When she had first spied it through the dusky gloom, she had been elated. A cottage! She was saved! The owner would take her in and give her food, warmth and shelter. But as she got nearer, she could see her hopes had been sadly misplaced. It looked cold and deserted. Its front door was hanging loose on its hinges, no smoke was coming from the roof, and now she looked closer, it had plants growing out of the small windows.

She pulled at the front door and had to jump back as it fell away, crashing down and splintering at her feet. She stepped over it and peered round into the gloom. As her eyes became accustomed, she could make out that there was vegetation everywhere, growing from the floor, climbing the walls and wrapping itself around the roof beams.

Ophelia set about making the place habitable; using the knife to cut away the vegetation and sweeping the dust and cobwebs off the surfaces with a particularly large leaf frond. A small pallet bed was revealed, as well as an old chest containing some blankets. She took these outside and shook them hard, coughing as they filled the air with dust and also released a fair few spiders. She went back in and noticed there was a thick woollen curtain pinned back behind the doorway, so she pulled it across the opening. The cottage became pitch dark, but at least it would be warmer.

Ophelia wrapped herself up in the blankets and lay down to sleep.

—o—

After three days in the cottage, Ophelia thought she was going to die of starvation.

She had found a small stream and drunk the water so her thirst was quenched, but her belly had been a different matter. It was used to the finest foods every day; meats, breads, vegetables, fruits, all washed down with excellent wines. But apart from a few wild mushrooms that had been nibbled raw and some leaves that looked vaguely edible, she had eaten nothing since the day she had been attacked. So, by the morning of the fourth day, she decided that even if

Scarhead and his men were not definitely gone, she had no choice but to set out again.

She had previously used the knife to cut a hole in one of the blankets and put it over her head as a cape. Another blanket had become a belt to hold her knife, and a third had been cut into strips to bind round her feet. So, feeling a little warmer and better able to walk, she left the cottage.

She had been going for maybe an hour, when she came across a well-trodden path. Checking the position of the sun, she headed west, and kept walking.

After another hour, Ophelia knew she had to stop for a rest; the hunger gnawing at her belly meant that what little energy she had started with was now exhausted. She stumbled to a stop, then slumped down to sit at the base of a tree.

It was not long before she drifted into a fitful sleep.

A loud barking and snuffling noise woke her, and with it the most disgusting animal smell. She opened her eyes to see an enormous boar was standing over her, blocking out the sun. It was snuffling at her curiously, its wicked tusks inches from her face. With a small whimper, she shrank back to the tree. The boar moved its head down and sniffed at her chest. Fortunately it seemed to be motivated by curiosity rather than hunger or malice, but this could no doubt change in an instant.

Keeping as still as she could, she whispered, "Begone! Begone, I say!"

The boar looked up, then it barked at her; a loud, angry bark that had her again shrinking against the tree and making small cries in the back of her throat. Its snout came up to her face and as she stared at the two black holes in its flat nose, it snorted. Its hot breath was the foulest thing Ophelia had ever smelled. Trying not to be sick, she whispered again, "Begone, beast, I beg of you!" She gripped the knife in her hand, ready to bring it up if the boar made any threatening move, although she had heard that a boar's hide was tougher than a suit of armour.

Suddenly she heard the unmistakable clip-clop sound of an approaching horse.

The boar raised its head and looked away. Then it barked again, before, thankfully, it loped away into the undergrowth.

Ophelia flinched. Was it Scarhead approaching? She felt as weak as a kitten and in no state to run. Then she breathed a sigh of relief as she saw it was just an old cart.

It stopped in front of her, and a man in a farmer's smock leaned down.

"Are you well, girl?" he asked.

"I thought I would be eaten by that beast," she whispered.

"Nay," he chuckled, "a boar is not likely to attack. Not like a wolf, mind. That is a creature that would have had your throat before you could raise a hand to defend yourself." He considered her a moment; a grey-haired old man with a kindly smile. "Can I take you any place? I am passing by the next town. I can set you down there if you wish?"

"Oh, would you?" she said. She struggled to her feet and climbed slowly up beside him.

He glanced at her sideways as he shook the reins to urge his horse on. "I have scarce seen a more ragged sight than you, girl. What has happened to you?"

Ophelia considered this old man and decided he looked honest. "I was attacked and robbed," she said. "My clothing, my horse and all else I carried were taken by brigands. It has been a few days and I am starving."

"By Heavens, that is unfortunate," he observed. "Lucky for you I happened by. We will be in the town in a couple of hours."

—o—

Ophelia thanked the old man, and climbed unsteadily down from the cart.

"The town is over there," he said, pointing down the road opposite. "Follow it to the end and you will arrive in the market square." Then he added, "You are in luck. Today is market day."

She looked up. "Thank you again," she said.

"Nay, it was a pleasure to have your company, child." He smiled. "May God go with you."

"And you," she replied.

"Although I would you find yourself some decent clothing as soon as you can, lest they think you a vagrant dressed like that. They will arrest you."

"Yes," she agreed. He flicked his reins at his horse and trotted away.

Ophelia looked down the road, that seemed to undulate in front of her like waves on a beach. 'I must eat,' she thought, as she started walking, 'or I will collapse ere long.'

But by the time she arrived in the busy market square with gulls squawking and crying overhead and what seemed like hundreds of people bustling between all the stalls, Ophelia felt so light-headed that she found it difficult to think at all.

As she walked between the stalls, she could not bear the sight and smell of all the foods on display; the cuts of meat, the crusty pies, the cakes and loaves of bread, that all seemed to move away from her as she approached them. How unlike it had been all those years ago when she used to go to the market with her mother. Then she had hung on excitedly to her mother's sleeve and chosen at will; the best cuts, the finest pies or the best cakes. Her mother would then fish in her purse to pay for whatever Ophelia desired.

Now here she was, dressed in a filthy shift and an old blanket, with not a single farthing to buy any food, despite her great hunger...

Ophelia realised she was standing by a bread stall. She glanced across at the baker, a fat old fellow who had all his attention on a woman as he sold her a fine loaf.

Something in Ophelia snapped. How could that woman have a loaf and she could not? Who had the greater need?

As the baker's attention seemed elsewhere, Ophelia reached down, took a loaf, and ran.

"Hey! Thief! Stop her! Stop that girl! Stop thief, I say!"

Ophelia kept running, although it seemed that the ground became as soft as mud as she ran, and she was sinking deeper and deeper, finding it more and more difficult to keep going, until a pair of hands suddenly wrapped around her and she found she could go no further.

"What is this?" asked a man's voice above her. She pressed her nose into a woollen jerkin. It smelled quite pleasant – like a summer meadow.

"She is a thief. And a vagrant, I warrant," came the baker's voice from behind.

"Is that the loaf of bread she has taken?" asked the man. The baker must have nodded, as the voice then said, "You had best return it, girl."

Ophelia silently held up the loaf and it was taken from her. Then she was thrust towards a plump beady-eyed man wearing a dusty-looking orange doublet. "Here, constable. She is all yours."

"A vagrant and a thief, eh?" asked the constable. "You are under arrest, my girl, and will appear before the Sheriff on the morrow."

CHAPTER TWO

Ophelia kept her head down as she was dragged into the courtroom by two burly guards. They stopped just inside the doors and kept her pinned so tightly between them that she could scarcely breathe.

She looked up and winced as she saw the portly constable in a faded orange doublet and brown hose; the one who had arrested her the day before. He was scuttling sideways like a crab up to the central table, his beady black eyes never leaving hers. "Next case, Master Sheriff," he announced to a severe-looking nobleman seated behind the table. "A girl who is both a vagrant and a thief."

"I see," replied the sheriff. "We will make this the last case for the morning session. Then we will adjourn for food and drink, before we resume in the afternoon." He peered at Ophelia down his unnaturally long nose. "And the name of this miscreant, constable?"

The fat man cracked his knuckles and gave a small unpleasant chuckle. "The churlish girl chooses not to give us her name," he said. Then he added quietly, although just loud enough for Ophelia to hear, "I fear she is not of sound mind, sir."

The sheriff nodded, as if this was as much as he expected. "And what did she steal?"

The constable gave one further glare at her, then transferred his gaze to the sheriff. "A loaf of bread from Simon the Baker's market stall yesterday, sir."

The sheriff nodded again, then looked around the room and asked loudly, "Is the same baker here to give evidence against her?"

"I am that, master," came a voice from within the crowd, who were sitting on benches three rows deep down one side of the room. She turned as the baker stood up, and pointed directly at her, his small, close-set eyes all but lost in his red, thread-veined face. "This brazen and thieving girl stole a loaf, then ran from my stall yesterday," he said. She looked down, trying to blot out the memory of this same man bellowing at her like an angry bull as she attempted to run away.

"Was it then recovered?" asked the sheriff.

The baker shuffled his feet and looked down. "Aye sir, that it was. She was seized by a good citizen when I called out the theft, and the loaf was restored to me."

"Do we have that citizen here?"

Another man stood up. "I stopped her, sir. She as good as fell into my arms."

Ophelia studied the man, seeing him for the first time. He was a grey-haired fellow wearing the same woollen jerkin as before, with an open, honest-looking face, for all he had a strangely hooked nose that seemed to split his upper lip in two. "Although I did feel she was most frightened herself," the man added. "She shook as I held her."

"As you say," the sheriff said dismissively. "But a thief nonetheless, it seems." He turned to the baker. "So you recovered your property?" he asked.

"Aye, but as you noted, sir, she is a brazen thief who had intent to steal. She must be punished."

The sheriff then addressed Ophelia. "What say you, to this man's accusation? He has made a strong case, I warrant." She shook her head and stayed silent. He raised an eyebrow. "You say naught in your defence? For all I will sentence you to a severe whipping in the market square?" He raised his gavel, and was about to bring it down, when there was the sound of a bench scraping back in the middle row and a tall, gangling boy stood up.

"I speak as her lawyer in defence," the boy said, in a loud, clear voice.

The gavel hung in mid-air a moment, then came slowly back to the table without making any sound. Ophelia gave the boy a curious look. He was above average height even for a grown man, and had long flowing brown hair that was pushed back behind his ears. She thought he had an open and friendly face, although that alone was hardly going to be sufficient to save her back from being flayed open like a cut of meat.

"And who might you be?" asked the sheriff, as the crowd muttered their own surprise.

"Robert Wychwoode, sir."

The sheriff looked him up and down a few times, then asked, "Andrew Wychwoode's boy?" At a brief nod in response, he added, "You cannot be above sixteen years by the look of you. What is this, that you have enough command of the law to speak for this girl?"

"I have observed the proceedings of this court on each and every occasion it has sat, sir," the boy answered. "I have not missed a single one of the sessions that have taken place here since I was but twelve years."

The sheriff pulled on his trim beard and said, "Now you say it, I do recall seeing you here on occasions. And I warrant you have a strong interest in the workings of the law. But that hardly suffices as a legal training." He sucked between his teeth a moment, then made a dismissive gesture with his hand. "But what e'er will be. We have heard a baker speak for the prosecution, I suppose it is all of a piece if we have a boy speak for the defence." He gave a small grunt, as if punctuating his decision. "If she agrees to have you speak for her, then we will hear you plead her cause. You could hardly make her situation any worse." He gave a thin smile and addressed Ophelia. "What say you? Do you allow this callow youth, who I suspect has no more years than you, to put your case?"

She gave a small, cautious nod.

The sheriff tapped his gavel lightly and said, "Then this court will adjourn early for our food and drink, so you can meet together and prepare such a defence as may be possible. We will finish hearing this case when we return. But I warn you, young Wychwoode," he raised his chin and frowned down his nose at the boy, "if you waste this court's time with spurious nonsense, then it will be the worse for you. I may even make you an accessory and have you whipped as well. You understand?"

Robert stood tall, swallowed hard and said, "I understand, sir."

"Good." The sheriff pushed back his chair and stood. "We will meet again in two hours." He gathered his heavy dark cloak around him and swept from the room, followed by the scuttling constable, then all the crowd from their benches, glancing curiously at Robert as they passed.

When the last person had gone, Ophelia was alone with the boy and her guards. She shook herself free of them and walked over.

There was a long silence as she stared up at him. He returned the look with clear blue eyes.

"I am unsure whether I should thank you for your intervention," she said eventually, "or scold you soundly for your presumption."

He glanced at the guards, and she turned to follow his gaze. They were paying close attention to the conversation as they leaned casually against the wall. "I would you hold your tongue from all talk of scolding," he whispered, "lest those fellows report it and you are fitted with a scold's bridle about your head as well as being whipped. Would you have a wound put through your tongue by its spike to match those in your back?"

"But you have offered to defend me," she said softly, glancing over at the guards. "If you do it well, then I will not have any such wounds – in my back, my tongue or anywhere else."

"True." He sat and indicated she should sit beside him.

"I would have you tell me why you do this thing," she said

as she sat. Then she twisted slightly so her back was to the guards and they could talk a little more easily. "What does it benefit you to defend me?"

He shrugged. "The reasons I do this are twofold." He leaned back slightly, pressed his fingertips together and looked at her with an expression that was more man than boy. "The first is that I would learn the practice of the law before I go to London to study it formally."

"So I am but the subject of your attempt at learning," she said with a thin smile, "so you can test whatever theories have been bubbling around inside that head of yours, like pottage in a cauldron?"

He seemed to ignore this. "And the second, is that I can see past the rough smock they have clothed you in, and the hair that hangs loose like rats' tails, to see that in truth, you are of noble birth."

She raised a challenging eyebrow. "And by what reason do you come to that conclusion?"

A self-satisfied looking smirk twitched at the corners of his mouth, then he nodded to himself. "When I saw you across the room, I could see that your hands are fine and cared-for. They are the hands of a well-born girl, not a vagrant, for all they are filthy." He nodded again, this time to her. "And when you stand, you stand tall and proud. I have observed many vagrants when I have attended this court, and it is clear that you are not one of them." Then he added, "And now I have heard you speak, my suspicions are confirmed."

"So you have eyes in your head, and ears that function." She glanced up at his ears, "Although to be sure, they do stick out most proudly."

"As may be," he said, his face flushing red, making her wonder with some amusement if this feature had been re-marked on by others. "In truth," he continued, "I wanted to know why you were brought before this court for theft and vagrancy, and why you would not speak or defend yourself?"

"And if I tell you?"

"Then I will do my best to get these charges dropped, so you may go free and unharmed."

She nodded slowly. "Very well," she said. "For all your youth, Master Robert Wychwoode, you are a clever fellow, and see things others do not." She leaned in. "So I will tell you all."

—o—

The sheriff settled himself in his seat and adjusted his fine black cap, adorned with an ornate brooch that signalled his elevated landowner status in this small rural Devon community.

"So, Master Wychwoode," he said. "Have you been con-firmed in your instruction to appear on behalf of this girl? Are we to hear her defence from you?"

Robert stood and grasped the edges of his overgown. "I have, sir."

"Then go to it, boy." The sheriff leaned back. "And it had better be good," he added. There was a slight ripple of laughter at this, and the sheriff gave a small, self-satisfied looking smirk.

Robert cleared his throat as he waited for silence, then looked over at Ophelia. She gave him a small smile and nod of encouragement, mainly to cover her concern that he might mess it up and make things worse.

"This young lady..." Robert began, but was interrupted by the sheriff.

"Does she have a name, boy?" he asked. "Have you been privileged enough for her to share with you what she will not tell us?"

Robert smiled. "Indeed sir. I can tell you her name is Mistress Ophelia Williams."

"Ophelia, eh? That is not a name I associate with a vagrant." The sheriff studied her, with a look that made her feel deeply conscious of how she must appear in her borrowed smock dress and filthy matted hair. The sheriff waved a hand vaguely in Robert's direction and said, "But 'tis no matter. Carry on, young man."

"She admits she removed the loaf of bread from the stall," he began again.

"Then theft is proven," the sheriff cut in. "We need go no further."

The crowd chuckled and muttered at this, but instead of responding, Robert turned and stared them down until, with a last few clearing of throats and coughs, they were silent again.

"I said she admitted removing it. I did not say she had intent to steal it."

The sheriff picked up his gavel and started turning it over in his hands. "I warned you, boy," he growled, "not to start giving us spurious nonsense..."

Ophelia held her breath for Robert's response. Was he going to make this work? Or would she end up being whipped?

He had seemed so confident in his plan for her defence when they discussed it earlier – but could he now present it with enough credibility to convince this bad-tempered sheriff?

"Sir," Robert said, looking the sheriff firmly in the eye, "the baker asserted earlier that Mistress Williams had intent to steal the loaf. I would like this court to know that she had no such intent."

"Come now, boy," the sheriff began, but Robert held up his hand for silence.

"Nay sir, please hear me out." As Ophelia chuckled silently at his insolence and the sheriff's mouth hung open, Robert continued. "This incident took place yesterday, which was a Thursday was it not?" The sheriff nodded slowly, his mouth still open. "And what occurs in this town on the third Thursday of each month?"

"Market day," said a voice from the crowd.

"Precisely," Robert agreed, turning to the men and women beside him. "It was market day." He addressed himself back to the sheriff. "And we are by the sea in this town, are we not?" Again, a silent nod from the man at the bench. "And as we all know well, there are many hungry gulls that come from the sea, drawn to the market by the opportunity of rich pickings, such as crumbs from stalls and offal from the butcher's table."

Robert gave a brief glance back at the crowd, and Ophelia could see they were now hanging on his words.

"And these gulls, that screech and squawk above us, when they have eaten their fill, what do they then do?" There were a few sniggers from the crowd, and an old man at the back muttered loudly, "they drop their shit on us." At this there was loud laughter from the rest of the crowd. Even the constable smiled briefly.

"For sure," Robert said, holding up his hand again, but this time to silence the crowd. Once the laughter had died down, he continued. "As this fellow so correctly asserts, they drop their shit..." he paused and nodded at the sheriff, "begging your pardon, sir. And what does a responsible person do, if they see a gull circling above a bread stall, looking as if it is about to foul the bread?" he paused again, "and so render it unfit to eat, and thus unfit to sell?" He transferred his gaze down to the crowd once more, and Ophelia was encouraged to see that he was getting nods and smiles in return.

"She removes the loaf before it is shat upon," said the old man.

"Precisely," Robert said. "She does that very thing. And when other responsible people who, like the baker, think she has stolen the bread – these people stop her..." he acknowledged the grey-haired man into whose arms Ophelia had run, "...she hands it straight back."

"Did she do this?" asked the sheriff of the grey-haired man. "Did she hand it back without protest?"

"Aye, that she did, sir."

"Do you agree?" he asked the baker.

The baker looked at the crowd and must have seen that the room was now more with Ophelia than with him. He nodded. "Agreed, sir."

The sheriff turned his gavel over once more, then placed it quietly back on the desk. "Then why did she not say that she had no intent to steal the bread, but to preserve it for sale, when she was first held?"

"Despite her honesty, she knew she had the look of a vagrant, sir," Robert replied. "Would she have been believed?"

The sheriff's eyes narrowed. "You say she had such a look." He glanced across at Ophelia. "As she still has now. Although I warrant she does stand taller and more assured than most such reprobates. Are you suggesting she is not such a vagrant?"

"That I am, sir," answered Robert. "Far from being a vagrant, she comes instead from a family of great means and status, and would not usually lack for food and drink, nor fine clothes."

The sheriff raised his eyebrows. "Then by what means does she come to be so attired?"

"She was robbed herself, sir, by brigands," Robert replied. "She was passing close to this village with two men hired by her father to protect her. She had been sent ahead to her father's house in Cornwall, and was journeying through the nearby forest when heavily armed thieves and cut-purses set about her party. Her two companions proved to be traitorous to her cause, and instead of protecting her, they were revealed as part of the gang that were robbing her."

Ophelia shuddered at the memory of Scarhead advancing on her with the knife.

"I see." The sheriff tugged at his beard a moment. "So these men hired to protect her planned instead to rob her ?"

"That seems to have been the case, sir."

The sheriff looked at Ophelia with what seemed almost like concern. "Her father will be most angered."

"As any father would be, sir," agreed Robert. "Mistress Williams was unclothed by the brigands for the high value of her clothing – even her stockings. She managed to get out of their grasp, and ran from these men wearing naught but her undershift. Terrified that they would find her, she hid in the forest for a few days in an abandoned cottage, eating almost nothing but occasional mushrooms and leaves as she found them. She was then brought to this town by a passing farmer. There she found the market was taking place and saw the bread stall and the gull above it." He paused. "The rest you know."

Ophelia lifted her eyes to Robert, and he smiled reassuringly down at her, which made her stomach give an odd little flip. It seemed so unusual to hear her own story being told aloud by someone else. There was no doubt he told it well, for all he could hardly know the full horrors that she had managed to live through.

"And why did she not tell us this tale of robbery and concealment herself when she was taken into custody?" asked the sheriff, glaring at Ophelia.

"I understand she tried, sir, but not only was she not believed, it was made clear to her that such a tale would only make her situation markedly worse."

Ophelia glanced at the constable. This man had shouted how she would be flogged, or worse, as he dragged her away from the market and threw her into his dark, damp cellar. Her protestations that she was a victim herself had only made him scream at her even more.

The sheriff raised an eyebrow at the constable. "Is this so?" he asked.

The constable shifted in his chair, looking as if it had

suddenly become very hot. "I saw only a vagrant girl caught stealing, sir," he muttered.

"I see," the sheriff said, "And did you, by any chance, suggest that her defence would, in truth, make things worse?"

"I might have suggested something of that sort," the constable replied, carefully picking at a piece of loose thread on the doublet stretching across his ample belly.

"I see," the sheriff repeated, giving the man a look that suggested to Ophelia there would be an uncomfortable conversation between those two later.

Robert continued. "So she wisely decided not to repeat the story, nor to give her name to this court as she feared the damage to her family's reputation would greatly anger her father. She hoped her father, when he eventually discovered she had not arrived at the house in Cornwall, would come for her and vouchsafe the truth of her tale, before any punishment was carried out."

The sheriff turned his attention back to Robert. "Has word been sent to him?" he asked.

"I will do so as soon as I can." Robert answered.

The sheriff looked at the crowd. "We have the baker asserting that this girl had intent to steal his loaf, while we have her young lawyer here, telling us it was to preserve the same against being sullied by gulls, and we understand from the baker that she returned it willingly when apprehended." He paused. "And we also learn that she is no vagrant, but the noble victim of an attack on her own person and possessions." He looked over at Ophelia, but she could see he was really addressing the crowd. "Should I then find you guilty of the crimes of which you are accused?"

The crowd shouted and booed, shaking their fists. Those that had staffs and sticks banged them on the floor. The sheriff held up a hand. When they were finally silent, he continued, "So, I hear the views of these worthy people, and find myself in full agreement." He banged his gavel on the desk. "Not guilty of all charges."

When the clapping and cheering had died down, he leaned forward and crooked his finger at Ophelia's guards. "Bring her here to me," he ordered. Once she was standing before him, he smiled, and it was like the sun coming out from behind a dark storm cloud. "I now understand why you kept silent, my child," he said. "You knew no-one would believe you, that the truth of your tale would make things worse, and that your situation might sully the good name of your family. You then trusted that your father would find you before any punishment was carried out." He glanced over at Robert, who was still on his feet. "In the meantime it was your good fortune to have young Master Wychwoode here speak for you so clearly today." He reached over and patted her hand. "You need to be bathed and dressed as befits your station, so I release you to the care of Master Wychwoode and his family, who can be your guardians until your father comes."

He sat back. "So go now, Ophelia Williams, and may God go with you."

3

CHAPTER THREE

Ophelia broke off a hunk of bread, stuffed it in her mouth and washed it down with a large gulp of ale. Then she speared a sizeable slab of beef and bit off half, chewed on it a moment, then added another swig of ale to the mix.

It was a couple of hours later, and they were in the parlour of the local tavern.

"You were indeed hungry," observed Robert from the other side of the table.

"Mmmm," she agreed, then pushed the other half of the beef into her mouth and sat back, chewing hard, as she studied the remains of the spread Robert had ordered. Her gaze stopped on a slice of hard crusty pie. She picked it up and took a bite.

In truth it was going to take all this bread, beef and pie to fill her stomach after many days with only mushrooms, leaves and spring water to sustain her. Certainly the small beer and hard cheese the constable's wife had given her the night before when they had thrown her into the foul cellar in his house had done nothing more than sharpen her appetite.

"This is good," she muttered, as she chewed.

"My mother always tells me not to rush my food," Robert observed. "Or she says I will make myself sick."

Ophelia swallowed the mouthful of pie, then paused with the rest of it halfway to her mouth. "Wise woman, your mother," she muttered.

"You will meet her presently, I have no doubt."

"Mmmm," she repeated, finishing the pie.

"And she will want you washed from top to toe, then clothed as befits your station."

Ophelia nodded. She could hardly wait to get out of the stinking dress the constable's wife had made her wear, and comb the tangles from her hair. But first she must finish filling the hole in her belly; a hole so big it had caused her such awful pain and even prevented her from thinking clearly – or why would she have tried to steal a loaf of bread so openly in a crowded market?

But the hole in her belly was the easiest problem to solve, compared to the much more pressing matter to be sorted before she could put the whole sorry business behind her.

She finished the ale and put down the tankard, as she considered Robert.

She had been fortunate that this gangling – but admittedly not bad-looking – lad had offered to speak so successfully in her defence. His idea about the gulls had been inspired; just plausible enough to sow the seed of doubt in the mind of the sheriff, and amusing enough to win over the crowd.

And now to the more pressing matter; she needed his help once again.

She needed him to undertake another task for her –and one with possibly as much risk to both of them as her defence in court.

"I am most keen to be washed and clothed by your mother, Master Wychwoode," she began carefully. "But there is something I need to do first – something we need to do together –before I can enjoy that happy event."

"We?" he raised an eyebrow. She nodded. "Which is?"

At least he was not questioning that he had a part in this.

She took a deep breath. "When I told you in court earlier of the brigands who stole my horse and my clothes, I did not tell you of another item that they tried to steal. An item with some value to them, but priceless to me."

"And this item?"

"A gold and jewelled pendant that my mother wore every day; given to me soon after she died some three years past."

She saw the understanding in his eyes. "I am sorry to hear of your mother," he said gently. "So for sure it was an item you could not bear to lose. And you say they tried to steal it?"

She nodded and told him how she had lost the pendant, then retrieved it.

"I see," he said. "And when you were arrested, you did not want it found..." He considered her a moment, "in case that grasping constable would not believe it was indeed yours. He would think you were even more of a thief."

"For sure," Ophelia answered. "So when they put me in their cellar, I hid it, along with the knife I took from the brigand. I wrapped them both in a strip of blanket and concealed them in a recess."

He gave her a knowing smile. "So you would look to retrieve this package without the constable having reason to arrest you once again?"

"Yes, I would."

Robert frowned. "But now he knows you are from a wealthy family, surely he will understand that the pendant is yours? He will see why you hid the piece and will simply return it?"

"Will he? I made him look a fool in that court. So he has every reason to cause me further trouble," Ophelia shook her head. "Belike he will still want to make enquiries as to its provenance."

"What then? Your father can give such reassurances when he arrives."

"Yes," she said, "But if the constable makes such enquiries before my father gets here, then I am concerned that the word will get out about the pendant."

"And?" he asked. "Why is that so bad?"

"Because the brigand who tried to steal it wants to take it again. Badly. And if there are enquiries, he may well hear of them, and come for it."

Robert's eyes narrowed as he appeared to think this through. "Belike he may already have heard," he observed slowly. "Those court proceedings were very public, and your story will be spreading across the county. If we do not get it back, and take you to the safety of my house, then you remain in very grave danger from the man." He took a deep breath. "I would say there is every chance he is on your trail even now."

Ophelia gasped; her memories of Scarhead were all too terrifying. The thought that he might come for her again was more than she could bear. "Surely not?" she whispered.

He gave a small shake of his head. "Perhaps not," he conceded, "but we have to accept it is a real possibility."

"So what are we to do?"

He leaned forward. "First we have to get back your pendant. Your knife would be useful as well. Which means we may need to spin yet more lies to get into the constable's cellar." He scratched his cheek. "And then get out again."

"Will you help me?" she asked.

"Oh, Mistress Ophelia," he said gently. "Of course I will."

She sat back in her chair. "Do you really mean that?"

"I do," he answered. He leaned in closer, his eyes clear and steady. "I have already started my legal career by having to lie to save you in court. This broke a promise I made to myself that I would only ever tell the truth in order to uphold the law." He leaned back and brought his fingertips together, just as he had earlier. "But now... now I have made my first win, and it is built on a lying conceit – about gull shit, of all things. So yes, I will help you retrieve your precious jewel, and if I have to bend the truth once again..." he sighed, "then that is what I will do." He shook his head slowly. "Now I am acting as your representative, Mistress Williams, I am most keen to ensure you remain unharmed." He nodded. "So I will do my all to protect you. I swear it on my oath."

She let out her breath. "I am most grateful. And that we can act on this together."

"Indeed. So let us find this constable's house."

"What will we do when we find it? How will we get into the house, and then to the cellar?"

He gave her a small frown. "I am not sure. But we will think of something."

—o—

The low afternoon sun made deep shadows between the tall houses as Ophelia and Robert walked from the tavern down towards the small harbour. She recalled that the constable's house was on a road going up a hill, and that she had caught a glimpse of the sea below before the constable had dragged her inside and led her down the dark stairs to his foul cellar. So Robert had suggested that they go to the harbour first, then start from there and work their way up through the town, to see if they could locate the correct road.

Soon they arrived at the dockside, and paused a moment to look out over the twinkling waves towards the distant horizon. Ophelia thought the sea was quite beautiful, and said this to Robert.

"Aye," he replied, "beautiful but deadly. A man can so easily be consumed by the waves if he chances to fall in."

She glanced across at him. "There are those who can support themselves in the water and swim through it without sinking," she observed.

"God save them," he answered, "but that is not something I am able to do." He gazed out over the water a moment. "Nor would I desire it, either." He said this with such finality that Ophelia felt there was no need to comment further.

She turned to look up through the town, trying to

remember which road the constable had dragged her along after she had been arrested in the marketplace. She scanned across the streets leading from the harbour to see if any particular landmark prompted her recall.

A fleeting movement in one of the streets caught her eye.

She let out a shocked exclamation which made Robert look sharply at her. "What is it?" he asked with some urgency in his voice. "What have you seen?"

"A man ducked into a doorway when I looked," she whispered. "Just there." She pointed at a building with a deeply recessed door, although now there was no movement. "I saw him only briefly but I would know him any place." She swallowed hard. "It was the man who attacked me. The one I thought of as Scarhead."

"Then it is indeed as I suspected," said Robert. "He has tracked you here already." There was a silence, then he added, "That is good."

"Good?" she squeaked. "What is good about it? 'Good' that you were right he would come for me, or 'good' that he will try to finish what he started?"

"Neither," he answered.

"What then?" she inquired.

"Good that this gives us a way to get into that cellar." He stared hard up the hill beyond where Scarface had hidden, as if looking for something specific. Then he nodded and grunted to himself, as if he had found what he sought. He took her hand and started walking quickly away. "Come," he said from the side of his mouth. "And I will tell all."

He led her across to the harbour buildings, then pulled her into a dark alleyway.

"Do you see," he said, when he had finished explaining his idea. "It covers all our needs. It allows us to retrieve your pendant, and also gets Scarhead away from us – forever, with luck."

"While I am the bait in the trap you are setting?" she asked. "I do not much like that part."

"It will all be good," he replied.

"So you keep saying." She did not feel particularly re-assured. "What if it goes wrong?"

"It will not. Trust me."

"Robert Wychwoode," she growled, "I have known you but a few hours. Why should I trust you?"

"Because I have already saved your back from a flogging, and I have sworn to protect you."

"There is that," she conceded with a more hopeful smile. "Then we had better not fail in this task."

—o—

A few minutes later, Ophelia walked back out onto the harbour alone.

Conscious that she still had the appearance of a vagrant in her dirty shift dress, she held herself as tall as she could and stared straight ahead, ignoring the curious looks of the sailors and dock workers as she passed.

She rounded a building, then took a deep breath to steady herself, before starting up the street where she had seen Scarhead, using the side of the street opposite to his hiding place.

Just before she came level with the doorway she stopped. Would he still be there? Had he found somewhere else to hide? The plan relied on him remaining there. But then she saw the toe of a dusty boot. Her heart quickened and for a moment she was back in the forest, staring down at those same boots as he prepared to stab her.

Now is not the moment to be afraid. This is going to work. It has to work.

Ophelia squared her shoulders and walked up level with the door. She deliberately turned to look into the dark recess.

He was leaning back with his arms folded; his hated face twisted into a nasty grin.

At the sight of him, she gave a loud, wide-eyed gasp and put her hand to her mouth.

Then she ran.

He pushed himself off the door pillar and started to run after her.

At first it was easy; she fairly flew up the hill. But soon the earlier lack of food, poor sleep and tension of the last few days took effect, not to mention the heavy meal she had just eaten.

Her legs started to feel as if they were made of wood.

Her breath rasped in her throat, and each step became harder and harder on the steep cobbles.

Keep going! Fear is the friend of the fugitive!

She could hear the pounding footsteps behind her getting closer and closer.

Now she could feel his breath on her neck.

There was a tall house just ahead, with wooden columns supporting the upper storey, creating a deeply shadowed entrance. It was the one Robert had said he had seen earlier.

She ran past it and on up the hill.

There was a shout just behind her, sounding like Robert. It was followed by a thud, then further shouts from Scarhead.

Ophelia staggered to a halt, then looked back down the hill.

Robert was sitting on top of Scarhead, just beyond the shadowed entrance where he had been hiding, and was pushing the man's left arm up behind his back. With his other hand he was pulling off his belt. "Quick!" he shouted to Ophelia, "take the belt!"

She slithered down to them and took it. Robert was clearly struggling to hold onto Scarhead, and she thought that at any moment the heavier man would throw Robert off his back. She tried to grab at Scarhead's left arm but he kept it moving and she could not get a grip.

"Tie his hands!"

"Then you hold him still!"

"He will throw me," grunted Robert, just as Scarhead got his free right hand down onto the cobbles and started to push upwards. When Scarhead's body was clear of the ground and all his weight was on the hand, Ophelia flicked the belt around his arm in a loop. Then she gave it a hard tug with all her weight. Scarhead gave a shout as his arm was pulled out from under him, and he fell heavily back on the cobbles with Robert clinging on like the rider of an unbroken horse.

"Now!" Robert shouted, taking the opportunity to push Scarhead's left arm further forward. Ophelia put her knee on Scarhead's cheek to hold him still, then leaned across as he struggled beneath her and managed to secure the belt round his outstretched right wrist. Then she pulled it across so she could bind his left as well.

"By Heavens, boy," snarled Scarhead, with his face pressed

to the cobbles under Ophelia's knee, "you will regret this. You both will."

Robert bent down. "I think not," he said. "For you are a thief and outlaw who will shortly be brought to justice."

Just then there was the sound of feet running towards them. Ophelia stood up, to see several townspeople gathering round. They were staring down at Robert and Scarhead with concerned faces. "What are you doing?" exclaimed a man wearing the garb of a merchant.

"We have apprehended a thief," answered Robert, as he climbed carefully off Scarhead's back. "This man attacked my friend here as she travelled through the forest. He took her horse and her clothes, and put her in real fear of being killed." He used the belt to pull Scarhead to his feet. "We will take him to the constable so he can be dealt with according to the law."

—o—

The constable answered the knock at his door with an expression of detached indifference. This changed to one of surprise when he saw Scarhead, bound and held between Robert and Ophelia, plus the merchant and other townsfolk who had gleefully accompanied them from the scene of the ambush.

"By all that is holy, lad, you have brought me Ned Carter?" He gave a broad grin as he studied the bound man's angry face, still red from the force of Ophelia's knee and now with a gag added by Robert to stop the shouting and cursing they had suffered on the way up. "I have sought this brigand for many a year, but he has always eluded me. And now you, a boy who would be a lawyer, have arrested him for me?"

"Ned Carter? Is that his name?" asked Robert. "Well, it was he who robbed Ophelia Williams here, whose case was heard earlier today. We caught him skulking around the town."

At this the merchant stepped forward. "Nay," he said, with a breathless air of one telling a most important tale. "It was more than that. The lad was concealed in a dark doorway when the girl ran past, being chased by this brigand. He had very near caught her, when the boy suddenly appeared like an avenging angel, and leapt upon him, knocking him hard to the ground. Then the girl came back and restrained the fellow further, before she tied him up." The merchant looked at the rest of the crowd, as if seeking confirmation. "I saw it all, constable."

The constable eyed Ophelia with some disfavour. "Ophelia Williams, eh? You seem to attract trouble, girl," he said. "And cause much annoyance. I should have you tried again – this time for a breach of the peace." At this Scarhead nodded, and grunted behind the gag. "But you have brought me Ned Carter, and for that I must overlook the nuisance you cause, and thank you instead. He has been sought for many a crime, and will surely hang for them."

Scarhead grunted and struggled against his bonds, then shot Ophelia a look of pure venom.

She shrugged, as if to say, 'You are the bringer of your own misfortune', which made him scowl even more, the scars on his bare head all a deep burning red.

"You will detain him for now?" asked Robert.

The constable nodded and said, "Aye. Bring him in and

I will secure him in my cellar before I have him committed for trial."

The excitement over, townsfolk melted away. Ophelia heard the merchant saying as they walked off, "I tell you, that lad flew through the air like an angel. Truly, 'twas a wonder to behold..."

The constable and Robert pulled Scarhead into the house. Ophelia hurried inside after them, trying not to shudder at the dreadful memory of being brought in only the night before, bound just like Scarhead. She took a deep breath and put her hand on a dusty table to steady herself.

Robert and the constable had Scarhead held close between them. The constable leaned over and opened a low door with his free hand. He took a candle from the table and held it high by the door, revealing the same dark stairway that Ophelia had been pushed down. She stood back and looked away, lest the sight of the stairs should bring back yet more painful memories.

"I thank you again, young fellow," the constable said to Robert as he pushed Scarhead to the door, "but I can take it from here."

"His hands are secured with my belt," Robert replied. "It has value to me. I would have it back."

The constable gave a small grunt, and said, "Very well. Wait here. I will secure him to the chain I keep down there and bring back your belt."

Robert shook his head. "I will come down as well," he asserted, "lest he try to escape while you change his bonds."

The constable looked as if he was going to refuse, then Ophelia thought he must have caught Scarhead's calculating eye, for he seemed to change his mind. "For sure," he said. "Follow me down."

They processed down the stairs, leaving Ophelia standing alone in the hall.

She looked around the constable's dusty little room and shivered, suddenly aware of the chill. She moved over to the fire opposite and held her hands to it for warmth. The flames were dying, so she picked up an old blackened iron poker from the hearth and turned the logs. Once she had some lively new flames going, she lent on the poker as she stared into the fire.

Would Robert be able to get the precious package while he was down there? She had given him precise instructions on where it was concealed, so with luck, he would find it. But would he be able to distract the constable while he slipped it out of its hiding place? If not, there would be trouble.

Robert. He was a well-meaning lad, of that there was no doubt. His promise on oath to protect her was welcome – although she did feel she had proved quite capable of protecting herself when the need arose. She gave a small nod of her head. Had she not stopped Scarhead from plunging his knife in her belly with a well-aimed kick? And managed to conceal herself high in the branches of a tree? So, for sure, his protection was to be valued, but her own abilities should not be dismissed. So why was it that Cressida and her father would dismiss them so readily? Did they not understand why that made her feel so rebellious, that she must act against their wishes so often? Why it made her feel so unwanted? Insignificant?

Ophelia pushed the poker into the fire again, moving it around in the flames until the logs crackled and burned even more fiercely. She lifted it out, and noted idly that the tip was now glowing with the heat.

There was a shout from the cellar.

She spun round, as there was another shout and the sound of feet pounding up the stairs.

She grasped the poker and dropped into a crouch, ready to see what – or who – was coming up the stairs.

She clenched her teeth. It was Scarhead.

He appeared in the doorway and paused a moment, his eyes glittering in the firelight.

He saw Ophelia by the fire, and he growled. It was the sound that a wild dog makes when it is about to strike. Or a man who seeks revenge.

Scarhead ran at her, his eyes fixed on hers; his grasping hands reaching for her throat.

If he had expected her to be an easy prey, then he was sadly mistaken.

The poker caught him squarely in the chest, its tip burning into his flesh before entering deep into his body through the ribs. With a gurgling sigh and a look of shocked surprise, he dropped to his knees. Then he fell slowly to his side, hitting the floor with a loud thud. A strong smell of burning flesh filled the air.

With a cry that was part disgust and part relief, Ophelia pulled the poker away.

The constable ran into the room, followed a few moments later by Robert.

"By Heavens, Carter managed to overpower us and get away..." the constable faltered to a stop as he looked at

Ophelia, standing with the poker and Scarhead lying still at her feet. "By Heavens," he repeated. "Is he...?"

"Dead?" she asked, trying to put a level of casual indifference into her voice that she did not truly feel. "I think he is."

The constable bent down and lifted Scarhead's arm. The hand flopped over at the wrist. He dropped it and looked up. "I should say he is," he muttered. He sniffed the air, and said, "What did you do to him?"

Ophelia silently held up the poker, its tip still smoking. The constable's eyes widened. "I should have you arrested for causing his death," he observed softly.

Robert said, "I take it you were defending yourself?" Ophelia nodded. "In which case, she has a strong defence in law," he observed. "And what is more, it looks like she has saved the court and the executioner their trouble. So I would argue the matter is closed."

The constable thought for a moment, his beady black eyes playing across Ophelia's face. He looked down at the body, then back up at Ophelia. "I agree," he said finally. "The matter is now closed. You are free to go, Mistress Williams."

Ophelia carefully put the poker back on the stone hearth and walked to the front door. "Come, Robert," she said, holding out her hand. He took it, and together they walked out into the evening dusk.

"Did you get it?" she whispered, once the door closed behind them.

"I did," he answered, pulling out the package and handing it over. She took it and peeled back the edge of the wrapping to reveal the pendant. He reached over and pulled it out, then held it up to spin gently in the moonlight. "A fine piece," he whispered. "Garnets are the stones of love, are they not?" She nodded, as he reached behind her neck and fastened the clasp. The pendant hung just below her chest.

"I shall never take it off again," she said, putting her hand over it. "Until the day I die."

"By Heavens, Ophelia, do not talk of death," he replied. Then he added, "Although, to be sure, you have just killed a man yourself."

"One who would have killed me otherwise."

"True."

She gave him a sideways glance. "The truth is that it was my good fortune he ran onto the hot poker."

"Indeed it was," he agreed with a grin. "But remind me never to leave you alone with such a weapon again." He chuckled. "But he was an evil, ungodly fellow, guilty of many crimes. You did God's work, and only hastened his certain journey to hell."

"Aye," she agreed. "Now let me see. First I near unmanned him, then I bound him, then I killed him." She made a small pout. "So you had better watch your step with me, young Master Wychwoode, now you have the measure of what I can do."

He snorted in amusement. "Is that a threat, Mistress Williams?"

"Do you want it to be?"

He stopped and turned to her, and she felt a little shiver run up her spine as his eyes held hers in the moonlight. "No," he said softly, "but I do have great respect for your talents. Belike it is not my protection you seek, but I yours?"

"Oh come now," she replied. "You are a man of action as

well as a planner. It was your idea to hide in that doorway and have me lead him past you, and it was you who leaped out on him." She laughed. "Like, what was it? An avenging angel!"

"But it was not the plan I conceived that worked in the end. I left much too much to chance. He nearly escaped from me and the constable – and it was only that distraction that allowed me to retrieve your package from the recess. I had not prepared for how I would retrieve it. I had to take my chance only when it was presented."

His eyes held hers. Even in the moonlight she could see how troubled they were. "You did your best," she said, hoping to set his mind at rest.

"Nay!" he said sharply, making her flinch. "I did not. My best is better than that. I was unprepared. I had not thought of all the possible eventualities. It will not occur again."

She dragged her eyes away from his, and carried on walking. "But we have the pendant, and Scarhead – Ned Carter – threatens us no more."

He sighed and she saw his shoulders relax.

"There is that."

She laughed. "So all is well."

He squeezed her hand. "I suppose."

"Then let us make our way to your parents' house. I would get out of this filthy dress and into proper clothes as soon as I can."

4

CHAPTER FOUR

It was a few hours later and they were in Robert's parents' house on the edge of the town.

Robert's mother had thrown up her hands in horror at Ophelia's condition the moment they had come through the door, and rushed the girl up the stairs 'to be cleaned and scrubbed and rendered fit for society'. Robert, meanwhile, had joined his father by the fire in the main hall, giving him a brief summary of the day's events and answering questions on some of the key points.

The men looked up as the door opened and Mother came through. She stood to one side, glanced back over her shoulder, then turned to them with a smile.

"I am pleased to present the true Ophelia Williams," she announced, "who has been sadly hidden from view during the dreadful events of the past few hours." She waved her hand beyond the door. "Come child, I pray you present yourself."

There was a pause, then a rustle of silks and an elegant young woman appeared in the doorway.

For a moment Robert looked past her in order to see where Ophelia might be, before the young woman grinned at him, and his breath caught in his throat as he realised who she was.

"By Heavens," he breathed, "I can scarce believe it."

Ophelia was dressed in a dark blue gown edged with cream silk, with a cream kirtle embroidered with fine golden thread showing through at the front. On her arms were pale blue sleeves that shimmered in the firelight. At her neck was the beautiful pearl and garnet pendant, matching the pearls that hung from her ears. Her pale chestnut hair flowed in a glowing wave to her shoulders, and instead of a hood she wore a jewelled circlet pushing her hair back. Her natural beauty was enhanced with only the smallest amount of rouge on her cheeks and lips, and a line of kohl around her eyes.

She walked slowly into the room and dropped to a small curtsey before Robert's father, Andrew Wychwoode.

"I must thank you, Master Wychwoode, for your kind hospitality and protection while I wait for my own father to collect me."

"Nay, 'tis the least we could do, child," Andrew Wychwoode replied. "You are most welcome to stay as our honoured guest for as long as may be necessary." He gave a small nod of his head. "I am very pleased that my son was able to help you today in court. It has been his ambition to practise the law almost since he first learned to speak. I have always encouraged his enthusiasm, but now I am proud to see that he has some ability as well."

Robert's mother said, "Mistress Williams has been telling me that there have been further developments since the court proceedings, involving the brigand who first attacked her."

"Aye," agreed his father, "I have been hearing this from Robert also." He glanced at his son, then at Ophelia. "I understand that the brigand who planned and executed the attack was brought to God's final justice by both your efforts? Is that not so, Robert?"

There was a silence, then Andrew nudged Robert in the ribs. "By the Heavens, boy," he hissed. "Say something." A moment later he added, "And close your mouth. Would you have this young lady think you a fish?"

With an effort Robert closed his mouth and bowed his head. He looked up again and tried to take in her beauty. It felt akin to staring at the sun, and he almost had to avert his eyes before they were burned by her radiance. Was this truly the same girl who had seemed such a vagrant but a few hours past?

"That is so, Father," he muttered.

"Come child," Andrew Wychwoode said to Ophelia, "pray sit with us and tell us of your life. We know naught except your name, and the unfortunate situation that led to the events of this day. I understand Robert made out that you were trying to prevent bread from being fouled by a gull." He indicated a chair by the fire for Ophelia.

"It is true, sir," she answered, then walked to the chair – no, she floated over to it like a lovely swan. "I was so hungry after days in the forest hiding from the brigands," she continued, "that I was not in my right wits, and took the bread with no thought that I might so easily be captured. Robert was most kind," here she glanced across at him, making his stomach squeeze like it was gripped in a vice, "to offer his service, and most eloquent in my defence."

Even the way she smoothed her skirts once she was seated and folded her hands in her lap made Robert catch his breath again.

"Then it was good fortune that Robert was first able to secure your release," Andrew Wychwoode observed, as he settled in his seat and stretched his legs to the fire.

"And you have said that your father was sending you on to Cornwall with some guards," Robert's mother said as she also sat, "who it seems were also outlaws?"

"Yes, that is so," Ophelia looked across. "We were at our house in Salisbury. My father had some business in London and was then planning to spend time at our place near Penryn in Cornwall, so I went on ahead."

"You have no mother, sisters or brothers to look to your care?" asked Mistress Wychwoode.

"I have an older sister who remains in Salisbury," Ophelia answered. "And I have two brothers. Jasper is in the North, working on the King's behalf, although I know not on what business. Thomas is in Oxford in the service of the King's Secretary, Thomas Cromwell, helping to arrange a census of church properties, so that they may better be taxed."

"No mother?" Robert's father asked.

"My lady mother sadly died of the sweating sickness three years ago."

"Oh you poor lamb," Mistress Wychwoode crooned, leaning across and holding Ophelia's hand. "God's will can be such a cruel thing. I am so sorry to hear that."

"It was God's will, as you say."

"And do you cleave to the new faith, that they call Prot-estant?" asked Robert's father.

Ophelia nodded. "Aye, sir, we do," she answered. "My father says it brings him closer to God."

"I agree – we also find the same," he said. "You are lucky to have such a wise father."

"Thank you," Ophelia said. She turned and smiled at Robert. "As are you."

Robert's heart was thumping like it would burst out of his chest. That smile! The way her mouth turned up at the corners – it was absolute perfection! How had he not seen it when they had spoken for so long before? Perhaps it was because she had been so filthy... But should he not be allowing for that? If a girl is perfect, as Ophelia so clearly was, then surely one should see this despite any grime and filth? Robert had never been in the presence of such beauty before, so this was a new experience for him. Should he allow himself to think her such a perfect being, if he had missed it when she was covered in a layer of dirt rather than cosmetics? Did it mean he could not appreciate her fully? That he was not worthy of her?

"I do believe Ophelia has asked you a question, Robert."

Robert broke away from his train of thought. "I beg your pardon, Mother," he muttered.

"Should she repeat it, boy?" asked his father, with a stern-looking frown.

"Hmm," he nodded.

"I was asking if you are set on a career in the law, Master Robert?" Ophelia said softly.

"Um, yes," he answered. "As my father has said, it has long been my ambition."

"And you attend the courts whenever they sit?" she asked.

"Aye," he answered. "I would see how they work, so I may better understand the processes of the law when I begin my studies in London shortly."

She smiled. "So I have such diligence to thank for my release this day." She paused, glancing at him from the side of her eyes. "Or else they would have flogged me in public."

"Where would the justice have been in that?" asked Robert's mother. "After all you have been through?"

"And have you got word to Ophelia's father?" asked Andrew Wychwoode.

"Yes," Robert answered. "After Ophelia's release I found a fellow travelling to London and expecting to pass through Salisbury, so I gave him a short note to carry to the house of Sir Francis Williams. Ophelia says he is expected back there tomorrow, so if he gets the message at that time, we should hope to have him here two or three days later."

"I see," his father said. "So we have the pleasure of Mistress Ophelia's company for a few more days." He nodded, eyeing Robert with a small smile. "I suggest you take her for a quiet walk around our gardens, modest as they are, before we sit for supper. I will instruct one of the servants to accompany you both as a chaperone for Mistress Ophelia." He waited until Ophelia had risen and walked over to the door, before he hissed quietly at his son, "I saw you gazing at her like a moonstruck calf, boy." He paused. "Have a care. You are sixteen years, and now an adult. You need to understand what it is to act as one."

5

CHAPTER FIVE

The sound of horses clattering to a stop from the other side of the house brought Robert and Ophelia to a sudden halt; their laughter stilled and their mid-morning walk through the trees immediately forgotten.

"Belike that is your father come to collect you?" Robert observed, finding it difficult to keep the disappointment from his voice. It was hard to think that if it was indeed her father, then the few days of blissfully relaxed companionship they had enjoyed were now at an end.

Of course, he had always known that Ophelia would soon be leaving him, but he had tried to put it from his mind. As they had walked together, talked together, laughed and played together in the few days since she had come into the house and been transformed by his mother, he had allowed himself the pretence that she would be with him forever, and that all was right with the world. Indeed, if she had not been chaperoned at all times by an elderly servant with a disapproving stare called Margery, he would have been tempted to make his feelings known to her, whatever might be the consequences.

But the truth of the matter could not be denied – which was that she was always going to leave him.

And then what? Would they ever meet again? The thought that they may not made him feel sick to the base of his belly.

She stared wide-eyed at him, her lips parted.

Did she also feel the same? Did she feel the horror of their separation? Robert hoped she did, if only because it meant that maybe, just maybe, she felt the same for him as he felt for her.

Then she smiled and said, "Yes, belike it is."

As they walked away from the gardens, she fell into step beside him and slid her hand onto his forearm.

Just as a wife holds on to her husband...

They stepped onto the path running around the house to the front door and saw two men dismounting. A couple of servants were scurrying forward to take both their horses, plus a third horse on a long rein with a side-saddle.

"Ophelia!" cried one of the men. He was wearing a dusty travelling cloak; tall and aristocratic, with short-cropped hair under his cap. "The Lord be praised," he exclaimed as he came towards them. "You are safe!"

"Father," she said, dropping into a deep curtsey.

Once he had lifted her with a hand under her chin, he said, "So, Philly, where is this Master Wychwoode, who sent me the note that let me know your situation and where to find you?" He looked over at Robert. "Is it your father I seek, young sir?" he asked. "Robert Wychwoode, I believe?"

Before Robert could answer, Ophelia cut in. "Nay, Father." She grabbed his hand and led him towards her friend. "This is Robert."

Her father frowned. "You, boy?" he said. "I had expected from the tone and style of the note that it was a man who had been the author."

"It was I, sir," Robert answered, keeping his voice low and steady, as if he were already the adult Ophelia's father thought him to be.

"Indeed?" Williams looked him up and down. "I see. Then let it be so. You do seem to have an air about you that belies your tender years." He turned to Ophelia and scowled. "But I know not what has happened, beyond the brief words this young fellow wrote in his note – that can hardly be believed! That you were attacked by brigands – and also by the very scoundrels I made responsible for your protection! And then arrested for theft and vagrancy! By Heavens, Philly, is this true?" She nodded with her head bowed, and suddenly his face reddened. "Those wastrels were expressly charged with your safety, girl!" he shouted at her, almost as if it was her fault that Nick and Edmund were turncoats. Then he put his hand to the hilt of his sword. "Once again your reckless and irresponsible behaviour has put you in danger, so that I must come and take you home! This has to cease, Philly!"

"You are mistaken, sir," Robert said, stepping forward. "Mistress Williams bears no blame in any of this. Were it not for the actions of the brigands and turncoat guards; actions which were in no way her fault yet to which she must respond, she would have arrived safely in Penryn as you wanted." He clasped his hands to his overgown. "I will attest that she behaved with courage, resource and integrity throughout, and has not weakened in her resolve at any time." Williams stared at him, as if unused to a challenge such as this, least of all from a boy of sixteen. "And I would add," Robert continued, "that when in court on a charge of theft, she maintained a complete silence on her identity, specifically in order to preserve the good name of your family."

Williams continued to stare silently at him, making Robert unsure that he might have gone too far. Then Williams took a breath and moved his hand away from his sword. His face started to resume a more normal-looking colour.

"Is this true, Philly?" he growled.

"Yes Father," she replied, giving Robert a small sidelong smile.

Williams pulled thoughtfully on his beard. "Then I find I must applaud your advocacy on my daughter's behalf, young man. You make a good case for me to be more understanding of her."

"I believe she deserves it, sir," answered Robert, and was thrilled to get a silently mouthed 'thank you' from Ophelia.

"Robert volunteered his services as a lawyer in court, Father. He spoke in my defence, and it was his advocacy that got me freed from all the charges. He wants to have a career in the law."

Just then the front door opened and Andrew Wychwoode came out. He hurried over to them.

"Sir Francis Williams?" he asked, bowing and sweeping off his cap. "You are most welcome, sir. It has been such a pleasure to have your charming daughter in our house these past few days, and we will be sorry to see her go." He replaced his cap and gestured towards the house. "Pray, come in and rest awhile. Let me offer you something to eat and drink before you leave."

"Yes, and I must hear the full story, especially of the remarkable conceit argued by your son," Sir Francis answered.

"Yes, you must," replied Wychwoode. "It is quite a tale."

"As it so often is where my youngest child is concerned, for trouble follows her like the closest of shadows," said Sir Francis, his anger now seeming quite gone, almost as if it had never been there at all.

Ophelia ran to Robert and kissed him quickly on the cheek. "You are truly my protector," she whispered, then added, "although what he will say when he finds out I killed a man..." then she ran after Wychwoode and her father and went inside with them.

There was a moment of silence as Robert watched them go.

That kiss... Somehow it seemed to have robbed him of all movement.

"You do not follow them?" came a strange voice.

Robert glanced over towards the willows at the edge of the lawns, to see a figure emerging. It was the second man that had come with Williams. He was dressed all in black, and had been hidden from view by the deep shadows under the trees, no doubt silently observing all that had passed. Robert had forgotten that he was even there.

The man walked into the light, so he could now be seen in full. He looked old; older than Robert's father, which made him at least in his late forties. He had small hooded eyes set into a fleshy face above the dark brown fur collar of his gown, which Robert could now see was the only part of his clothing that was not totally black.

Robert was about to answer with a question of his own – who are you and why were you hiding in the shadows? – when their eyes met and a small shiver ran up his spine. The man gave off such an air of power and authority – and of such menace – that the words seemed to stick in his throat.

Eventually he was able to find his voice. "I will go in shortly," he said. "I just needed a moment first."

"To prepare yourself to part from such beauty," the man observed. "And it will not be easy. It pierces your heart." A statement, not a question.

Robert did not answer. How could this man know his feelings? It was not natural.

"Then you wait, take a breath and stiffen your resolve, as the girl you love transfers her loyalties back to her father, for all she frustrates him and he in turn causes her upset." The man took a step closer. "You have now observed that he is quick to anger; something I have known this many a year. His feelings rise and fall like a flame in a breeze. But for all that, he is still her father." The man gave a small shake of his head. "It is hard for you, as the girl once again becomes his de facto property, rather than the free-spirited individual you have fallen in love with." Again Robert did not respond. Was this man using some sorcery to see directly into his soul, and read what was written there as if it were the plainest book?

"You claim to know what is in my heart, sir," Robert said. "How is this so?"

"It does not take the wisdom of Solomon to know this,

boy," the man said. "You were staring at the girl with the look of a lovesick swain, and when you spoke up for her to Sir Francis Williams, you looked on him with obvious disdain. Then, when the girl gave you an affectionate peck on the cheek, it was as if you would faint on the spot. Your feelings could not have been plainer than if they had been written on parchment and called out by the town crier."

"I was not aware I was being so obvious," Robert said, trying to put a touch of the same disdain into his voice.

"Nay lad," the man answered, "and if you would be a lawyer, as I heard Ophelia say, then you must learn to control these boyish feelings." He came closer. "You are able to make a persuasive argument, as was clear when you spoke on the girl's part. But your feelings must be kept hidden from sight, so your enemies know not what you are thinking." He nodded, almost to himself. "Aye, then you have power over them, for this is the element of surprise you need for success in the law."

"And invention," Robert said sharply.

The man frowned. "I do not understand."

"I originally won the case in court by the invention of a conceit."

"Ahh." The man nodded. "I have no doubt you did. But conceit is the very basest currency of the law. Without it, we lawyers are as naught. I would expect no less."

"I will always seek to defend the innocent, and will do my utmost to ensure that the guilty are justly punished." Robert pulled himself to his full height. "But I vowed to myself that I will do this without resorting to untruths – and already I have broken this vow. I will not do so again."

"A worthy ambition, young man – but I fear such a noble ideal will be hard to maintain as you progress through your legal career."

"Why so?"

"Because life is about solving practical problems, not about maintaining high principles. Save those for Church. And for the law, be prepared to use whatever trickery is necessary. That is the only way to get any form of justice, believe me."

Robert considered the man a moment. "Then you are also a lawyer?"

"That I am. But I am more than that; I have certain responsibilities directly to our noble King Henry." The man stepped back, still holding Robert's gaze with his black eyes. "I am not only a cousin of Sir Francis Williams and his daughter Ophelia. I also have the honour to serve the King as his Lord Privy Seal and as his Principal Secretary. In truth, I was on the King's business with Sir Francis when your note was delivered."

He bowed, swept off his cap, then replaced it and stood to his full height.

"Thomas Cromwell, sir, at your service."

6

CHAPTER SIX

The Cornish sun was casting bright beams of dawn light across the narrow corridor, as Ophelia tiptoed up to the bedroom door. She knocked softly, then stood back, chewing her lower lip in excited anticipation.

There was a long silence, so she knocked again. Eventually a muffled voice came from within. "Who is it?"

"It is me, you goose," she answered. "Let me in."

The door creaked open and Robert Wychwoode's tousled head poked out. He scratched his cheek as he squinted down at her. "I was asleep," he muttered. "And it is most irregular you coming here. A girl should not be unaccompanied in a boy's room. And particularly not when that boy is a guest."

"Even when it is by the girl's great powers of persuasion that he is invited to her house?"

"Even so."

She smiled. Robert joining them on the journey west had

been very much at her own insistence. Although to be fair, once she had decided he was to come, her father and Andrew Wychwoode stood little chance against her.

So it was not only Robert who could make a compelling case if needed.

It had been when she, Sir Francis and Thomas Cromwell had mounted their horses to depart. Cousin Thomas had announced that he was not going to accompany them to Cornwall, but was going to make his way back to London on the King's business. As Ophelia had settled in her saddle and adjusted her reins, she had looked across at Robert.

He had been standing a little way off, as still as a statue. Looking at her with eyes so full of sorrow that she thought her heart would burst.

Suddenly she knew with total certainty that she was not yet ready to be parted from him.

So, ignoring her father's call that they should be away, she slipped down from her horse and walked over.

"Farewell once more, Mistress Williams," he said softly. "I shall recall our adventures and our time together with great pleasure."

"Robert, this is not right," she said fiercely.

He raised an eyebrow. "What is not right?"

"Us parting after only a few days. We need more time. To get to know each other better."

Robert's eyes crinkled as he smiled. "I would say the same for sure, Ophelia, but..."

"Then that is settled," she cut in. "We are of one mind." She nodded to confirm the point. "You will come with us to

Cornwall and be our guest for a few weeks. At least until you need to go to London and begin your studies."

"But your father..." He glanced across at Sir Francis and Thomas Cromwell, their horses skittering impatiently under them.

"He will agree."

Robert raised an eyebrow. "Without becoming enraged?"

"I will persuade him. You will see."

And she had. Her initial appeal to him as an indulgent father had been unsuccessful, so she had switched to a suggestion that Robert could act as her guardian and protector – giving her father some peace and quiet from any of her girlish pestering and wilful behaviour. This seemed to have a better effect, and he agreed to invite Robert to stay.

Her approach to Andrew Wychwoode had been more overt, and had involved the use of big eyes and even bigger smiles. The poor man had been as soft clay in her hands, and the whole thing was quickly finalised. So, after some swift packing of bags and a horse being brought out, they had all set off.

Now it was a few days later, and they were settled in the house on the hill overlooking the little harbour town of Penryn.

Ophelia hopped up and down outside Robert's chamber. "Let me in," she hissed. "Before someone sees us."

"But..." he tried again.

"Let me in!"

With a small sigh, he stood back and she scuttled into the room.

"What is it?" he asked, after he had glanced briefly out

into the corridor to check no one had observed her, then shut the door.

"The May Fair is taking place in Penryn this day, and I thought we could slip out and go." She looked up at him with wide eyes. "I have never been to the fair before, and always wanted to see what it is like. I am sure it would be such fun. I thought with you to come with me...?" She looked up at him with her most appealing look.

"But this was discussed last night at supper," he said. "You can scarcely have forgot that your father expressly forbade us from attending the fair when you asked him." He frowned, and for a moment she could see how he might look as a grown man. Strangely, she found this rather pleasing.

"I am sure he was not really serious," she answered with a brief smile.

"He seemed most serious to me," he said. "If I recall correctly, his words were, 'You are not allowed to go to the fair, Ophelia'. Did he not also add, 'under any circumstances'? And did he not also enjoin me not to allow you to go?" He frowned again, as if he could not quite understand why she did not recall what had been said only a few hours previously. "Did I mistake him?"

"Where is the harm?" she answered. "I am sixteen, and you are tall and look older than your years."

"But I am here as your father's guest, and specifically enjoined to prevent you getting into any mischief. I would not go against his express instructions, nor abuse his hospitality." Nor, she thought, risk her father's legendary sudden temper – even as a guest he was not exempt. But she kept that to herself.

"He trusts you to look to my safety."

"After you had made that suggestion." He frowned. "And after you had made me promise my own father I would take such responsibility seriously."

"Your father also thought it was good for you to come here," she observed. "He agreed it would help you learn better responsibility."

"You gave him little choice to disagree."

"He could have done so," she said.

"What, with the prettiest sixteen year old in all of Christendom fluttering her lashes at him? The poor man did not stand a chance."

"I thought he agreed most readily," she said with a small pout.

He smiled. "Aye, he had to, or he knew my mother would take him to task for encouraging such unseemly behaviour towards himself."

"And Master Cromwell – he too thought it an excellent idea," she said. "I made no such fluttering at him."

"Nay," he answered, "but that would not have had any effect on him, I warrant."

She paused. "You know he had two daughters, both lost to the sweating sickness, like my own mother? His wife also."

"No, I did not. How sad for him." He bit his lip. "And I am sorry for you as well. I should so like to have met your mother."

"As she would have wanted to meet you."

He considered her a moment. "Tell me of your mother," he said softly.

Ophelia took a couple of breaths as she looked up; seeing

not the high beamed ceiling above them, but her mother laughing and scooping her up in her arms. How to describe her? Her beauty? Her smile? Or how she made you feel like you were being wrapped in a warm, safe and secure blanket; a blanket of love and of laughter? How she was always ready to offer a word of advice or support? And always there for her youngest daughter – from baby to child to young girl?

That was until that final, fateful, dreadful day three years before, when God had decided so cruelly to take her mother away.

It was a day that had started like any other, with not the slightest indication that God had such a dreadful ending planned. Mother had been her normal, happy self in the morning, then at lunch she had started shivering as if cold and complaining of feeling unwell. Before she had even eaten a morsel, she had risen from the table and taken herself unsteadily up to bed. And then – then the unimaginable horror that night, as she was finally covered, stiff, grey and unseeing, by her sweat-soaked sheets.

Ophelia shuddered at the awful memory.

They had tried to stop her seeing the body, but she had run in and caught sight of her mother's face before they could pull the sheet up over it, and it had taken all her father could do to stop his thirteen-year-old daughter from throwing herself onto her mother's lifeless body. Eventually her oldest brother Jasper had carried her kicking and screaming away, and stayed with her until her howls and sobs had finally drifted off, leaving her in a fitful and troubled sleep.

Life had been very different from that day on.

Ophelia's older sister Cressida had marched into the

position of lady of the house, immediately assuming control. And not just of the household, but of Ophelia's life as well. Where Mother had been warm and loving, Cressida had been quite the opposite; ordering tasks to be done – and re-done when she was not satisfied. And Father had let Cressida assume such powers, taking her side when Ophelia had complained; often becoming angered when Ophelia refused some instruction or other.

Ophelia might have hoped her two brothers would offer their support, for she had always had a loving and friendly relationship with them. Especially Jasper, who would often take her to one side when she was crying over some hurt from Cressida and tell her she had to be his 'big brave girl'. Indeed it had been Jasper who had insisted she have Mother's pendant, and taken her part when Cressida had tried to take it for herself. He had made it clear if he ever found Cressida had stolen it, his action would be 'swift and decisive'. Thankfully Cressida had said no more on the matter.

But Jasper and Thomas were no longer there to look out for Ophelia, and particularly not when she had become more and more wilfully disobedient, running off to Salisbury or deciding to make her home in a stable until her absence was finally noticed. That was because both brothers had since been called away on the service of the King. It seemed that her father's cousin Thomas Cromwell was behind this, now he was in a position of such influence at Court. Thomas had joined Cromwell's service in Oxford, while Jasper had been sent up north on some business that appeared to be such a secret that no-one would tell Ophelia what it was.

Cromwell had become a regular visitor to the house in

Salisbury. He would spend hours in front of the fire in the solar room with her father, deep in discussion on matters that, like Jasper's business, young Ophelia was not allowed to know anything about. And often, when Cromwell had visited, her father had then gone away on some matter or other, staying away for many days, before coming back and resuming his life with Ophelia and Cressida as if nothing had happened.

Ophelia recognised that for her father, she was but a distraction and a nuisance to be tolerated, rather than a youngest daughter to be loved. In her mind, that was why he had allowed her to travel to Cornwall with Nick and Edmund, two almost unknown guards.

So if he cared so little for her safety, how could his insistence that she could not attend the May Fair hold any real weight?

"You were going to tell me of your mother," Robert repeated, pulling her back to the present. "But you seemed lost in thought."

She smiled. "My mother was always happy and always laughing," she said. "When she was with me, I was her little girl. Now she is gone, I must grow up, and become the woman she would have wanted me to be."

"A woman who attends the town May Fair expressly against her father's wishes?" he asked, with a cheeky smile.

"Ah yes," she agreed, "but this woman does so with a tall, protective young man. A man who would be a guardian of the law, and has already proved himself in a court and has given his word to be her own noble guardian." She raised her eyebrows. "And of course," she added, with her head on one side as she smiled at him, "if the young man in question refuses to accompany her to the fair, then he will be, of necessity, the one to explain to her father why he was not able to prevent her going alone."

7

CHAPTER SEVEN

Ophelia and Robert came to a halt at the top of the lane. The little town of Penryn appeared below them, clustered around the harbour, which had several small boats tied up to the quay. A single, much larger coastal vessel with two masts and a raised section at the rear was moored out in the wider stretch of water shimmering in the distance beyond the harbour.

But it was not the ships that held Ophelia's attention; it was the fair, spread out in the spring sunshine, and seeming to be a glorious patchwork of movement, music and fun.

"Come Robert," she said, "we should go down and join in!"

He shook his head. "We will stay here and only observe. It is not safe that we go down…" he waved vaguely at the activity below. "Down there."

"For sure it is safe," she responded with a little stamp of her foot. "We will raise no comment, for as I planned we are dressed exactly as all those people down there." Her plain brown dress had no adornments, and she had a matching brown linen coif over her hair. She glanced back at Robert; he was wearing the black woollen jerkin and dark green hose she had found for him, tucked into a pair of old black leather boots.

He turned his sharp blue eyes on hers. "That is true," he said, "but I do not need to repeat the arguments as to why we should not be here. I can only imagine your father's anger if he discovers what we have done, so I would we return now, before we are missed."

"Let us stay here a little longer and observe, as you said," she answered.

"Very well, but that is all. You have seen the fair, as you wanted. We do not go down the hill."

She nodded, deciding not to argue. Let him have his way for now; she would have hers in good time. Meanwhile, she continued to take in the sights and sounds down the hill.

Townsfolk were dancing around the maypole on the green, keeping perfect time to the music being played on the lute and whistle by a couple of men. Their movements were creating a bright weave of ribbons that worked its way downwards, as if the post was being eaten by a many-coloured snake. Circled about the pole was a ring of other townsfolk, two or three deep, who were clapping in time and cheering as the dancers moved around each other.

"See," she observed to Robert, "how charming is the maypole! The pattern is most pretty – quite beyond belief!"

"Belike," he muttered, his eyes roving across the crowds. He glanced briefly at the pole. "It is simple geometry; each person passes inside or outside the fellow coming the other way, creating the layering you see with the ribbons they hold."

She punched him lightly on the arm. "Well, I think it is pretty, even if all you see is the 'gommetry' or whatever you call it."

"Geometry."

"As you say." She looked around at the rest of the activity taking place. While some of it was spilling out into the fields beyond the town, most of it was on the green. A few tents had been erected to one side, near to a little copse of trees that separated the green from some houses. In front of one tent she could make out some mummers on a small stage, who were performing a play to a small, but appreciative crowd – to judge by the hoots and waving of arms as the mummers strode around the stage with exaggerated movements.

On the other side of the green an archery butt had been set up, and she could see men taking turns to loose off their arrows at the straw targets. Between the butt and the maypole some morris dancers were performing; the jingling of their bells lost in the wave of music and happy laughter drifting up the hill.

Some movement beyond the trees and houses caught her eye, and she pointed at a crowd who were running around in a field. "What do you suppose is happening over there?" she asked.

He squinted at the activity for a moment, following the ebb and flow of the people as they ran back and forth on the field like waves washing up and down the beach. "I believe it is a game called 'football', where the aim is to kick a pig's bladder full of air between two posts." He watched for a few more moments. "See, those on the right of the field are trying to kick the bladder between those posts on the left, and the others are trying to kick it between the posts on the right." He watched a little longer, then observed, "It looks like a disagreement has now arisen between the two sides. See, they have abandoned the bladder and are just fighting with each other."

"I do believe they are," she observed. "Belike you should go down there and see if they need the services of a lawyer to resolve their dispute?"

"I do not think that would be in their best interests," he muttered. "Or even in mine." He turned to her. "Although I appreciate your thought that I may be able to help."

Ophelia was about to respond that it had been but a light-hearted jest, when she saw he was smiling. So he had understood her jest, but responded in his own way. She put her arm through his and looked back down at the green.

The mummers had left the stage, and now there was a procession of couples dressed all in green, each stepping up and bowing to the throng, then stepping off again. "Oh!" Ophelia exclaimed, "I have heard of this – it is where Robin Hood and Maid Marian are selected by the Lord and Lady of the May." She turned to him, her eyes bright. "They then lead more dancing round the maypole! Now I insist! We must go down and see!"

She grabbed his hand and before he could resist, pulled him stumbling, tripping and protesting down the lane, until they reached the bottom and came up to the back of the crowd. Still holding his hand, she started making her way through the townsfolk towards the stage. Once they reached it, she pushed to the front for a better view.

"By Heavens," he hissed into her ear, "we must go back up the hill this instant!"

"Shh!" she responded. "You have agreed to protect me, so I would you address yourself to the task!"

"Yes, but how can I possibly do so, when you..." he tried, but she shushed him again.

"Look," she said, "they have chosen the winners!"

A fellow all in green was being pulled to the front of the stage by a man wearing a long robe and a wooden crown, while a woman in a similar crown was pulling a girl in a green robe with flower-garlanded hair forward as well.

"I give you Robin Hood and Maid Marian!" called the man, who Ophelia supposed was the Lord of May. There was a great cheer from the crowd, and some of the men threw their hats into the air. "They will be leading us in dancing at the maypole most presently!" The Robin and Marian characters held hands and bowed to the crowd, causing another great cheer to ring out.

"We are delighted to accept the honour you give us this day!" Robin called out, in a voice that was strong, although marred by a throaty rasping sound that made every word sound like a sneer. "And we would have you join us soon at the maypole!"

"What fun this is!" Ophelia said to Robert. "I thank you for agreeing to come."

"I do not think I had much say in the matter," he muttered, "but now we are here, I will submit to your will for a short while, before you accept mine, and we return home."

"Of course," she answered, but only to keep him quiet on the subject. Then she added, "although I have a hunger now, as we did not break fast before we slipped out of the house this morning. Can we not find something to eat?"

"For sure," he said, then started looking around over the heads of the crowd. "Aha," he exclaimed after a moment. "I see a gaudily coloured tent over there, where it looks like there may be food to be had." He led the way to the last tent in the row and they went inside.

As Ophelia's eyes adjusted to the gloom, she made out a table laden with pies, breads, cheeses and bowls of pottage. The smell was heavenly, with cooked meats vying with rich spices, while the strong aroma of mature cheese combined with freshly baked breads. It was enough to make her stomach leap in anticipation.

She pointed at a sumptuous-looking meat pie, set within a thick crust of pastry.

The seller followed her direction. "A farthing for two slices," he said.

Robert fished in the purse at his belt for a coin, which he handed over. They emerged again into the sunshine clutching their wedges of pie.

"Should we sit in the shade?" he asked. "The sun is becoming quite hot."

Ophelia glanced about. "How about over there?" she asked, pointing at the small copse behind the tents. "We can sit in the shade under that thick tree on the edge."

They walked over to the copse and settled themselves on the ground with their backs to the tree. Its broad branches gave them good shade, and behind the row of tents it was peaceful and quiet, with only a slight breeze in the tops of the trees and the occasional cawing of some rooks. Ophelia shuffled slightly closer to the trunk to get deeper into the shade.

Robert settled himself next to her, with one leg extended out fully and the other bent beside it.

There was a companionable silence as they both ate.

Ophelia finished her pie and was about to suggest they go back to the maypole, when there was a rustling noise from inside the copse behind them, then the sound of a twig snapping. A voice came from quite close by.

"Art certain we are quite alone?" It was a man's voice.

There was no mistaking that sneering, rasping sound; it was the fellow who had been declared the Robin Hood character.

"Yes," came another voice, which Ophelia thought sounded like the Lord of the May.

"Good. We must be brief, Jack. I will need to be back to the maypole soon, or folk will start to wonder where I am."

"Then be brief, for this is a dangerous subject we discuss. If we were to be overheard, then both our necks could be stretched."

Ophelia glanced quickly at Robert, who put his finger to his lips. She nodded, then looked down at her brown robe, then at his black jerkin and green hose. Those dark, earthy colours must have blended seamlessly into the shadows under the tree, which meant they had not been spotted.

At least not yet.

She kept as still as she could, hardly daring to breathe.

"The changes in religion by this king are beyond acceptable," Robin said, his voice making his words sound even more sinister. "If we do not act, then where will it end? The man throws aside the Pope, which is the basest heresy. Our church and our faith – and, by God, our immortal souls – are under the gravest threat, and I, for one, am not prepared to stand idly by."

"Then what is your plan?"

"There are men of Cornwall, good, worthy Catholic men, who think the same as me." There was a pause. "I have been approached by a nobleman – Sir John Bowlby – and he is raising an army. He already has upwards of two hundred men pledged as an advance party, while a larger army is being gathered to march on London."

"When does this all start?"

"At midnight tonight."

"And the meeting point?"

"The Smugglers Inn."

"Then what?"

"This monster that calls himself king must be struck off the throne, and the concubine Anne Boleyn he has falsely taken to wife must also be removed."

"And then?"

"His daughter Mary will become Queen. Her catholic nature is well known, so all the heretical acts of her monstrous father will be reversed." There was a pause. "Are you with me on this Jack? I need to know."

There was a further silence, then Robin's voice came again, now with an edge of cautious concern. "Jack? What is it? What have you seen?"

Ophelia's blood turned to ice in her veins.

She looked again at Robert's long leg, which was still

extended straight out as he sat. Was his boot visible to the man Jack? She glanced at Robert; her own fear reflected in his eyes. She flicked her gaze down at his boot, and he nodded.

Do not move! she mouthed at him.

No! he mouthed back, shaking his head. When I say, run!

"Are we not alone, Jack?" came Robin's voice, almost a whisper.

It sounded closer.

There was still no answer.

Then a hand touched Ophelia's shoulder.

She screamed, and Robert yelled "RUN!"

Ophelia leapt to her feet, forcing the hand to let go as she sprinted away round the tent. Picking up her skirts, she glanced to her side. Robert was running with her, his head down and his long hair flying out below his cap, as they headed towards where the crowd was thickest.

"Do not look back!" he yelled, "lest they see your face!"

Then they were in amongst the crowds. He grabbed her hand and started to push through. Once they were completely surrounded, he raised his head and briefly glanced back.

"They are close behind," he said, "but I think they have not seen us, as they look in all directions." He glanced down at her coif. "Is that lined?" He peeled back one corner by her ear. "Good," he pulled it off her head, punched it inside-out and pushed it back on. "Different colour." Then he pulled his own hat off. "A shame," he muttered, as he led her deeper into the crowd. "No lining." He stopped by an elderly man in an old red cap. "I like your hat, good sir," he said with a small grin. "Would you care to exchange? Mine is newer and cut from a finer cloth." Before the man could respond, he whipped the red cap off the old fellow's head and swapped it for his own. "Good day to you, sir," he said, then pulled Ophelia quickly away, leaving the man smiling as he examined his fine new cap.

A few yards further on, he suddenly turned Ophelia round, and started pulling her back the other way.

"No!" she yelped, tugging on his hand. "Not back towards them!"

He glanced round at her, his face still red from the running. "They think we go ever forward," he said. "If we circle round, we will be able to get clear. They will not think to look behind them."

Ophelia could see the sense in this, so she hurried behind him as he pushed on through.

Just as the crowd began to thin out, he came to a sudden stop. She came up beside him. He was looking back the way they had come. "I see them," he said. "They are pushing forward as I thought. Come on, quick."

They reached the food tent again, then he led her back into the copse where they had first overheard the plotters. "I recall these trees gave onto a row of houses," he said as he stepped over some roots and pushed past a branch. "Once we are in the streets of the town, we will have a clear path back to your house."

"For sure," she muttered, lifting the hem of her dress as she tried to stop it snagging on the shrubs and sticks that were in her way. She glanced up at Robert ahead, striding easily across such obstacles with his long legs. How nice it would be if she had the freedom to wear hose and boots like him!

A few minutes later she emerged into a small cobbled lane,

to find him waiting for her with his hands on his hips. "It is easy for you," she muttered, as she tried to pick a length of briar off her skirt. "You do not wear a robe that would catch on every twig."

"Nay," he answered. "But you are here now, and we must keep moving." He gestured up the lane. "We go that way to get to your house," he said as he started walking. She managed to free the briar from her robe and threw it back into the copse, then trotted after him. "And we must decide what to do with the information we have learned," he said as she caught him up. "If we are to foil this dreadful plot against God's anointed and rightful King."

8

CHAPTER EIGHT

Robert watched Sir Francis Williams stride away from where he and Ophelia were standing at one end of the Long Gallery. Sir Francis's steps reverberated like thunderclaps off the ornate plaster ceiling, making the fine porcelain vases rattle ominously on their marble plinths. Then he turned and strode back, his features set into a look of barely concealed anger. Robert thought it made each of the stern-faced ancestral portraits Sir Francis passed seem almost relaxed and happy in comparison.

"By the Lord's wounds!" Sir Francis snarled when he was before them again, his face red and his chin jutting out ominously, "I know not how to punish you, my daughter, for yet another piece of gross disobedience, and you, young Wychwoode, for abandoning your sworn duty!"

Ophelia whispered, "Robert is our guest, Father."

"He has made a promise to keep watch on you, my

daughter!" Sir Francis snapped. "And to prevent your disobedience." He stared at Ophelia. "And this is my house, where I make the rules. So if I wish to punish this boy for breaking that promise, I will do just that!"

Robert said nothing, but tried to maintain a steady gaze at the older man, while noting from the corner of his eye that Ophelia was now studying the toes of her slippers with exaggerated care.

"I accept we were perhaps a little foolhardy, sir," Robert began.

"A little?" Sir Francis exploded. "Foolhardy? I would say that barely begins to cover the matter!" He turned and walked a few strides away, then stopped and marched back up to Robert. "You have both been unseen for several hours, and then you appear dressed as common peasants and tell me that you have visited the fair, when I had made it clear – most clear – that this was not to happen! And what is more," he jabbed a finger into Robert's face to emphasise his words, "you then tell me that you had to flee from a couple of half-baked Catholics that you overheard concocting some fanciful notion to depose the King."

"As you say, sir," Robert said, "but it cannot be denied that while we were in some danger had we been caught by these men, what we learned before they became aware of our presence could be vital in order to thwart their plans."

"Plans you cannot verify, other than by a few words overheard behind a pie tent at a fair!"

"We know what we heard, sir," Robert answered, "and it seemed most real. Some plan to meet at the Smuggler's Inn at Penryn this night." He paused. "Had you been there also, I am certain you would view this threat with as much concern as we did."

Sir Francis did not reply immediately, but scowled silently while chewing on his lip. Eventually he said, "Somehow I doubt it." He took a deep breath, and Robert noted his face was starting to assume its more normal colour. "Do you know what I do to serve His Majesty, boy?" Robert shook his head. He suspected it was something of importance that involved Thomas Cromwell, but beyond that he did not know. Perhaps he was about to find out.

Sir Francis stepped back a pace. "I will tell you, boy," he said, his voice dropping to a more level tone, "and what I say must go no further, do you understand? Not even Ophelia has been told this, but as you have both heard what you think is a plot, I will let you know why I give it no credence." He nodded, as if confirming to himself what he was about to do, then said, "I have much to tell, so I suggest we sit before the fire, rather than stand here."

—o—

"The last time there was a plot coming out of Cornwall was in the reign of the late king, in the year of Our Lord fourteen ninety-seven." Sir Francis Williams began, once they were seated by the fire with glasses of wine. "It got as far as London, but the rebels were defeated at the Battle of Deptford Bridge."

"But what was the cause of their rebellion, sir?" asked Robert.

Sir Francis put his fingertips together and observed Robert

for a moment. "As you find this of interest, young man," he said, "I will tell you." He settled in his chair and took a sip of wine.

"The men of Cornwall were heavily taxed by the present king's father, Henry Tudor. Not only did he levy taxes to finance his wars with the Scots, but he also removed concessions that had been in place for nearly two hundred years on the mining of tin – a major source of Cornish income. Two men led the subsequent uprising. They were Michael Joseph, also known as An Gof, who was a blacksmith from St. Keverne, and Thomas Flamank, who was a lawyer of Bodmin. They led a force of some fifteen thousand men up through Devon, Somerset and on to London. On the way they were joined by Baron Audley, who became a leading figure in their rebellion."

"So, did they aim to depose the King?" asked Robert, imagining this column of men snaking through the countryside, full of zeal to end the reign of a king who had forcefully taken the throne himself only twelve years earlier.

"Nay, that was never their object," answered Sir Francis. "They sought mainly to restore their mining industry, and to secure the persons of King Henry's tax collectors, Cardinal Morton and Sir Reginald Bray. But after the defeat at Deptford Bridge, the leaders were executed as traitors. They were hung first, which, let me tell you is not a pretty sight. The man has the rope put about his neck, then the stool he stands on is kicked away and the rope tightens, taking all his breath..."

"Father! Please!" Ophelia exclaimed, her face going white. "I do not wish to hear such things!"

Sir Francis smiled. "Pardon, Philly," he said. "I did not mean to upset you, but these are the ways of the world, and this is what happens to traitors." He took another sip of wine. "After they were executed, these men had their heads removed and displayed on London Bridge as a warning to others."

"Father!" Ophelia yelped. "That is worse than your talk of hanging!"

Sir Francis smiled again. "Further pardons, Philly. As a young girl, it is not for you to hear how a man may meet his death."

Robert glanced at Ophelia, wondering if all this talk of a man's death had reminded her of what she had done to Scarhead. But she gave him a small wink and he smiled to himself. Her outrage was more for show; to help keep what she had done a secret from her father.

"But even after such punishment," Sir Francis continued, "we have always known that the men of Cornwall could rise again, and we have been prepared to ensure this does not happen."

"How so, sir?" asked Robert.

Sir Francis said, "Before I answer that, let me tell you of the work I do." He settled further in his chair, all trace of his earlier anger now gone. Indeed, Robert wondered if it had all been put on for show. Although he was sensible enough to know that he and Ophelia could still be in a lot of trouble.

"As you know," Sir Francis continued, "I am cousin to Thomas Cromwell, the Lord Privy Seal and King's Secretary, who was travelling with me when we heard of Ophelia's situation a few days ago. Master Cromwell has long been mindful of the threat of any new Cornish rebellion, so he has charged me with establishing a network of intelligencers in this county. I have therefore recruited men to my cause; men of the fields, those who drink in taverns and the like. They keep their eyes and their ears open and if they hear talk of sedition, it comes back to me, and thence to Master Cromwell. It is a comprehensive system that has served us well – several instances of loose or treasonous talk have been picked up, and the guilty parties brought swiftly to justice." He stared hard at Robert, "So you see, boy, if there is a rebellion stirring, with a nobleman at its head as you have told me, then I would already know of this. Believe me," he added, "if an army of even a few hundred rebels was planning to set off in only two days, this would not be news to me." He paused. "And you say these men named Sir John Bowlby as the main mover behind the plot?"

Robert nodded. "That was the name we heard, sir."

"Then all the more reason to dismiss this as fanciful nonsense. I know of this man Sir John, and have even met him on some occasions in London. I can assure you he has not a traitorous bone in his body." He sat back. "Which means, what you heard was either the fanciful chatter of a couple of malcontents, or a deliberate ploy to deceive you."

"Then why should they give us chase, father?" asked Ophelia.

"To give their conceit some form of credibility, my child."

Robert asked, "But if those who have talked of treason in the past have been brought to justice, why would you not do the same for these men we heard?" He looked at Ophelia and she nodded back her agreement. "Their words were the highest of treason in themselves."

"Robert," the older man replied with a sickly smile, "how could I possibly convict men on the testimony of two such young people as yourselves, who did not even have sight of such men at the time these words were uttered? I am sorry, for I know you have given much credence to what was said, but I repeat, they are but empty ramblings." He patted Ophelia on the knee and Robert saw her flinch slightly. "Believe me, a Cornish mouse could not make a genuine plot against the King, but I would quickly hear his squeaking."

"And you are certain these men were not plotters?" Robert asked.

"That I am." Sir Francis stood and turned his back to the fire to face them. "Indeed, the only plotters I know of just now, are you two before me. You conspired to visit the town fair against my express instructions, and for that I must issue a suitable punishment." He put his hands on his hips and glared at each of them in turn. "You can be thankful that I will not have you beaten. Instead, I have decided on this, that you will remain confined alone within these walls." He nodded. "Apart from once a day when we eat our supper together, you will each stay locked within your chambers. This will continue until I decide you have learned your lesson and are prepared to behave as I instruct."

9

CHAPTER NINE

Ophelia smiled weakly at her father as she smoothed her skirts and sat down beside him at the high table for supper that evening.

"I trust you have spent the time alone in your chambers reflecting on your situation, and are truly sorry for disobeying me in such a fashion?" he asked, as he threw a napkin over his shoulder and washed his fingers in the small silver saucer offered by a servant. "Or have you passed the time with embroidery or some such?"

"That I have, Father," she muttered as she also washed her fingers. Then she asked, "Will Robert be joining us?"

"I believe so," he answered. "I have just now sent a servant to unlock the boy's room and fetch him hither."

The door opened and Robert was ushered in. He walked up to the table with a sombre expression, then squeezed behind Ophelia and her father to get to his seat. As he passed, he put a hand on her shoulder and leaned forward. "I hope you are well, Mistress Williams," he said into her ear, loud enough for her father to hear as well.

"That I am, Master Wychwoode," she answered, trying not to gasp as she felt him pushing something down between her back and her gown. "I have been reflecting on our disobedient behaviour."

Her father nodded. "I am pleased to hear it," he observed, as Robert sat on his other side. "It gives me no pleasure to make such a punishment, but I cannot be disobeyed."

"No, Father," she said levelly, trying to subdue her rising excitement. What had Robert given her in such a clandestine manner?

The meal proceeded at a snail's pace; every set of dishes seeming to take an hour to be served, although in truth it was probably only a few minutes. Ophelia could hardly sit still; whatever it was that Robert had given her kept pressing and scratching at her back, like a kitten eager for attention. She wondered if she should feign sickness and excuse herself so she could get to the privacy of her room and see what it was, but decided it could wait just a little longer. So she smiled and made small talk with her father and Robert, while trying to contain her excitement.

When the meal was finally finished, Sir Francis Williams pushed back his chair. "You will both return to your chambers," he said. "Until the same time tomorrow."

A few minutes later, Ophelia was back in her room. As soon as she heard the key turning in the lock behind her, she ripped off her sleeves and started clawing at the lacing of her gown. Finally she managed to get herself free, so that the heavy garment fell in an ungainly heap on the floor. She lifted it up by the shoulders and shook it out, then gave a squeak of excitement when a small square of folded paper skittered away towards her clothes chest. She grabbed it and jumped up onto the bed. With her heart thumping Ophelia unfolded the paper and smoothed it across the blanket to read.

I plan to go back to Penryn this night to find those men. I must determine their plot, and prevent it if I can. I might be going into danger, and as you know, I have pledged to keep you safe – so I need you to remain here. You must raise the alarm if I am not back by morning. Burn this note once you have read it. RW.

Ophelia read and re-read the note, then threw it onto the dying embers of the fire. It sat there unaffected for an agonisingly long time, until finally a small flame started in one corner, then flared up, consuming the whole piece.

So Robert was planning to go to Penryn.

Without her!

In order to keep her safe!

How dare he leave her out of this? Did he not recognise her capabilities? That she was perfectly able to look after herself?

Ophelia went to the window and eased it open. She scanned the grounds to assure herself that he was not yet crossing on his way to the lane that led to Penryn. Then she went to one of the clothes chests by her bed. The brown dress was where she left it, together with the coif. She put them on, then arranged the bolsters under her bed covers to look like she was sleeping there; a trick she had used successfully on one of her past excursions into Salisbury. Then she hurried back to the window to keep watch.

—o—

Robert eased the corner of a blanket under his door, then used the tip of his knife to push the key from the lock, so it fell softly onto the blanket on the other side. Then he pulled the key back under the door and turned it gently, hoping it would not make any creaks or rattles.

Picking up his boots, he slipped out into the corridor in his stockinged feet, then re-locked the door. He paused to listen for any sounds or indication he had been heard. After assuring himself that all was quiet he tip-toed down the stairs, taking care to stay at the edge of each tread where creaks were less likely – although he did still test each one with his weight before committing to it.

When he got to the bottom – thankfully in silence – he gently opened another door and padded down the stairs into the kitchens. He went past the grates with their red glowing embers, then over to the back door. He lifted the latch as silently as he could, then slipped out into the herb garden.

He pulled on his boots, then paused again. The expanse of gardens lay before him, the grass looking grey in the moonlight. The distant gate which led onto the lane to Penryn was at the far end of the lawns – so he would be exposed as he ran to it. He glanced back at the house to check there were no candles alight in any of the windows to suggest someone was awake and might observe him. Apart from one window which was open, there were no lights to be seen.

The chance must be taken.

He waited until a cloud obscured the moon, then ran as fast as he could.

Arriving at the gate, he stopped, listening out for any sounds that suggested he had been seen. Thankfully, there was nothing but the trees rustling in the breeze and the distant hoot of an owl. He turned back and waited for the moon to reappear, so he could study the gate and see how it opened.

A sound came from the house.

He spun round. All was dark while the moon stayed hidden.

There it was again! A sound like a foot on gravel.

He stared hard, trying to make out any movement in the dark. Then the moon came out from behind the cloud, and he saw a figure running across the lawn towards him.

There was no mistaking who it was.

"Ophelia!" he hissed when she got to him. "What in Heaven's name are you doing?"

"I am coming too, you goose," she whispered back.

"No, you most certainly are not." He put his hands on his hips and squared up to her in the moonlight. "This might be dangerous."

"And?" She put her hands on her own hips, so they were facing each other as if in a mirror. "Have I not proved myself able to take on danger? Did I not get the better of Scarhead, not just once, but twice?"

"Belike you did, but your father was most clear..."

"Oh pshaw!" she said.

There was a silence. "Did you just say 'pshaw' to me?" he asked.

"Yes I did. And I will say it again," she replied. "Pshaw to you, Robert Wychwoode. And to my father, too. He cares not a jot for my safety. I am but a nuisance to him."

"You certainly are if you keep disobeying him," Robert said.

"And I will continue to do so, if it suits my purpose."

"By Heavens! And that purpose is…?"

"As yours, to stop the rebellion by that man Robin."

"Not his real name."

"I care not what his real name is. I just want to stop his treachery."

She raised her eyebrows, as if challenging him to come back on this, and he noted just how determined she looked in the moonlight. Still, there was no possibility of her coming with him, so he needed to end this nonsense now.

"Go back, Ophelia. I will not let you come with me," he said. "And that is final."

10

CHAPTER TEN

It was a few minutes later, and they were walking hand-in-hand along the lane into Penryn.

"I cannot believe I let you talk me into bringing you," he muttered. "I am such a fool."

"Not at all," Ophelia answered brightly, squeezing his hand to reassure him. "Most sensible."

And in truth, did he have any choice in the matter?

"Would you really have woken the whole house to say I had gone?" he asked.

"Of course. There is no sense in making a threat unless one is prepared to carry it through."

"You are quite impossible, Ophelia," he said.

"That is all part of my charm," she answered. "Which is why you enjoy my company so."

"Belike," he muttered.

"Now, pray tell, what is your plan?"

He stopped, and faced her. "We need to hear what this rebellion entails before we can do aught to stop it. We know it involves the Smuggler's Inn at the harbour, so we need to be there tonight if we are to hear anything of use. I have been thinking just now; we should claim to be a brother and sister in search of their father if anyone asks what is our purpose." Then he added, "Our father is Silas Webster. He is a sailor, which is why we seek him in such a place."

"Silas Webster? Why that name?"

"I thought it unlikely to belong to anyone known at the inn, but it still sounds plausible."

"I see. Then you are..." she was silent a moment as she thought, "...you are Remus Webster, and I am... I am Rema Webster. Father Silas lacked imagination when he named us."

"By Heavens, Ophelia," he snapped. "This is serious. It is not one of your mischievous excursions into Salisbury. We are walking into an inn where a traitorous plot is being put in motion, by people who already mean us harm."

The moon went behind a cloud again, sending them into pitch darkness.

"So, how will we find this inn?" she asked, putting the chill of the night into her voice. He was right, of course, but it was not what she liked to hear.

"I am unsure," he answered, and she breathed a sigh of relief that they were back on the mission. "Penryn is not a large place – and we know the inn is by the harbour, so I am sure we will find it soon enough."

They stumbled along the lane, until Ophelia became aware that they were now walking up quite a steep rise. If she re-called correctly from that morning, the lane opened out onto a grassy hill, where one could see the whole of Penryn spread out below, with the sea beyond.

The morning seemed so long ago. And so much had happened since – it was hard to believe it was only that a few hours since they had set off for the fair, with its coloured maypole in the bright spring sunlight...

"Lights. We can look for the lights," she suggested.

There was a pause, then his voice came out of the darkness. "The lights?"

"For sure," she answered, as the thought became clearer in her mind. "A tavern will be lit by many candles and maybe some braziers also. It should be clear to see any such inn among the poorly lit houses as we stand on the hill above the town. And it will be close to the black of the sea, where there are no lights at all."

"Yes, well, I am sure I would have thought the same when we got there," he muttered.

Ophelia stopped abruptly and let go of his hand. "Yet I thought of it and I voiced it," she pointed out. "You are not the only one with a head for planning, Robert Wychwoode."

She heard him stop also, just as the moon reappeared from behind the cloud and lit him up as a ghostly blue figure. He had his hands on his hips once more.

"I planned the gull-shit conceit that secured your release from that sheriff," he said, "as well as the ambush trick to capture the man Ned Carter, and I got away from a locked room earlier. He frowned. "Given your head for planning, I assume you have brought the knife you took from that Ned Carter fellow?"

Ophelia did not reply immediately, but tapped her foot in

annoyance. The knife! In her excitement to climb down from her window, she had quite forgotten it.

Then best to hope she would not need it.

"That is of no matter," she muttered.

"Yes it is. I would feel better if I knew you had it to defend yourself if you get into danger."

"Well, we will just have to make sure that does not happen, will we not?

"Which means our plan needs to be sound," he said. "And it is I who has come up with a plan to learn more of this treacherous rebellion," he continued, his voice sounding higher than usual, and with an edge of annoyance, "so we may demonstrate the reality of the thing to your father."

It was good that he was again worried for her safety. But that did not warrant him acting as a petulant little boy.

She glanced up at him. He still had his hands on his hips, with a scowl that suggested he was waiting for her answer.

"Such planning as yours has its place," she said, trying to get away from her forgetfulness over the knife. "But we face this danger together, so we must work together to overcome it." She paused. "You did not consider looking for the lights of the inn, and I did. You should welcome a good idea from wherever it comes, and rejoice that you associate with those who think at least as well as you do." She smiled coldly. "So I suggest you stop behaving like a spoiled child, Master Robert Wychwoode, and become the man we both need you to be this night."

Then before he could answer, she marched past him and on up the hill.

—o—

The Smuggler's Inn had been easy to spot by the bright lights spilling from the windows, as well as a brazier illuminating the hanging sign that swung lazily above the door. It was also close to a wide expanse of darkness that must be the sea. She had silently pointed it out as they stood on the top of the hill, but Robert had merely grunted his acknowledgment before striding off down to the town. She had been forced to trot along to keep pace with him.

Arriving at the inn, Robert found a shadowy side street nearby. He slipped into the darkness, pulling Ophelia in with him.

"We must be prepared before we go in," he whispered. "So, Mistress Williams, what is your scheme? Let us trust it does not require a sharp blade."

"Do not be such a goose," she hissed. "You are the one that came up with a plan, Master Webster, so let us now put it into effect."

"I see," he muttered. "So we will use mine?"

"Of course."

"Good." He nodded. "Then remember, we are the brother and sister who are looking for our father, a sailor. Nothing more."

He grabbed her hand and together they went onto the harbour. They had to stop and wait as a couple of men walked past them and clambered down a jetty onto a small rowing boat, where a number of other men were already seated. It pushed off onto the open water, then there was the sound of oars splashing as it headed out. Ophelia looked across at where it was heading. The coastal sailing ship she had spotted earlier that day was riding at anchor; its lights shimmering on the still night waters.

She turned back and saw Robert was also staring at it.

"Men rejoining their ship," he muttered. "Not unusual for a port such as this, and at this late hour."

Ophelia followed him into the Smuggler's Inn, holding her breath as they stepped into the brightly lit room. She kept her head down and avoided looking at any of the men sitting at the rough wood tables. Their combined smell was bad enough – it was fouler than a sty full of pigs.

Robert led her to a table that had two empty seats at one end, and they settled themselves beside a couple of heavy-set men in rough woollen smocks, who had been talking quietly. Ignoring their curious glances, Ophelia took her seat and put her hands demurely in her lap.

"Well met, young sir," one of the men muttered. "For all 'tis near midnight. Should you and the young mistress not be abed?"

"We seek our father," Robert answered.

The man nodded, took a swig of his ale, then asked, "And who might such a fellow be?"

"A sailing man by the name of Silas Webster," Robert answered, his voice different from its normal tone. Rougher. Coarser.

The man shook his head. "Nah," he said, "I know of no person by that name."

Ophelia let her breath out gently, as the man resumed his conversation with his companion. A serving girl came over, and Robert ordered a couple of ales.

The two men finished their drinks, then walked over to a door at the back of the room; reappearing a moment later, each with a canvas bag slung over their shoulder. Then they left through the front door. Two more men came in and sat silently in the empty seats. These two looked much like the previous ones. Ophelia was surprised to see that they did not even order drinks, but also got up after a few minutes, walked over to the room at the back, then left with similar bags.

The ales arrived and Ophelia took a tentative sip. It was nothing like the quality beer brewed by her father's servants, but not overly unpleasant. Even so she could not help wrinkling her nose as she took a longer drink.

"The young mistress likes not the ale?" asked another man, as he and a companion took the now empty seats at the table.

"My sister is unused to such drink," answered Robert. Again, Ophelia had to avoid reacting to the unusual roughness of his tone.

"Then what is your purpose here?" asked the other.

"We seek our father," answered Robert. There was a silence, so he added, "He has told us to meet him here at this hour."

The man nodded. "Then I expect he will be along soon." He looked at his companion. "Come, let us be away." Like the others, they went to the back room, re-emerged with canvas bags and left.

Ophelia watched them go. "It is curious, is it not," she whispered, "that all these men come in, stay but a few minutes, pick up bags from the room at the back, then leave hurriedly? They seem like rough fighting fellows, too."

"I had noted the same," answered Robert softly. "This must be some part of the plot." He tapped his fingers briefly on the table. "This is our best chance to find out more. I must go into that room myself and see what is in there."

Ophelia took a small sip of ale, as her mouth suddenly seemed very dry. "You are the one who talked of danger," she observed. "Is that not the highest risk? There could be men in there who are part of the plot."

"I think not," he answered. "I have heard no voices from in there. And those that go inside are out again in only the time it takes to pick out a bag." He stood up. "Stay here. I will see if I can secure one for myself, so we can determine what is within."

Before she could say anything, he marched across to the room and went inside. The door swung closed behind him.

Ophelia found she was biting her lip as she waited for him to reappear. If he was right and there was nothing but bags in there, he would be back out as quickly as all the men.

She glanced across at the door, but it remained firmly shut.

Then a couple of burly men in smocks walked over, opened the door and went in.

Ophelia bit her lip again as the door opened, but it was not Robert who walked out. It was the same two men with bags over their shoulders, talking casually to each other as they walked over to the front door.

The back room door remained shut. Should she go in? See if he was still there?

Ophelia began to realise that this was now very real. She was a sixteen-year-old girl alone in an inn full of rough fighting men. At midnight.

Even if they were not traitorous rebels, she was in the gravest danger.

With no-one to blame but herself.

She sucked in through her teeth as she stared at the door, willing it to open and Robert to reappear.

But those men had made no indication of anything amiss, which meant he was probably no longer there. Or maybe that he had quickly hidden himself when they went in?

She drummed her fingers on the table.

The door was still closed.

Now what? Should she run back home as fast as she could, and seek help? But if she left and he came out, he would find her gone and think she might be in danger.

Ophelia looked wide-eyed at the door. It remained resolutely closed.

Her bench moved as a man sat down, but she ignored him; her focus still on the room at the back.

"I thought so," came a soft voice from behind her. She shuddered as she caught a familiar rasping edge to it. "The girl who ran so swiftly from us today at the fair." A hand grabbed her wrist and forced it up her back, making her stand. "You are the girl who spied on our conversation at the fair, are you not?" he growled.

"I know nothing of this," Ophelia answered over her shoulder, trying to put some surprised indignation into her voice. "You have me confused with another."

"You think I am a fool?" he snarled. "I saw you and that tall lad in the crowd. I recognised you by the brown dress you wore then, and you still wear now. And I find you sniffing around the Smugglers at the very hour we put our plan into action – how can I think it is aught but a result of your spying?"

"That is for you to think on," she answered, "not me."

There was a silence, then she felt the chain to her pendant being pulled away from her neck. "Oh! What do we have here? Gold, I warrant?"

"Leave it!" she snarled over her shoulder, but to no effect. He pulled it some more.

"I wonder what hangs from this." She flinched as she felt his free hand flick the clasp, then the pendant was pulled off her neck.

"No!" she snapped. "Give it back!"

"I think not. A fine piece indeed. Gold and garnets, eh? Plenty of pearls as well, for all they are small. Worth a pretty penny, I warrant."

Ophelia tried to kick back at his legs, but he must have stepped aside, for she kicked only at air.

"Enough of that, or folk here will start to talk." He gave a small snigger which turned her stomach. "For all that none in here would dare to tell tales on me."

Ophelia looked desperately around the room, trying to catch the eye of any man who might come to her aid – but they were all seeming to ignore her plight, their heads turned away or carefully studying their ale. "No, you are coming with me, young mistress," the voice snarled. She winced with pain as her hand was forced higher. "And be sure, you will not be informing any man what you have seen in this inn tonight. Not now..."

There was a pause, then the voice added, "And not ever."

11

CHAPTER ELEVEN

Robert crouched down behind a pair of old barrels at the back of the room, concerned that the men who had thrown open the door and come in to collect their bags could hear his heart pounding like a blacksmith's hammer. He did not think they had spotted him, as he had leapt for cover as soon as the door had started to open.

He heard movements as bags were picked up, then after a short moment – yet one that that seemed to stretch out forever – the sound of boots thumping and the door swinging shut.

He waited until his heartbeat eased, then slowly raised his head above his hiding place.

There was no-one in the room. Opposite him the pile of bags glowed like a ghostly white mound in the candlelight.

He pulled himself to his feet and moved out from behind the barrels. With a glance at the door to make sure it was not opening again, he went over to the pile of bags, grabbed one, then dropped back into his hiding place with his prize.

The bag was about as long as his arm, wider than two hands and made of rough canvas. It was tied at the neck with a piece of rope, with the ends looped for carrying. After a brief fumble, he managed to untie the rope and ease it open.

Inside were several waxed linen packets, a drinking costrel and a piece of grey material. He shook this open and spread it out on his knee. It was a simple tabard. He turned it over; it had a black rectangle with a white cross sewn on both sides. Robert nodded to himself. The flag of Kernow – of Cornwall. These men would be fighting as Cornishmen when they attacked the King. He opened one of the linen packets to find some hard cheese and tack biscuits. Provisions. This would be each man's initial rations for their journey. He prised the stopper off the costrel and sniffed. As he suspected – watered rum.

He put everything back in the bag and re-tied the cords.

So the vessel they had seen earlier in the harbour was not just a ship going about its usual business; it was taking on an army of men this night. An army of men who each had a kit bag containing provisions and Cornish fighting colours. If that was not a suspicious plot, then Robert did not know what was.

Time to go. Time to tell Sir Francis that this plot was real; a clear and present danger from rebellious Cornishmen planning to sail around the coast and on up to London. According to the conversation he and Ophelia had overheard at the fair, this was the advance part of the force, while a larger land army was being assembled to march on the city.

He stood up, stepped round the barrels, then walked to the door. As he put his hand to the latch and was just about to turn it, it moved by itself.

He stepped back sharply. The door swung open and a single man came in.

This time there was nowhere to hide.

Robert quickly slung the bag over his shoulder and with his best confident swagger, began to stride towards the door. He caught the man's eye and gave a small nod, as if acknowledging their shared enterprise.

But the man put out a hand and stopped him.

"You seem a young lad for this venture," he growled. "Who sent you?"

Robert thought a moment. "Jack," he said in his best rough tone. It was the name used by the rasp-voiced Robin Hood to the Lord of the May at the fair.

"Jack Ingleby?"

Robert nodded. "Aye, if that is his name."

"He called me also." The man frowned. "He spoke not of a boy."

"I have a passion to end the heresy of this King," Robert replied, with what he hoped was an easy smile. "So here I am."

"Well, he will not want you in the fight," the man answered. "A lad of your years with a pike or a blade will be naught but a liability to us all." He studied Robert a moment. "And you do not have the voice of a true Cornishman. Did he say what task he has in mind for you?"

"Nay, but I am sure he will tell me in good time."

"For sure." Then the man suddenly grabbed hold of Robert's wrist, leaned across and picked up a bag with his free hand, before opening the door and pulling Robert forward. "You need someone to look out for you, lad," he said. "You can come with me."

"But, I am not..." Robert began, feeling his heart starting to thump again.

"Nay nay, 'tis no bother." The man interrupted, looking back. "A lad such as you needs a man beside him. A true man of Kernow. Come."

Robert thought quickly. Boarding the traitorous vessel was not part of his plan. How was he going to get out of this? And what was Ophelia going to do when she saw him being marched out like a prisoner? As soon as they were in the tavern, he would grab her and make a run for it.

But when they walked back into the main room of the inn and Robert looked across to where he had left Ophelia, he felt his stomach clench in even greater fear.

She was not there.

He glanced quickly around the other tables, but there was no sign of her.

"Come, lad," the man said, pulling sharply on Robert's wrist. "The tide will not wait."

All thought of running vanished from his head as the man dragged him out into the night air and across the harbour. They were headed to where another small rowing boat was tethered to a jetty, already crammed with similar fighting men. Robert looked about him with increasing panic as they walked, hoping to catch sight of Ophelia somewhere. Anywhere.

But there was no sign of her among the various sailors and men moving around the harbour.

For the first time in his life, Robert felt total despair as he was pushed down the slimy steps and into the boat. It was rocking from side to side and he nearly stumbled as he took one of the last seats.

He slumped down and stared at the black water slopping around his boots – although he was not seeing it, nor feeling the cold on his feet.

Ophelia was taken – and it was all his fault! He should never have let her come – whatever her threat. And even when she did, he should not have left her alone! What had he been thinking?

The thought of his own danger suddenly disappeared as he realised that losing her was more than he could bear. Ophelia, who he had saved from the sheriff; who had walked into the hall at his parents' house looking like absolute perfection; who had taken such delight in the simple pleasures of the May Fair, even joking about silly names on the way to Penryn – she would now be at the mercy of treacherous rebels...

Robert looked up as the oarsmen pulled the boat away from the jetty and the growing wind flicked black spray into his face.

If he ever got out of this, and he got Ophelia out as well, then he would never leave her alone again.

The hull of the coastal vessel seemed like a black cliff as they drew alongside. One of the oarsmen grabbed at a rope ladder that slapped against the wooden planks in the increasing swell. While the rowing boat knocked against the hull with the regularity of a church bell chiming, the men each chose their moment and clambered up the ladder.

When it was his turn, Robert's companion pushed him forward and Robert took hold of the wet rope.

Boarding the ship seemed the most sensible option now he was here, rather than trying to overcome the oarsmen and get away in the small rowing boat.

Or throwing himself into the water to drown, because of his inability to swim.

With luck he could decide once aboard how best to get back ashore, and then work out how to find Ophelia.

Climbing up was not easy as the ship lurched one way then the other, but he gritted his teeth, grasped the side ropes with all his strength and took care to ensure his feet were well placed on each slippery rung before committing his weight. Eventually he got to the top and clambered over the side, dropping heavily onto the deck. The other men from the rowing boat were standing by the rail beside him, clinging on as the ship moved under them.

There was a thump as his companion landed behind him, then he felt a hand on his shoulder.

"Well done, lad." Robert turned to find the man standing close behind. "You ever been at sea before?"

Robert gave a weak smile. "No, that I have not." The ship moved suddenly to one side, then sharply back again, and Robert was forced to grab at the rail to stop himself being flung onto the deck.

"Me neither." The man returned the smile as he also grasped the rail. "But it will be worth it to rid us of this ungodly king, eh?"

"Amen to that," Robert muttered, shifting his grip to make it more secure.

Just then a thick-set man strode over and stood before them, his face ghostly pale in the moonlight. "Well met, good Cornishmen all," he said. "I am Ed Carveth, and you are welcome aboard."

Robert noted how Carveth was not holding onto any part of the ship for support; instead he kept his knees bent and allowed the movement of the swell to be absorbed by them, while his upper body stayed still. Robert tried to bend his own knees, and found it seemed to help – although he kept hold of the rail for the moment.

"We have a few more men to come aboard this night," Carveth continued, "and our leader also. He will bid you all good welcome, and say some words about our venture when he arrives." He paused as a loud gust of wind blew across the deck, then added, "Meantimes, I suggest you spread out around the rail on both sides of the ship. It will not do to have the weight of you all to one side."

Robert looked across the deck and saw a space opposite. "I shall go there," he said, pointing. His companion nodded and they made their way over, supporting themselves by holding on to various bits of rigging and structures as they went, although Robert was pleased that he managed to stand unsupported for a few moments, using Carveth's soft-knee stance.

They arrived at the far rail.

"You look as you are already getting the hang of being on a ship," the man observed. "Are you sure this is your first time, lad?"

"Yes, I am sure," Robert answered. "And it is Robert... er, Rob... not 'lad'."

The man smiled. "Aye. And I am Tristam, although all men call me Tris."

"And what makes you want to join this venture, Tris?" Robert asked.

Tris didn't answer immediately; instead he gazed out across the ship to the lights of Penryn flickering in the distance. Robert looked at him, as if seeing him properly for the first time. He was a tall man, almost as tall as Robert, but with broader shoulders. He looked in his mid-twenties, with sandy hair and a hooked nose that reached almost down to his mouth. It seemed to cut his moustache neatly in two above his thick beard.

Tris turned back. "The main reason?" Robert nodded. Tris shrugged. "I am ordered to do so by Squire Linton, and through him by Sir John Bowlby, whose land I till and whose tithes I pay."

"Sir John Bowlby?" Robert asked. It was now the third time he had heard that name; first from Robin at the fair, then being dismissed as a true loyalist by Sir Francis Williams. And now from Tris, confirming that this Bowlby was indeed an instigator of the rebellion. "Is he aboard the ship?"

"Nay, he would not come aboard, for all he is indeed the owner of this vessel, The Flying Cloud. I have heard tell that his part is to raise a large army and lead them in a march on London, so we have an attack from both land and sea."

Robert nodded. So Bowlby was not just an instigator – he was the instigator; the man behind the whole enterprise, using his position to recruit men like Tris – giving them little option but to join his treasonous venture. Which made it all the more important to get off this ship and get word to Sir Francis so that Bowlby could be stopped.

But only once he had found and saved Ophelia.

"It is not only that you are ordered by your master aboard this ship?" Robert asked. "You do so willingly for your own reasons?"

"Aye." Tris's eyes glittered in the moonlight. "I have attended mass every Sunday and every holy day for all my life. I pray to the Lord for the sake of my immortal soul, and that of my wife, my little son and my baby daughter." He looked across at Penryn again. "And now I see the King's men sniffing about the Priory, and there is talk they will close it down and cast out all the holy men. And if that alone is not the devil's work, there are those that say the King has cast off his allegiance to the Pope in Rome, so that maybe soon we will not be able to hear mass anymore." He stared at Robert. "Do you know what I think of that?" Robert shook his head. "I think that means the gates of Heaven will be closed to me and I will burn for eternity, all because this godforsaken King says I must."

"So you would risk death in battle, or that of a traitor, if you fail?"

Tris shook his head. "Nay, Rob. Men of Kernow do not fail."

Robert raised an eyebrow. "Not even in the rebellion of fourteen ninety-seven?" he asked, recalling the short lecture on that subject from Ophelia's father.

Tris turned on him, with a face of thunder, "That is not true," he growled. "The men of fourteen ninety-seven did not fail – for in ten years or thereabouts, their demands were finally met. Cornish mining was restored."

"Yet that was not the only aim of the rebellion," said Robert. "As I have been told, it was also to kill or capture King Henry's tax collectors, Morton and Bray, who had been taking high taxes on his behalf to finance his wars. Those men kept their lives and the rebellion was defeated at the Battle of Deptford Bridge."

"You know much for a young lad," observed Tris, looking impressed despite his earlier outburst.

Before Robert could respond, there was a series of thumps from the far rail. Robert looked across to see a few more men clambering over the side. Then one of them leaned back over the rail and seemed to be reaching down to grasp at something. He pulled a small figure up by the arms, and onto the deck. It had a sacking hood covering its head and a large cloak obscuring its body. The man then pulled its hands behind its back and tied the wrists together. Another man appeared next, looking very like the traitor who had been declared as 'Robin', although it was hard to be sure in the moonlight. He jumped down onto the deck, before pulling the hooded figure over towards an open hatch near the steps up to the raised stern cabins. Robert narrowed his eyes. There was something familiar about the way the figure moved... Something about the height and the general shape...

He drew a sharp breath.

It was Ophelia!

Then Robin picked her up and, without a moment's pause, dropped her down the hatch and climbed down after her.

It was all Robert could do to stop himself running across the deck and leaping down the hatch – but he did stop. Assuming – nay, hoping – it had been a short distance to fall and a soft landing, then God willing she was still in one piece. So it would be best to keep his head down and bide his time until he could work out how to get her safely away. If Robin had gone to the trouble of bringing her out to the ship and taking her below, then maybe it was because he wanted her alive and in one piece. And he had put her in a hood, which was presumably as much to stop her seeing where she was as it was to stop the men on the ship realising there was a woman on board. Robert had heard of a superstition by sailors that a female on a ship was bad luck.

Robert pursed his lips. Best to keep his head down for now and decide what was to be done.

Almost immediately, a door opened from the rear cabins and it was definitely Robin who stepped out on deck again. "You are all well met, noble men of Cornwall," he called out in his rasping voice. "On our venture to rid the realm of this godless king." There was cheering from the men around the deck. "Indeed," Robin shouted above them, "God is on our side in this venture, as we fight for the true faith!" The cheering grew louder, until he held up his hand for silence. "Now I would have you all go below deck, find yourself a hammock and get good rest this night. In the morning we will sail up the coast. The following day we will dock at the port of Weymouth to take on more food and water. Meantime, I would have you come up on deck in groups of ten during the day and we will practise combat in preparation for our glorious victory when we arrive in London!"

When the cheering that followed this speech had died down and Robin had gone back inside, Tris put his hand on

Robert's arm. "Come lad," he said, "let us find a hammock each and get our rest, as the man has said."

Together they headed over to a hatch at the bow, and filed down into the darkness.

1 2

CHAPTER TWELVE

Ophelia shuffled backwards on her bottom in the darkness, and immediately bumped into something smooth, hard and curved. A barrel?

The whole room lurched suddenly, slamming her head onto the object and causing stars to appear in the blackness.

The room lurched back again, and this time she leaned her head forward, so that the next movement caught her on the shoulder blades. It still hurt, but much less than before and without the stars.

By Heavens, how had it come to this? To be bound and hooded, and thrown into some prison full of painfully hard objects on board a ship? To be transported to who knew where? Certainly further and further from Penryn.

And from Father. Not that he would particularly miss her.

She growled to herself in her frustration. How vexing for a girl to be so unappreciated by her own father! He would be angry of course, but as ever, it would be anger at her disobedience rather than because she might be in any danger. For she was in grave danger – of that there was no doubt.

And it was all her own silly fault! How stupid could a girl be, to put herself in such a situation?

Robert had been most clear when he told her how desperate these men were. "This is not one of your mischievous excursions into Salisbury," he had said. "We are walking into an inn where a traitorous plot is being put in motion, by people who already mean us harm."

Well, Robert had not been mistaken. The danger was real. So when the man she thought of as 'Robin' had sat down beside her at the table and spoken in that grating voice of his, she had been truly terrified.

But then he had forced her arm up her back and made her stand.

And stolen her pendant.

Ophelia felt a cold chill that was nothing to do with the thin brown linen dress she was wearing.

Robin had then marched her out of the inn and over to another small building, before forcing her into a room full of sails and ropes that smelled of mustiness and rat droppings.

He had thrown her down onto a pile of sails and stood over her. While she lay back beneath him, he had started to run his hand up and down her legs through her dress – first one leg then then the other. With a look of grim concentration he patted her upper thighs, inside and out, then moved down to her calves. Ophelia was initially too shocked to react, then she gave a small yelp and hissed, "What are you doing?"

He finished and stood back a couple of paces. "Good," he

said, "you have no knife or other weapon concealed about you. Which would have been the worse for you if you had."

"I am but a girl," she answered, breathing a silent prayer of thanks that she had forgotten the knife. "Not a spy."

"Even a girl can be such a thing." He took a step closer. "Who do you work for?" he demanded.

She said nothing, staring up at him in sullen defiance.

"Tell me!" he snarled. "Or it will be the worse for you."

"I do not answer to a thieving dog like you." She tried to kick her leg upwards towards his crotch, but had little space to move and the kick landed with poor force on his shin.

"Think you to try and unman me, you little bitch?" he snapped.

"I would if you were a man in the first place."

He leaned forward and suddenly she felt as if her head had exploded, as he hit her across the side of her face with his open hand. "Silence, girl!" he shouted. "I will not have you answer me that way!"

Ophelia did not respond immediately. Instead she brought her hand up to her cheek and held it there to try and stop the pain that radiated around her jaw. "You would strike me?" she whispered. "My father shall hear of this."

"I care not if your father is Cromwell himself." Robin snorted. "You will tell me what I need to know, or I can assure you, you will not leave this place alive."

"The King's Secretary Cromwell is my cousin," Ophelia heard herself saying. "And he shall also learn of this."

Robin stood back, and she could see in the dim light that he was frowning; his mouth working as he considered what she had said. "Is that so?" he said. "Then you are a well-connected young bitch, are you not?" He tapped his fingers against his thigh. "Belike your father is one Sir Francis Williams? Cromwell's man here in Cornwall? So that is who you work for."

Realising she may have given too much away already, Ophelia just nodded.

Robin laughed. "By Heaven, we made every effort to keep the man unaware of our plans, and it is his child who has uncovered our secret!"

"You kept him unaware?" Ophelia asked, curious to know how her father's seemingly solid ring of intelligencers and informers had been broken. "How?"

Robin smiled thinly. "Oh, it was not difficult. The man who has instigated our rebellion has met your father on occasions and gained his confidence, such that your father has grown quite careless with his talk. So our leader has known for some time who your father's informers are, and we have made sure they were kept well away from any talk of our plans." He nodded, seeming pleased with himself, and it was almost as if he wanted to boast to her how he had outwitted her father. "The man is a fool if he thinks he can better us. We were always ahead of him."

"Then he will be sure to change his ways when I tell him."

Robin laughed again. "Oh, no, mistress," he said. "You are not going home this night, believe me." He paused, staring at her. "The good news for you is that I will not kill you here as I planned, for now I know who you are, you are more use to me alive than dead. I will take you with me to London as my hostage, and if we fall foul of Cromwell's men, and you are indeed his cousin, then you will be a valued bargaining counter for our freedom."

He took hold of her arm, then picked up some rope and pulled her wrists together behind her back. "Let us be sure you will not run away," he muttered, as he tied her hands together. Then he secured the free end of the rope to a roof beam, while he rummaged around the store for something. "Yes, this will do," he said, shaking a small sail out of a canvas bag, then coming over. "We will put this on you so the sailing men do not see you and invoke their foolish superstitions about a woman on a ship being bad luck." He put the bag over her head and immediately everything went black. She tried not to gag at the smell of musty canvas and seawater as he used the bag's own rope ties to secure it round her neck.

"You will wear my cloak to help hide the shape of your body," he muttered. She felt it being thrown over her shoulders, before her hands were pulled out behind her, and she found herself stumbling out backwards after him.

And then he had brought her onto this vessel, thrown her carelessly down a hatch and cast her into this cupboard or store, or whatever it was.

She decided it would help if she had a picture in her mind of the space she was in.

So there was a barrel; a hard one that had hurt her head most painfully when she had hit against it.

Trying to work with the movements of the ship, she made her way round in what she thought was the opposite direction to the barrel, then inched across the rough boards. Almost immediately she came up against something flat and smooth, but which moved slightly as she slammed against it with the next lurch of the ship. A door. She pushed against it, but it moved no more than an inch. Locked, of course.

She kicked forward with her outstretched legs, but did not need to stretch them far before she felt the barrel once again. She moved her legs to the left, and almost immediately came up against another object; something tall, square and smooth. As she felt it with her leg it vibrated, then there was the sound like a chain moving inside.

Ophelia grunted to herself. So she had been thrown into a tiny room; her hands still bound behind her back, the hood still on her head, while the ship tossed her about like a pea in a drum. This revelation made her feel nauseous, and every subsequent movement of the ship made her feel as if she was about to retch into the hood.

A sharp pain in her knee made her wince – her nausea briefly forgotten.

That must have been when she had fallen forward at the bottom of the hatch after Robin had thrown her into empty space. The memory of falling without knowing how soon she would land – and if it would break her legs at the very least – made her want to blaspheme the Lord in her anger. It made her vow that if she had a chance to make that thieving Robin pay, then that was what she would do.

The vile man had stolen her pendant! Ophelia balled her fist in frustration. Look at what had happened to the last man who had tried to take it! How would it be to push a hot poker into Robin, just as he had pushed her into this place without a word, ignoring her muffled pleas to have the hood removed?

Well, she would soon see about that.

With her back against the door, she dropped her hands down, then clenched her teeth as she started wriggling them under her bottom. Once they had reached the underside of her thighs, she moved round until she was parallel to the door. Then she lifted her feet so they were pointing straight up and worked her hands further along under her legs. Eventually she reached her ankles, then, with a small cry of triumph, she passed the rope under her feet.

Now she had her hands in front of her body, she was able to get them up to the knot securing the hood, and after some fevered fumbling between movements of the ship, she undid the knot and pulled the base of the hood open. Then she eased it up over her face – until it fell off behind her and she could look around.

Unfortunately there was very little change in the darkness. The only light was coming from under the door, and that was very dim. She peered around her space while trying to rub away the pain in her knee, seeing if she could make anything out. Maybe there might be a store box with some form of blade inside so she could free her wrists? As her eyes grew more accustomed to the low light, she made out that there was nothing in the room other than two barrels, some rope coils in the corner, and a few unstoppered pottery jars.

She shuffled across to the jars, picked one up and shook it. It was empty.

She struggled to her feet and leaned across to grab one of the barrels as the ship tried to throw her backwards. It had a large cork bung in the top. She winkled it free and cautiously sniffed the contents, then recoiled at the acrid, oily smell. She recognised it from when some men had been repairing the roof of the stable at their Salisbury home. Pitch.

She worked her way across to the second barrel. This one was different; a sulphurous smell of rotten eggs that made her feel immediately unwell.

She quickly replaced the stopper and staggered over to the smooth column. She grabbed it with her hands, and again she felt the vibrations, with the sound of a chain moving inside. What could it be? The chain sound came again, and almost immediately the ship lurched to the right.

So there was a chain that moved, followed by change of direction in the ship. Ophelia thought back to the pictures she had seen of ships as a young girl. Was there not a man at the back who turned a great wheel to steer it? Then perhaps the wheel was connected to a chain – and she was directly below it!

Feeling strangely pleased with herself for working this out, she shuffled back to the door again, then sat with her back to it.

The feeling of nausea re-appeared, and she swallowed a few times to stop herself being sick.

"Ophelia Williams," she said aloud, and it felt good to hear her voice. "You may have been clever about the wheel, but this is no time to feel pity for yourself. Maybe Robert has gone to get help. Maybe he has already alerted Father, and he rides even now to your rescue." She thought a moment, then grimaced. "Or maybe Robert really was taken in that room as you thought, and he is even now another captive." She shook her head. "No. He is brave and resourceful, and if Father is not coming to my aid, then Robert will."

She rubbed her knee again, helping to ease the pain just a little.

So now she was being tossed about as a hostage in a small storeroom at sea; her stomach churning with the movement of the ship.

And with fear for her fate. "Come now, Robert Wychwoode," she said aloud. "You have saved my life once before; now I need you more than ever." She stared round at her dim, moving prison. "I am sorry for tricking you into letting me come on this venture, but I need you."

The ship gave another lurch. "I need you to come and save me once again."

13

CHAPTER THIRTEEN

Robert lay back in his hammock, his hands behind his head as he stared up at the dark beam above him. Sleep was, of course, quite out of the question; not only were the snores and grunts of the men around him as loud as the howling wind and creaking timbers, but the hammock was unable to absorb all the sharp movements of the ship, which meant he was constantly being swung one way then the other. Not that any of this had stopped Tris from sleeping; his snores from nearby were some of the loudest of all.

Then there was the dreadfulness of his predicament.

It was bad enough that he had been pressed into an army of men embarked on a treacherous rebellion, and could there-fore end up with either a pike in his guts or hanging from a noose. But he felt sick to his stomach at the thought that he had also caused Ophelia to be in the same predicament and a captive somewhere on the ship. If only he had not written that note; then she would never have followed him. Even now she would be safely asleep in her chambers.

He moved his hands down and gripped the sides of the hammock. No – he was Robert Wychwoode, an aspiring lawyer and consummate planner. He had got Ophelia into this, so he would have to find a way to get her out of it.

But how? Even if he could find her and free her, how could a boy and a girl alone stop a ship full of armed fighting men?

One step at a time. First, he had to concentrate on finding and freeing Ophelia.

Robert smiled to himself in the dark. She had challenged him to let her make plans as well – so yes, he would give her just such an opportunity. He would find her and together they would work out a way to get safely off the ship.

But how to find her? He could hardly just wander around below decks calling her name. That would be of the highest risk, in case he called at a door that was not concealing Ophelia, but instead held Jack or Robin.

Robin. A vile man with the most unpleasant voice, coming out of the cabins and giving his traitorous speech.

Robert took a sharp breath.

Had Robin not reappeared almost immediately after throwing Ophelia down the hatch? He would scarcely have had time to walk the length of the ship below decks and back.

So that must mean the place where he was holding her was likely very close to the hatch itself.

Robert nodded to himself. That was good thinking; it meant he had narrowed her whereabouts down to one section of the ship.

How to narrow it further? What would be an indicator of

exactly where she was held? They would not bring her out of such a place, for fear she would scare the sailing men with her very presence, so they would keep her locked away until they needed her for whatever was their purpose. That meant she would not eat with the men, but instead would have her food brought to her...

Her food!

Some fellow would need to bring her food! So all Robert had to do was follow any person carrying provisions such as for a prisoner, and see where he went!

Which would mean being in the right place at the right time to observe this man... He sighed. A small chance indeed.

But it was the best that he could do.

Resolving to find a way to loiter near the hatch the next day, and at a time when they would most likely be bringing Ophelia something to eat, Robert put his hands back behind his head, and started to empty his mind for sleep.

—o—

Ophelia smiled at Robert as she put her arms around his neck, then closed her eyes as she leaned forward and opened her mouth.

Robert thought his heart would burst as he smelled the sweet scent of her breath. But when their mouths came to-gether and he savoured the softness of her lips and the gentle caress of her tongue, he thought he was wrong – his heart had burst already and he must now be in Heaven.

After what seemed like an age, she gently pulled away, then smiled up at him again.

Her mouth moved and she whispered something – but he couldn't catch it. Perhaps it was a declaration of love? He needed to know for sure.

"What say you?" he asked. "I heard it not."

Then she did something quite unexpected. With a deep, manly voice that was wholly unlike her own, she said, "Get up, you lazy dog!" and punched him in the shoulder.

"Nay," he answered, puzzled as to why she should behave so. "I would know what you said just now."

She frowned. "I said, get up, you lazy young dog! We must go on deck this instant!"

Then she started to disappear from view, as if being pulled sharply away by a rope down a long dark tunnel.

"No!" Robert cried out. "Come back!" But she was gone, leaving only a whistling wind and creaking of timbers as she became but a small dot in the distance.

He opened his eyes to see Tris standing over his hammock.

"Come on, we must be up and on deck for training," Tris said. "I could not leave you sleeping like a babe and smiling as if a soft-headed fool. Although you did give a shout just now. Were you dreaming?"

Robert shook his head. "Nay," he muttered, as he swung out of the hammock and dropped to the deck. "I was not. Let us be away."

They climbed the ladder and emerged into the bright sunlight.

Robert glanced briefly around, the last dregs of sleep being cleared from his head by the fresh wind that was blowing in from the open sea. Small, fluffy clouds dotted the blue sky, and although there was a wind, it was nowhere near as strong as the night before. The ship was under full sail, rising to meet each small wave like an eager puppy jumping for a stick, before lowering its nose for the next. Men were pulling on ropes and scurrying up and down the rigging, while a broad-shouldered fellow was holding on to the ship's wheel with bunched muscles and a red face.

On one side was the open sea, stretching away to the far horizon where it merged into the blue sky. On the other was the coastline; looking much the same, except that it seemed as if someone had taken a piece of charcoal and drawn a thick dark line between the two.

The hatch they had come up was in the centre of the ship's deck, just forward of the main mast. The one that Ophelia had been thrown down was further backward, with the hatch itself lying open on the deck.

"Come, lad," Tris said. "Stop gazing about like an idiot. We are bidden to train for combat. You should take part, in case you are indeed called on to fight."

Robert followed Tris across the deck, bending his knees as he had learned the night before to absorb the regular movements of the ship. A few men were gathered on the deck not far from Ophelia's hatch, and he made sure he was at the end of the line nearest the opening.

Ed Carveth was standing facing them, holding some pikes under one arm and a couple of cutlass swords in his other hand. Now he was seeing the man in daylight, Robert noticed he had an angry red scar running down one side of his face. "Come, now," Carveth barked. "Draw closer." As the line shuffled together, Robert glanced over at the hatch. It was hard to see into it from where he stood, but he did get a brief impression that there was a corridor running below it.

If only he could get closer for a proper look!

Then he narrowed his eyes as a plan started to form itself…

Maybe there was indeed a way he could get down there…

"You, lad!" Carveth snapped. "Close up and pay attention!"

Robert moved up to the line, and saw he was standing beside Tris.

"Now, to business." Carveth began. "I am the one that will have you trained and ready for the fight to come." He scratched at the scar on his cheek as he scowled at each of them in turn. "I care little where you come from. I care even less whether you have a trade or if you till the land. I care not at all if you have wives and children at home. All I care about is that you are fighting men under my command. We work together and we battle together to rid the land of this heretic king. Are you with me?"

There were nods and grunts of agreement down the line. "I heard you not," Carveth said. Then he raised his voice. "I say again, are you with me?"

"Yes!" the men shouted back. "We are with you!"

Carveth gave a small smile that moved only the unscarred side of his face. "Good. Then know this. I will school you and shape you, so that we come before the heretic's troops as a single body of men. We will be well trained and well disciplined." He held one of the pikes forward. "You will be equipped with one of these."

Robert did not think he had ever actually seen such a weapon up close before. It was a wooden pole, about eight feet long, with a wicked-looking barbed metal point at the tip. "You have all been trained on its use?" Carveth asked. Everyone except Robert nodded and grunted agreement.

"You, lad?"

"No sir."

Carveth scratched slowly at his scar. "I see. For sure, I have not the time nor have I the mind to hold up these men while I train you alone, young lad. You can step aside for now, and I will talk with Master Ingleby. We will see if we can determine some other use for you."

"As I said," Tris muttered from the side of his mouth.

Now the plan was fully formed – and here was the ideal opportunity to put it into action...

Robert nodded and took a couple of steps away from Tris. Then he waited a moment to time his next move. As the ship pitched up to a wave he staggered forward slightly, as if losing his balance. Then, as it pitched down again, he stumbled a few paces back with a look of shock on his face. It was artfully done, and only someone observing his soft knees would have spotted that his moves were quite deliberate. But everyone was looking at his shocked expression, which became a look of surprised horror as he stepped back into the hatch and disappeared down into the void.

After he had dropped softly to his feet, Robert took quick stock of his surroundings. He was indeed in a corridor, lit by a single oil lantern swinging on a bracket on one wall. A thick wooden ladder ran down from the hatch to the floor, with a small space behind that was deep in shadow. There was no time to look further, before he had to make his next move. He turned his back to the nearest wall and sat against it. Then he stuck one leg out so it was in the pool of light from the open hatch, and grasped his ankle firmly with both hands.

Almost immediately a couple of heads appeared silhouetted at the hatch. From the shape of them it was Carveth and Tris.

"By Heaven, lad, that was unfortunate," Tris said. "Art hurt?"

Robert grimaced up at them. "I think I have twisted it," he said. "I landed hard upon it."

"Can you move?" asked Carveth.

Robert felt his ankle, then winced. "Nay," he muttered.

"Belike it is broken?" This was Tris.

Robert felt it again and gave another gasp, as if in pain. Then he looked up and smiled weakly. "I think not."

"Stay as you are for a time, until you are able to move," Carveth ordered. "And be sure to keep out of the way if any man needs to pass," he added.

Robert waited until the heads had disappeared, then permitted himself a small smile of triumph. Once again a Wychwoode plan had worked!

Although it was yet one more nail in the coffin of his quest to uphold the truth.

With a sigh, he crawled across the corridor to the ladder and wriggled into the dark space behind, where he could hide deep in the shadows unseen. With luck, some food would be brought to Ophelia soon, and he could determine where she was being held.

Robert settled against the wall and prepared for his vigil.

14

CHAPTER FOURTEEN

Sir Francis Williams sat impassively behind his desk as his informant was ushered in. Wordlessly he indicated a chair before the desk, but the man – a small, blond fellow with a thin, straggly beard and tousled hair escaping from under his cap – remained standing.

"Well?" Sir Francis asked. "What do you have to report that is so pressing that it could not wait?"

The man took his cap off and twisted it in both hands, as if it was wet and he was wringing it out. Indeed, Sir Francis noted how the fellow was sweating so profusely that perhaps there would be some liquid expelled all over his fine Persian rug. Forcing himself to look the fellow in the face, he repeated his demand. "Well Jago? What have you to say?"

"For sure, Sir Francis," the man called Jago said as he put his cap back on. "You asked me to report anything of suspicion, and that I must." He pinched his beard and pulled at it a moment. This seemed to give himself the confidence to continue. "It appears that overnight half the menfolk of Penryn and the surrounding villages have... just disappeared."

"Disappeared?" Sir Francis repeated, not sure he had heard correctly.

"Aye, sir, that they have. Gone sir. The womenfolk and the older men are tight-lipped on the matter, and none will tell me aught, but from what I can understand, two or three hundred men have... well – gone." He paused. "Fishing boats lie idle, sir, forges are cooling, and flour remains un-ground. The men are just up and away, sir – that is the truth of it."

"What age of men?" Sir Francis asked. "You indicated it was the older men left behind?"

"Aye, sir. Those that are gone are of fighting age, if that is what you mean."

Sir Francis felt his heart sink. Was this a militia being mobilised for some traitorous purpose? No – surely not! If it was, he would have heard – no man had a finer circle of informers than he. It was as he said to Philly and the Wychwoode boy; if any rebellious action was being planned, it would not escape his notice.

Philly and Wychwoode! They had been so sure they had heard some men at the May Fair concocting a plot to depose the King, but he had dismissed their wild imaginings.

Except that they had been so convinced – what if there was some truth to it? What if somehow a plot had been actioned without any of his men hearing? What if youngsters had been the ones to discover what his men had missed?

Sir Francis frowned. Where was it they said the plotters were to meet? He searched his memory, then nodded to himself. The Smuggler's Inn, was it not? He knew of it; a base, ramshackle establishment by the harbour frequented mainly by sailors.

Sailors – who put to sea...

Sir Francis looked up at Jago. "Men do not just disappear. Belike they boarded a ship? Have any ships put to sea this day?"

Jago pulled his beard a little more, then said, "Aye sir. I made some enquiries to that effect, and have discovered that The Flying Cloud, a coastal vessel, was put to sea in the early hours of this morning."

"The Flying Cloud? I have heard of her; she is one of Sir John Bowlby's ships. And I assume she is capable of carrying that number of men?"

"That she is, sir."

Sir Francis drummed his fingers on the desk a moment. "Thank you, Jago," he said with a thin smile, "you have done well. You may go, but please keep your ears and eyes open for any further intelligence on this matter."

Jago nodded his head and scuttled out.

Sir Francis sat back and pressed his fingers together.

Sir John Bowlby? Could he truly be behind a plot? It could scarce be believed.

But if so, and there was indeed a plot of some colour; it was one that had somehow escaped the notice of his intelligencers. But not his feisty daughter and young Wychwoode! They had somehow heard the basis of it while disobeying his strict orders and attending the fair. Well, perhaps their disobedience was in truth his own good fortune!

Sir Francis stood up and walked to the door. It was now

clear that the girl and boy were being punished without good reason, so must be released.

—o—

Sir Francis stood back from Ophelia's bed and stared silently at the vaguely body-shaped line of bolsters revealed when he had pulled back the blankets. Damn the girl! How had she got away from a locked room? And where had she disappeared to? He glanced at the window. It was pushed closed but not locked. Had she escaped that way? He went over and pushed it open. The ivy leading down from the window to the ground was partly pulled from the wall.

With a series of ever-stronger curses muttered under his breath, he marched down the corridor to the boy's chamber. The key was in the lock – so for sure he was still inside?

Sadly not. There was no boy there, and when he pulled back the bed curtains it was clear that nobody had even slept there that night.

"By the Lord's Wounds!" he shouted as he threw the curtains back. "These confounded children!" He paused a moment. The two of them must have gone down to Penryn and observed the men departing from the Smuggler's Inn, then boarding The Flying Cloud. But surely once the ship had weighed anchor and set sail they would have come swiftly back to report on their findings? No doubt Ophelia would be wanting to show her father just how deeply he had been mistaken? He could imagine her triumphant and cheeky smile as she told him what had passed.

But The Flying Cloud had sailed many hours ago, so why were his daughter and the boy not back already?

"By Heavens!" he said aloud. "They are taken! They are on that godforsaken ship!" Then another thought occurred. "My daughter at the mercy of a group of brigands! In the gravest danger of her life!" His eyes widened. "Or at the very least her honour!" He took a couple of short, sharp breaths. "By Christ, young Wychwoode, what have you got her into?" But in his heart he knew there was every chance that it was as much Ophelia's doing – that it was the wilful young woman who had dragged the poor boy along. But at least they were together. Probably. "You had better look to her safety, boy," he muttered, "for if any harm befalls her, by all that is holy, I will hold you responsible."

Sir Francis stamped down the stairs back to his study. Once inside he headed straight for his shelves, turning over papers and throwing neat stacks of documents onto the floor as he searched for something.

"Aha! Here it is!" He held up a large folded paper. He took it to his desk and spread it out; a map of the southern and western counties of England. He put his finger to Penryn. "A day's sailing," he muttered, as he traced it across open water to Salcombe, then on up the coast. "It is a coastal vessel full of additional men. They will need to put into a port in a day or so for provisions. Where might they first put in?" His finger stopped further up the Dorset coast. "Bridport? No, too soon. Swanage? Bournemouth? Maybe too far? Weymouth? Possibly. He looked out of the window at the trees swaying in the summer breeze, but in truth he was seeing Ophelia's fair face smiling up at him; laughing as he swung her around playfully as a small child; holding out some flowers for him that she had picked specially; looking solemn as they prayed for the soul of her dear departed mother...

"Weymouth, it is," he said. "If that is where I can find my wayward daughter. It's as good a place to head for as any other."

Sir Francis picked up a small bell and rang it. After a minute or two a small woman in a black dress and a white cap came in.

"Joan, get me Simon, if you would."

She nodded and left. A few moments later a young man with sandy hair put his head round the door. Sir Francis looked up from the map, "Simon? Good. I need a note taking to London with the utmost haste."

"London, Sir Francis? If I ride hard and change horses at Fleet, I can be there in a day."

"Good." Sir Francis pushed the map to one side, reaching for a piece of paper and his quill. He scratched out a short note, then blotted and folded it, sealed it with hot wax and pressed it with his signet ring. "Take this to Master Cromwell, who you will find in the Palace of Whitehall." He held it out to Simon. "His hand and no other – you understand?"

Simon took it and put it carefully into a small leather satchel hanging from his shoulder. He nodded. "Yes, Sir Francis."

"And I would have you wait for Master Cromwell's response, then bring it to me with the same haste. I shall be heading for Weymouth. Look for me there. I will most probably be at the harbour."

Simon nodded. "Very good, Sir Francis," he said, then marched out.

Sir Francis rang the bell again. After a moment, the woman came back in. "Yes, sir?"

"Joan, please have my horse made ready and a satchel with provisions for a half-day's ride. But I may be away a few days."

Indeed, Master?" Joan asked. "Shall I allow Mistress Ophelia and Master Wychwoode out?"

Sir Francis took a deep breath. "They are escaped, Joan." Her eyes widened and she put a hand to her mouth. "I am riding out to find them," he added.

"Then may God go with you, sir," she replied. "And help you find them with good speed!"

He nodded as she hurried out. "By Heavens, Philly," he said as he stared again at the trees outside. "Once again I must look to your safety, you wilful child!"

15

CHAPTER FIFTEEN

Ophelia sat with her back to the door and stared into the darkness, bracing herself with her feet against the movement of the ship.

Her stomach was settled now; she no longer felt as if the constant motion was about to make her violently sick, although it had been a close call for the first few hours of her imprisonment. She had even been able to sleep a while, and guessed it was now a new day. Not that she had any way of telling in the darkness, other than the level of hunger gnawing at her belly.

Of course, she would not have had such a hunger if she and Robert had remained at home, safe from rough-voiced rogues bent on overthrowing God's anointed King. Securely locked in their rooms with nothing more pressing to concern them than how soon they would be called down to eat...

To eat! What would they be offered? Roasted meats. Crisp vegetables. Fine puddings...

Ophelia's mouth actually started to water at the thought.

Do not think of food! Father will have to dine alone this day...

Father! What of him?

Ophelia bit her lip. How would her father react when the servants came down and told him that both she and Robert were gone? In truth, it did not take a soothsayer to know how great would be his anger at this news...

But then, would he reflect on why they had gone? Would he wonder why they had been so sure that the plot was taking place, that they must do something about it? Would he understand that their motives were good – for all they had disobeyed his orders? That on occasions, it was best to do what was right, not what one was told?

She sighed. No – Father was so sure that the reports of his intelligencers were correct, that he would not accept there was even a plot in existence.

Well, he would find out soon enough, one way or another. Either she would tell him, or...

...Or sweet Jesus! He would not hear it from them, for they would have failed to stop it and would have perished in the attempt...

Then again, would he even care?

Ophelia grimaced in the darkness. For sure he would not care. Indeed he would most likely be pleased that the thorn in his side that was his wayward daughter Ophelia was no longer there to trouble him.

Now she felt sick again.

There was a thump on the door.

"Stand aside, Mistress Williams," barked a voice.

She struggled to her feet and went to stand by the barrel. There was the sound of the bolt being drawn, then the door opened and Robin came in. He was holding something before him. In the dim light of the doorway, she could just see it was a wooden platter with what looked like a hunk of bread, a piece of cheese and a large beaker of some sort.

"I see you have removed the hood," he observed. "Very well – you have saved me the bother of doing it myself so you can eat." He put the platter down on top of the barrel. "But know this – I will make sure it is back on your head when I bring you ashore."

"What do you want from me?" she asked in what she hoped sounded her most confident voice.

He shook his head. "That is none of your concern right now." He went to the door, then turned back. "Just be thankful I do not put you to death, but I keep you fed and watered, for all I hold you secure as my hostage." He paused. "I will even release your hands. Although," he added, "I will be quick to change my mind if you do aught untoward," She held out her hands and he undid the bonds. Then he went out and closed the door. She heard the bolt being pushed across again as she rubbed her wrists to restore the circulation.

Ophelia stared at the shape of the platter in the nearly total darkness. It was certainly no feast – but given how hungry she was, it would have to do. She took a small bite of the bread, then the cheese. Both were almost completely tasteless, but she ate them anyway, then took a sip of the liquid in the beaker. It was a foul-tasting ale, so she drank only enough to wet her mouth.

When she had finished, she felt her way back to the door and slumped down again with her back to it.

What was it to be held a hostage? She had no real idea what that meant, but guessed from what Robin had said earlier that it was this: if the rebellion went wrong, then she might be used by the rebels to bargain for their freedom.

In which case Father would be compelled to make a choice between her life and that of the rebels. And given how angered he would be with her for disobeying him, would he sacrifice her to ensure their execution?

Or maybe he would not even have this choice – maybe she would be seen as complicit in the plot by her very presence on this ship. Would she then be horribly executed herself as a traitor? Would she also be hung then have her head removed, as they would be? Ophelia shivered in the dark, remembering her father describing the fate of traitors. She tried not to think what it would be like to be led up the steps to the hangman's noose, to be standing on a stool and have the rope put about your neck, then to have the stool kicked away and the rope tightened till you could not breathe...

"No!" she said out loud. "I bear no part in this plot. Father will see to it I am pardoned. Cousin Cromwell will ensure it!"

Somehow, as she sat in the dark being swayed by the motion of the ship, this seemed of little help.

But then, maybe it would not come to such a dreadful conclusion? Maybe Robert would come for her, and together they would get ashore and raise the alarm before the rebels carried through their foul scheme?

If only Robert would indeed come for her...

Ophelia stared into the darkness, trying to let the motion of the ship lull her back to sleep.

Another thump on the door behind her made her jump. She grunted in annoyance. Presumably Robin was back to take away his platter and tie her hands again.

She stood and felt her way back to the barrel. The bolt was pulled back and the door swung open, revealing the slightly less dim patch of darkness. A figure slipped in, then the door closed.

"What now?" she asked, her voiced edged with resignation. "Art come to tie my hands once more?"

"Nay," said a familiar voice. "I am come to rescue you."

Her heart skipped a beat and her breath caught in her throat. "Robert? Oh Robert!" she gasped.

And then she was in his arms, her head held close to his chest, her heart now thumping with the joy of the moment; the joy of having him with her once again.

"By Heaven!" he said, stroking her hair. "It is good to find you!" She felt him place a soft warm kiss on her forehead. "When I saw you bundled aboard last night and thrown down the hatch, I have thought of naught but how I could determine where you were held." He paused. "Are you well?"

"I am in one piece," she said. Then she added with a small sob in her throat, "That man we know as Robin. He stole my pendant."

"Oh no!" He pulled her even tighter to his chest. "That is one more thing we have to sort out."

"Yes. He is as evil as that Scarhead."

"A madman for sure." He stroked her hair again. "Anything broken or hurt when he threw you down?"

She reached up and cupped his cheeks in both her hands. "Nay, I was fortunate to land softly on my feet, before Robin came down the ladder and snatched me up, then threw me in this place." She felt a twinge in her knee, but decided not to mention it.

"Do you know what purpose they have for you?" he asked.

"Robin has said that I am a hostage, to be used as a bargain for their lives if needed."

There was a silence, then he said, "So they know who you are? They know your value to Cromwell?"

She nodded, then realising he could not see her, she said, "Yes."

"I understand." There was another silence. "We need to stop this thing, Ophelia. We need to find a way."

"Indeed. What is your plan?"

He chuckled. "You mean you have not passed the time in this place dreaming one up yourself?"

"Nay, you goose!" she responded. She paused, then muttered, "I have been too... too concerned with us being accused as well."

"Not if we do all we can to stop it," he said. "You can be sure of that." She felt him grip her arm and she nodded.

Just then there was the sound of the moving chain and they felt the ship turning. "It is the room below the ship's wheel," she explained. "I have worked that out by the sound of the chain moving inside this pillar here."

"For sure," he agreed. Then he said, "Is this a place of storage? Perhaps there are things in here that might be of use."

"I have noted two barrels; one of pitch and the other of something that smells most rank – like rotten eggs," she said. "Plus some rope and empty jars."

"Hmmm." He let go of her arm and she heard the cork being withdrawn from one of the barrels, followed by the sound of his sniff. Then the other cork and a further sniff. "By Heavens," he said, "I know what this is! Most opportune indeed." She heard him chuckle under his breath. "I have some thoughts already..."

—o—

It was a short while later that Robert slipped out of the storeroom and locked Ophelia back into her confinement, before climbing the ladder and stepping back on deck.

Inside the room, Ophelia took some deep breaths as she sat against the door. It was good to have hope. It was good to have a plan, and especially as it was one they had worked out together – for all it was mainly his, and she had just added some details.

All they had to do now, was to make it happen.

16

CHAPTER SIXTEEN

Robert limped carefully back towards the sleeping quarters, running through the finer points of the plan in his head. He was therefore unprepared for the tense stand-off scene that greeted him when he climbed down from the hatch and ducked inside.

Tris was on one side of the room, holding on to the rope that secured his hammock to its beam; his knuckles clearly white even in the dim red light of the flickering lanterns. A group of ten or twelve other men were surrounding him in a menacing-looking semi-circle, like a crab's claw that seemed ready to crush him at any moment.

Tris looked over briefly as Robert stopped in the doorway. "Hello, Rob lad," he said, his voice sounding tight and strained. "Art able to walk now, then?"

Robert glanced from Tris to the men, who seemed to be

inching closer. "Aye, that I am," he said levelly, "but what passes here, Tris?"

"You know this fellow well, boy?" snarled one of the others; a short, thick-set man standing in the middle. He had long side-whiskers and droopy eyes that gave him the look of a bulldog.

Tris shot Robert a wide-eyed look of caution with a very small shake of his head, as if to say that a swift exit would be the best option.

Robert stayed firm. "I do," he said clearly. "We collected our bags and came aboard together." He stepped forward, remembering at the last moment to drag his other foot. He looked at the bulldog man. "What has he done, that you must address him with such menace?"

"'Tis no concern of yours," Bulldog replied. "And I suggest you make yourself scarce, lest we string you up with him."

Robert took a deep breath and let it out slowly. Then he took another step into the room and grabbed the nearest beam to steady himself against the rolling of the ship. He certainly did not want to fall over while saying what was clearly the right thing.

As a lawyer, it was his duty to defend any accused man.

"Whatever he has done, I will speak for him." Robert said. "No man should be condemned without a defence being heard."

"Think you a leech-mouthed lawyer, boy?" snarled Bulldog. "Art scarcely old enough to wipe your own arse."

"I have the years and enough experience to make an argument, sir," replied Robert. "And do indeed aim to follow the noble calling of the law when I am older." He raised his chin and looked down his nose at Bulldog, trying to emphasise his considerable height advantage. As if that would count for anything if it came to a fight; the man looked as if he was made of solid oak. "I say again," Robert continued, trying to steady his voice and hoping it did not betray the nerves that were now clutching at his stomach like ivy strangles a tree, "tell me what he has done."

It seemed to work. Bulldog glanced briefly at the men on either side and appeared to come to a decision. "This man has spoken so ill of the good Cornishmen who marched on London in the year fourteen ninety-seven," he said, "that we can scarce believe him a true son of Kernow. Instead we think him a traitor to our cause."

With the feeling in the pit of his stomach becoming even worse, Robert asked, "Why, what said he on this matter that led you to think so?" Although, as he recalled the conversation he had with Tris the night before, he could easily guess what the answer would be.

He was correct. Bulldog replied, "He said they were marching to remove the king's tax collectors Morton and Bray and restore mining that had been banned, when it is well known that in truth they marched for a higher purpose – to remove the tyrannical Tudor usurper from the throne." He paused and looked again at his fellows for affirmation. "My own father fought at the final Battle of Deptford Bridge. Indeed he was one of those that took hold of the usurper's lackey commander, Lord Daubeny, but then let that man go unharmed." He nodded. "Which is a good thing, else my pa might have been cut down or strung up himself, and I would not be here."

Resisting the temptation to observe how helpful such an outcome might have been, Robert said, "And why might the thought that the march was only to remove the tax men and restore mining be so wrong?"

Bulldog gave a short, barking laugh. "For sure, 'tis well known."

"Is it? I, too, have heard different," Robert responded, trying to soften his voice in order to disarm Bulldog. "I wonder how you came by this knowledge?"

"From my pa, as I said, you cloth-headed fool," sneered Bulldog. "Although I call you a fool, yet perhaps I should say 'traitor' also?"

Several of his fellows sniggered in apparent agreement.

"Indeed," said Robert, trying to ignore the ever-tightening grip of nerves. "And how many other men who were there also supported your father's version of the event?"

Bulldog frowned, then shook his head. "Why should I need others? I said my pa was present. His word was enough."

Robert nodded, then addressed the rest of the aggressors. "So, my friend Tris here has been accused on the basis of one single opinion – that of this man's father." He glanced across their rugged faces. "Is that enough to mark him a traitor, worthy of your retribution?" There were a couple of dubious-looking head shakes. "And here is a further question," Robert pressed his advantage, "how came this man's father to form such a view of the rebellion? He was in the middle of the action, so understandably he was not privy to a wider understanding of the aims of the whole venture." Robert paused to let the point sink in. "And what is more, we learn that he was part of the band of men that captured the enemy's commander, yet who allowed that commander to escape. Which meant that instead of perishing on the field of battle, he came home hale and hearty." There were a few small nods and murmurs of agreement as Robert continued, "And if you were part of a band of men that came home alive, would you not want to tell the most glorious tale of the venture; especially to your own son?"

There were more nods and murmurs of agreement. They were definitely coming round – or at least less willing to think Tris a traitor.

Robert turned his attention back to Bulldog. "I understand why you hold your view, but I repeat, I have heard a contrary one, based on the stated aims of the rebellion's own commanders, Baron Audley, An Gof and Flamank. Can you truly call Tris here a traitor to Kernow for expressing the views of such well-informed men?"

Bulldog growled, but said nothing.

Robert looked back at the others. "I put it to you, good fellows all, that Tris is no traitor, but he is as true a man of Kernow as any of you."

More of them nodded in agreement.

Robert delivered his summation. "So, what say you? Do we fight as one, with all division forgotten in this glorious new venture? Do we not have our own battles to fight, rather than repeat those of our forebears?" He let go of the beam and raised both his voice and his hands to encourage them. "In faith, can we not rely on every man when the time comes?" Then he gave them the final blow. "Are we not one, united body of men?"

"Aye!" they roared back, although Bulldog did not look up and scowled at the floor.

"Then we are agreed?" Robert asked, lowering his voice back to its more normal level. The tension in his stomach disappeared as if the ivy had withered away from around the tree – to be replaced by the sweet feeling of success.

"Aye!" they repeated, also more quietly.

"And to be sure, Tris is no traitor?"

"Nay!"

Robert looked directly at Bulldog. "Then I thank you for hearing me speak in his defence," he said. "It shows your generosity of spirit as a good Christian."

Now all the men were smiling and cheering, and some came over and shook his hand, congratulating him for his presence of mind and clarity of speech. Finally the last man moved away and joined one of the little groups now congregating round hammocks, talking quietly and easily.

Robert looked over at Tris, who had not moved.

There was a moment as the older man nodded slowly, as if acknowledging not only the skill with which Robert had turned the men's anger, but also the bravery it had taken him to do so. Then he walked slowly over and grasped Robert's hand and let out a soft laugh. "By Heavens, Rob," he said, "that was quite something!" Suddenly he pulled Robert towards him and enveloped the boy in a sweaty-smelling bear hug. "You have the gift of speech for one so young!" he said in Robert's ear. Then he stood back and grinned broadly. "Had I not seen such a performance I would not have believed it possible." The grin faded, and he shook his head. "If you do not become a true lawyer as a legacy of this day's work, then there's no justice in God's kingdom. None at all."

"Happy to help," said Robert.

Bulldog came over. "A fine performance, young fellow," he growled, the sneering expression on his face suggesting he thought otherwise. "But I want you to know it has not moved me as it has moved these others." He waved his hand at the other men. "I find myself wondering if you really are as true to our cause as you claim. I am watching you, boy. Get on the wrong side of me just one time, and it will be the worse for you. I will see to it." With a last glare at both Robert and Tris, he stomped away across the deck to his own hammock. Robert took a deep breath. "I suppose you cannot win over every man," he muttered. He paused. "Now, let us share some rum, Tris." He shook his head slowly. "For after that speech and what I have just heard, I find I have a deep and burning thirst."

17

CHAPTER SEVENTEEN

It was noon the following day. Robert stood at the rail and shielded his eyes from the sun as he watched the sailors scurrying up and down the rigging, furling and securing the sails. The ship was heading for the docks, and Robert could appreciate how well the men's actions were slowing her speed as she passed by Melcombe Regis and into Weymouth harbour.

It was truly incredible to see how they climbed, as nimble as spiders scuttling across a web, then balanced without a second's hesitation on the ropes that ran under each spar, tying up the sails so the canvas no longer caught the wind.

Robert smiled to himself. While he was full of admiration for the sailors' bravery and skill, their life was not for him. No, his own future was as Tris had said; to be a worthy and successful lawyer. A leading defender of the wronged and merciless prosecutor of those that wronged them. And naturally, Ophelia would be by his side; his beautiful wife and the mother of his children, supporting and loving him as much as he loved her.

Assuming, of course, the plan worked, and they could get off this accursed ship safely.

Robert took a deep breath. It had to work. It just had to. Or they would die together in the attempt – of that he was certain.

As each sail was rolled up and secured to the spar, he felt the ship slow her pace through the water. He looked across at the approaching dock, and could see how expertly the steersman was judging their approach. They would be going at no more than the pace of a slow walk when they came up to the dock side.

Robert pushed himself off the rail.

It was time to put his plan into place.

With a quick glance around to ensure he was not being observed, he walked over to the stern hatch. Although he made sure to limp heavily, just in case.

Reaching the hatch, he looked about him a moment, seeking a necessary implement for his plan. With a small grunt of satisfaction, he spotted a handle attached to a windlass. It was a slim piece of metal held in place by an iron peg. "Perfect," he muttered, before slipping off the peg. Holding the handle tightly, he took another quick look around, then dropped lightly out of sight. Pausing a moment after he landed to allow his eyes to adjust to the dim light, he reached up and unhooked the nearest lantern, then carried it along the corridor to Ophelia's door. He knocked gently; two quick taps followed by two slower – their agreed signal.

"Who goes?" came her soft response.

"Robert," he said, as he pulled open the bolt and let himself in. "As well you know from my signal."

She seemed pale and grey in the flickering flame of the lantern, but gave him an excited-looking smile. "Yes, but I needed to be certain," she whispered.

"Is all ready?" he asked. She nodded, and handed him one of the ropes.

"Good. Then let us make our final preparations." He put the lantern down by the door and took the rope. Then she gave him one of the open jars. "'Tis full of the weak ale Robin has been bringing," she said. "I have poured as much of it in here as I could.

"You will have a thirst," he observed.

"For sure," she answered. "But it is a small price if we succeed."

He lowered the rope into the jar until it was fully inside, then he picked the jar up and shook it in circular motions.

"We need to be sure it is wet all through," he said, putting it on the floor. "I will leave it a moment to soak."

After a minute or so, he gave the jar one more shake, then fished out the end of the rope. "Yes, that is good," he muttered, squeezing it between his fingers. "As wet as we could hope, given there was not all that much ale."

He pulled out the full length, which was around three feet in total. He removed the stopper on the barrel containing the sulphurous substance. "We are fortunate this was here," he said. "A full keg of gunpowder – which naturally has the smell of rotten eggs." He looked back at Ophelia. "I suppose the ship's powder store was a secure enough place to put you. They did not think you would be found, and a plan put in place."

He pushed the rope down inside the barrel, coating it liberally in the powder. "Now," he whispered, "let us make it into the fuse we need."

"How long do you think it will last?" she asked.

He shook his head. "In truth, I know not," he muttered, "as I have never done this before. But I hope that by wetting it first, it will burn more slowly, giving us good time to get away." He pulled the rope out and examined it carefully. "Now it is coated liberally in the powder," he said.

"For sure, it smells of the most rotten eggs," Ophelia said, wrinkling her nose.

"As you say," he agreed, pushing one end into the hole in the barrel, then jamming it in place with the stopper. He picked up another of the empty jars and placed it carefully on the top of the barrel so it protruded clearly out over the edge. Then he draped the rope across the top of the jar, so it hung down clear of the curved side of the barrel. "We cannot have the fuse fouling on the side," Robert observed, "or it might stop the flame."

He stood back. "Are we ready?" She gave him a small, wide-eyed nod. "Good. Then let us light this and be gone."

He opened the little glass door in the side of the lantern and held the end of the rope against the flame. There was a moment where nothing happened, and Ophelia started to say, "What if...?" but then the rope suddenly caught alight with a fizzing and crackling blue flame of its own. Robert let it fall so the rope was once again hanging down, the flame now working up its length. He observed it for a few moments.

"I would say it moves at just over an inch each minute," he said. "So I reckon we have a half hour before it reaches the powder."

"Now I see it for real," she whispered, "I fear we will be responsible for many deaths."

"Nay, I think not," he answered. "The gunpowder will blow a hole in the timbers, and the pitch beside it will set the ship aflame, but we are in port, so I warrant every man will have time to get ashore before she sinks. It is not as if we were at sea, where all would drown."

"But what if a man is directly above the explosion?" she asked.

"Then he would not be so fortunate," Robert answered. "But we must not forget, these are godless men who would commit the basest treason. Our duty is to the King and thus we must stop their plan by whatever means we have at hand." He took her face in his hands. "And God has seen fit to put gunpowder and pitch in this place, has He not?" He gave her a small kiss on forehead. "Then we are doing God's work if we put them to good use."

She gave a small nod, then a more confident one. "Yes, you are right," she said, as he took his hands away. "Come," she pointed at the flame. "It is already an inch higher. We must be away."

She opened the door slowly and peered each way, before stepping into the dark corridor. Robert followed, then slipped the bolt to lock the room, before taking out the windlass handle and levering it hard against the protruding end of the bolt, bending the metal out wide, so it could no longer be withdrawn.

—o—

Ophelia clung to the ladder, her face level with Robert's calves. "All clear," she heard him whisper down to her. "We go on my mark." She nodded, and waited for his command. In her mind she rehearsed their plan; a run across the deck and a leap over the ship's side down to the dock just below, then a hard run for some crowded place like a tavern where they could find help – and be far away when the gunpowder blew and put The Flying Cloud beyond the rebels' use. She took a few deep breaths and flexed her fingers ready for the climb.

Then she heard a shout and suddenly Robert's legs were whisked upwards, as if they were those of a bird that had launched itself into the sky.

She looked up into the light, just as a head appeared over the edge of the hatchway.

"You too, Mistress Williams."

With a sick lurch of fear clutching at her belly, she saw a pair of hands came down. "Come on, take them," said Robin. "Take them now, or it will be much the worse for you." The hands gestured upwards. "I already have your young man. Take them."

With a resigned sigh, Ophelia gripped Robin's hands and found herself being lifted up out of the hatch.

As soon as she was set down on the deck, another pair of arms grasped her from behind, pinning her close. Her immediate reaction was to struggle to get free, until a voice hissed in her ear, "I have you Missy, so struggle ye not." There was a sickening smell of foul breath, then the voice added, "Lest I might enjoy your movements too greatly, eh?"

Ophelia was immediately still, fighting down the overwhelming urge to spew up what little there was in her belly.

She caught a movement out of the corner of her eye, and glanced to her left. Robert was also being held, by a stocky man with long side whiskers and drooping eyes.

Robert caught her eye and gave the tiniest shake of his head, as if to tell her to keep silent about the gunpowder below. She returned an equally tiny nod of agreement.

"Now, I understand from Jake here," Robin nodded towards the man with the whiskers, "that this young fellow sees himself as some sort of man of law, for all he is hardly yet pulled from his mother's breast."

"Let us go," said Robert. "We will have no part in your treason."

"Nay," growled Jake. "I recall well how you enjoined us all to 'fight as one, with all division forgotten in this glorious new venture of ours'. Was I mistaken? And when you asked us if we are not 'one united body of men' – did I hear wrong?"

"It was of the moment," muttered Robert. "In defence of my fellow, Tris."

"But if Tris is your fellow," Jake said with a sickly smile, "and you showed so clear that he is on our side in this venture, then that makes you truly committed to our cause as well."

"I agree," said Robin. "So you will take him below, and keep a close eye on him. Then, when we launch our initial attack on the King's men, he can be in the vanguard. And if he is hit by an arrow, a blade or a ball – as no doubt he will be – then he will take his final breath knowing his life has been given in a most noble cause."

"You would have me lead your advance?" Robert asked, with disbelief in his voice.

"Indeed," said Jake, "if you stop a ball or a blade, it could save the life of the man behind – a true man of Kernow. That makes you a valued asset."

"A shield is all," muttered Robert, "and a poor one at that."

"Whatever you say," replied Robin. Then he turned to Ophelia. "And what shall we do with this young woman, eh, that tries to escape when I would have her held secure?" He gave her a sickly grin. "As I have said before, I will not kill you, but I do need to keep you as my bargain if all goes wrong. In that, you will be of value to me." He glanced around at what Ophelia could see was a growing audience, consisting of both sailors and rebels. Ophelia hung her head, wishing she could disappear from the sight of all the rough, ugly staring faces. She was hardly sure which was worse; the sailors regarding her with what seemed like fear and loathing, or the rebels, scowling at her with open enmity.

"If I had some stocks," Robin continued, "I would put you in them, on display for all to mock and jeer in punishment, but I do not..." He stopped. "But I have it!" he cried. "Tie her to the wheel instead! That is like a stock, and all can mock her for as long as we are in port. A few hours there will teach this little madam not to attempt another escape!"

With rising terror making her breath catch in her throat, Ophelia felt herself being marched towards the wheel. And although she tried to press her heels against the deck, she could not stop herself being pushed up to the spokes, her hands forced through, then tied tightly to the structure. The man who had been her captor then stood back and gave her a twisted grin. "There you go, missy," he laughed. It made one side of his face crinkle up, while the other side, that had a large scar running down it, remained unmoved. "You stand there for a few hours and learn your lesson!" Then he stood back again, his mouth working a moment. She stared in horror, not sure of what further terror he was preparing to inflict on her.

Then it became clear, as he spat directly in her face.

While she was left reeling in shock, he swaggered over to a group of rebels. "Treat her as if in the stocks," she heard him say. "That is what I have done."

Ophelia looked around at the groups of men on the deck. But it was not their leering grins or angry scowls that made her almost faint from fear. It was not the man's spittle running down her cheek like a slimy crawling slug. It was not even the shame and degradation of being on show to all these men.

It was the barrel of gunpowder just below her feet that was set to explode in less than thirty minutes.

18

CHAPTER EIGHTEEN

Jake, or as Robert still thought of him, 'Bulldog', threw Robert roughly down the forward hatch, so he landed off balance and sprawled across the dark wooden deck below.

"Get up," snarled Bulldog, jumping down beside him. Robert felt his collar being pulled tight, then he was lifted to his feet as if he weighed no more than a mouse. While he tried to catch his breath, Bulldog took hold of his wrist and twisted it up behind his back.

"Unhand me, you traitorous cur," Robert growled over his shoulder.

"I take no orders from a young shit like you, who lies like a poisonous rat," Bulldog snarled, pushing him forward towards the line of hammocks swinging from low beams.

Some had men lying inside, while further men were sitting around chests, playing at cards or backgammon. Robert felt all eyes were on him as he was forced up to one of the beams.

Bulldog held Robert still a moment. "Oi!" he called over his shoulder to a man who was in a nearby hammock. "You, fellow! Look lively and pass me some rope."

The man rolled out of the hammock and went over to a pile of kit bags in the corner. Robert watched him untie the rope from one of the bags, then bring it over to Bulldog.

"Think of this as your stocks, just like that girl is lashed to the wheel." Bulldog said, as he pulled both of Robert's wrists around the beam and tied them tightly together. He stood back and gave a thin smile. "That will keep you secure until we get to London." He went over to a rough wooden chest and rummaged a moment, then came back with a length of dirty sacking. "And this will keep your silence." He reached up and forced the foul rag into Robert's mouth, then secured it behind his head with some more rope. "No more of your weasel words and lies, eh? I will not have you talking your way out of this."

Robert tried to breathe as best he could through his nose, and to keep his tongue away from the rag, lest he taste its foulness. He watched with narrow, angry eyes as Bulldog stood back and addressed the room.

"Now hear ye all!" Bulldog shouted. "This boy has proved himself false to our enterprise, and would thwart us if he could."

"How so?" asked one of the men. "We heard him clear! He was urging us to fight together."

"We thought him a true son of Kernow," said another.

"Nay," answered Bulldog, "he is no more a son of Kernow than the King himself."

"But how is this known?" asked a third.

"Our leader had sight of him at the May Fair." Bulldog said. "He saw this boy and a girl running off like spying rats after learning of his plans. He captured the girl when she was skulking around in the tavern, and had her held secure on the ship as a hostage. So he knew for sure that the boy would appear sooner or later." He looked over at Robert, who narrowed his eyes even more, as if that alone could communicate his disgust. "True enough," Bulldog continued anyway, "our leader came on deck not ten minutes past, and happened upon this young fellow's head appearing at the stern hatch." He reached over and ran his hand slowly through Robert's hair, making the boy want to vomit. "These long, flowing locks were all the identification that was needed," he said with a sickening smile, "for he said he had seen a boy with just such hair changing caps with an old fellow in the crowds at the fair. And not many boys have both unnatural height and hair like this. He was indeed the spy who would prove us false."

"Fie!" said one of the men, "we thought him true to our cause!"

"Nay indeed," Bulldog continued. "As false to our cause as he could be. And what is more," he added, "the boy was caught in the very act of releasing the hostage girl as well."

"God's wounds! What of her?"

"She is tied to the wheel for a few hours as if it were a set of stocks, so any man who wishes to, can show his displeasure."

"And this boy?"

"Feel free to show him the same."

Robert flexed his wrists to try and relieve a little of the constriction, but it made no difference. He could feel his fingers start to tingle, such that they would no doubt blacken and die from the pressure of the bonds within a few hours.

Not that he had a few hours until the powder would blow – taking the ship to the bottom of the harbour.

And sending poor Ophelia straight to Heaven.

—o—

Robert had always felt he was a pretty good judge of how quickly time was passing. He had long been able to predict accurately the passage of an hour hand on a clock, or the speed of sands running through an hourglass. So his mind was fixed on the thirty or so minutes counting down to the flame hitting the gunpowder keg, rather than the constant procession of men that came up to punch him in the belly, slap him in the face or pull at his hair. It was almost as if these things were happening to someone else, while the true Robert Wychwoode was standing to one side, noting instead the passing of each minute.

Setting the fuse with a half-hour to burn – call that 'minute one'.

Assessing its speed and leaving the powder store – 'minute two'.

Leaving the store, bending the lock and making their way to the hatch – 'minute four'.

Being taken and Ophelia being tied to the wheel – 'minute eight'.

Being dragged to the sleeping deck and tied up – 'minute twelve'.

The procession of abusers ill-treating him thus far – there had been many of those, so call it 'minute twenty'.

Which meant there were but ten minutes remaining...

"I trusted you as a friend!" said a familiar voice.

Robert re-focused on the next man to appear in front of him. It was Tris, coming up and putting his hook-nosed face so close that Robert nearly went cross-eyed looking back.

Unable to speak through the gag, Robert merely raised his eyebrows and shrugged.

"I was grateful to you for defending me before those fellows."

Robert nodded and crinkled his eyes, as if he was smiling.

"And now I hear you are in truth a traitor to our cause."

Robert shook his head and rolled his eyes – as if to refute this accusation.

"I have observed these men come up and vent their anger upon you, which is as God would have it, for you – and the girl presently tied to the wheel – have played us false." He paused. "And I have been told you will be placed in the vanguard of our attack, so you will almost certainly be done to death."

Robert shook his head slowly, while looking hard into Tris's eyes.

"You would say nay to this?" Robert nodded. Tris stepped back. "Then 'tis just fancy. I can scarce credit it in your position."

Minute twenty-one. Nine remaining.

Suddenly Tris staggered sharply sideways; pulled away by Robin, whose face was so red that Robert thought he might soon explode like the barrel below.

"What have you done in the powder store, boy?" he snarled. "I went to check on it, and the lock is bent so I cannot enter."

Robert raised his eyebrows and shook his head, as if to say he had no idea what Robin was talking about.

"By the Heavens, no man bends a lock so none can enter, unless there is something he would keep hidden!" He shook his fist in Robert's face. "Tell me!"

Robert shrugged and rolled his eyes down to the gag. Robin looked at it, almost as if seeing it for the first time. "God's blood!" he muttered, then reached up and, after a few fumbles with the rope, got it off.

"Now tell me!" Robin barked.

Robert ran his tongue around his mouth a few times to try and rid himself of the dry foulness of the gag. "I know not," he said.

Minute twenty-two. Eight left.

There was a sudden blinding pain in his jaw and his head snapped round like a branch in a gale. For a moment Robert had no idea what had happened, and could see nothing but flashes of light, but then they cleared and he turned back to see Robin holding his fist. Robert took a couple of careful breaths to try and clear the pain, moved his tongue again to make sure it had not been bitten by the force of the punch, then rotated his jaw. Nothing seemed to be broken, thank the Lord.

After a few moments the pain started to mute down to a dull throb.

"I shall not tell you."

Robin's eyes narrowed. "So you do know, but will not tell?" He held his fist up to Robert's face again.

"If you will hit me once more," Robert stated, "belike I will not tell because my jaw is broken." Then he added carefully. "In which case it will be too late."

Robin gave him a sideways look at these words. "Too late? Too late?" he snapped. "What is too late?"

Minute twenty-three. Seven left.

Robert stayed silent, letting Robin work it out for himself. After a moment the man's eyes widened.

"By the Lord!" he gasped. "By the Lord! It is the powder store! You have set a flame to the powder!" He stepped forward and grasped Robert's shoulders. "Is that so, boy? Is that what you have done? Is that what will happen before it is too late?"

Robert gave him a slow smile, and the slightest nod of his head.

"You will blow us all to Heaven!" Robin shouted.

"Or to Hell?" Robert replied quietly.

Robin ignored this, pacing away across the deck with his hands on his hips. Then he turned back. "How long do we have?"

"As the fuse burns," Robert said. "I would say between ten and fifteen minutes."

Minute twenty-four. Six remaining.

"By the Holy Cross!" Robin yelled. "Ten to fifteen minutes? We have to pull the flame now!" He looked across at Bulldog. "You, man, come with me. We will force open the door!" Leaving Robert without the gag, he ran over to the hatch, closely followed by Bulldog. Together they scrambled up the ladder and could be heard running across the deck above.

There was a brief moment of silence. Tris raised his eyebrows and slowly exhaled. "You have planned this so?" he asked. Robert nodded. Tris looked around at the men who were all now listening intently. "In truth boy, how long do we have?"

"Five minutes, maybe a little more, maybe less." Robert answered quietly.

"Christ's wounds!" Tris yelled. "But five minutes? Then we must get away now!" He looked at the men. "Come all!" he shouted. "We must be off this ship before she explodes!"

There was a moment's pause as they all stared at him, then suddenly there was frenetic action. Some tried to grab their bags, while others ran straight for the hatch and scrambled up. A few made it up the ladder and away across the deck, while some only made it half way up before being pulled down by those behind and falling into the throng.

Tris was one who ran for his bag. He almost made it to the hatch, when Robert yelled, "Tris!"

Tris checked a moment and glanced back, then shook his head, and pushed on into the crowd.

"TRIS!"

With an angry frown, Tris turned and ran back. Robert shook his bound wrists in the man's face. "Please Tris, help me! I did as much for you!"

"I should leave you to burn, you traitor," Tris growled, glancing back at the hatch. There was still a crowd of men below it. Still too many to get out quickly.

"Please!"

Tris took a knife from his belt. "I still say you are a traitor," he said, slicing through the ropes.

"Thank you!" Robert said, as they ran together to the hatch.

Four minutes remaining.

Four minutes till the powder would blow, taking the ship to the bottom of the harbour. And hopefully send Robin and Bulldog, as they tried to open the door that was only a few feet from the blast, straight to Hell.

And poor Ophelia to Heaven.

Four minutes, more or less.

Maybe less.

Robert pulled one man out of his way, using his extra height and weight. Then another.

Ophelia would be screaming in terror.

He had to get to her. Now!

He pulled another man away from the ladder, and suddenly there were empty rungs before him.

He started to climb.

His head came up into the air and looked to the stern.

Ophelia was still at the wheel.

Two more rungs.

Something grabbed his ankles. Suddenly the daylight disappeared as he was pulled down. He landed in a heap on the deck below.

Three minutes.

Robert stood up. A man was half way up the ladder. Robert grabbed him by the legs and pulled hard, stepping aside as the man came down.

Again he started to climb.

This time he was ready for attempts to dislodge him and

lashed out with every step. He felt hands trying to grab his ankles, but managed to kick them away and keep climbing.

Robert hauled himself out of the hatch and crawled onto the deck. He picked himself up and sprinted over to the wheel.

"Robert!" Ophelia screamed as he got to her. "Untie me!"

Two minutes.

He looked at the rope binding her wrists to the wheel. It was thin, so the knots were small and very tight.

"Come on!" she yelled. "It could blow at any moment!"

Robert's fingers felt like great clumsy sausages as he fumbled with the knot.

"Were you molested?..." he asked.

"THAT IS NO MATTER!" she screamed in his ear. "COME ON!"

He took a breath, then studied the knot carefully, looking for the best strand to pull. There it was – the one curled round the top of the knot. He tried to grip it with his nails, but it would not move.

Ophelia said quietly, "Please, Robert."

He nodded, then tried the strand again.

It moved.

Quickly he picked at it, trying to open it out, but it seemed stuck once more.

"Are we going to die?" she asked.

"Nay," he muttered.

One minute.

Robert took another breath, then gave a determined pull on the strand. It moved again, and he was able to open it out, and with it came the rest of the knot.

Ophelia was free.

Together they ran hand-in-hand to the side of the ship.

As Robert grasped the rail ready to jump down to the harbour just below, it suddenly seemed to move away by itself, breaking apart and splintering under his hand, causing him to fall forwards. The deck below him then bent and flexed, curling down so he was no longer standing on it – rather it was pushing him away from the ship's side. A burning blast of hot air punched him hard in the back and he was lifted off his feet and thrown past the broken rail. Then it felt like his head had been hit by a blacksmith's hammer as an almighty crash of sound exploded out, making even the air itself shake and his ears feel as if they had burst. Then he was clear of the ship, flying through the air, still holding Ophelia's hand as all sound faded into a ringing silence, and now there were no more minutes to count; it seemed that time itself had almost come to a standstill. The harbour came up slowly to meet them, and Robert could see they were flying towards a pile of sails and bags. Then everything seemed to speed up again, so he had no time to prepare himself as he let go of Ophelia and the pile of sails came up and slammed hard into him...

—o—

The silence continued for a few more moments as Robert lay buried under the sails.

Peaceful. Quiet.

Suddenly sound – and heat – and pain – came back with such force that he wondered if he had been killed by the blast, and they had landed in Hell itself.

They?

Him and Ophelia.

Ophelia!

He pushed his way out from under the sails and bags, and looked over at her still form.

She was lying face down with her arms out wide; her brown linen dress blackened and scorched.

He took her hand and squeezed it. "Ophelia?"

Nothing.

He moved closer, lifted her head gently and turned it towards him. Her eyes were shut.

"Ophelia?"

Nothing.

He turned her body until she was lying curled on her side, like a sleeping babe.

He could see by the rise and fall in her chest that she was still breathing, but her breaths were shallow and ragged.

He leaned across and took her head in his hands. "Ophelia?"

Her breathing became shallower, and more ragged, until, with a long breath out...

...it stopped.

"Ophelia! NO!"

Robert gave a cry like a wounded animal, and gathered her into his arms. "No!" he sobbed. "No!"

Then it was as if all his pain faded away; all the hurt from the men who had punched him while he was tied up; the blow from Robin to his jaw; the scramble to get out of the hatch; the blast itself and the landing on the harbour – it all drifted into a numb stillness as he cradled her body and rocked it like a mother comforts a child, tears streaming down onto the stillness of her face.

"Rob?" asked a voice.

Robert looked up, to see Tris standing over him. Then he saw beyond Tris what he simply had not noticed before; that the ship was burning like a massive bonfire, leaning away from the harbour as she filled with water, the ropes tethering her to the dock straining and cracking as she tried to get away from them so she could finally sink. As he watched, the ropes gave way, each snapping with a report like cannon fire. This allowed the ship to sink quickly below the sea with a massive 'whoosh' of steam and bubbling sprays of water, until there was nothing but one of her masts standing above the dockside, its tip just above the level of the great bollards that she had been tied to.

The ship was gone.

Robert wiped his eyes on his sleeve. What did it matter, when he had lost Ophelia? The first girl he had loved; the only one he would ever love.

He turned back to Ophelia, and brushed a stray hair off her face. He looked up. "Go away," he whispered to Tris. "I would be alone with my loss."

But Tris crouched down. "I am sorry," he said. "Is this the girl that was held hostage and tied to the wheel?"

"Aye."

There was a moment of silence, then Tris said, "I see now I was wrong about you, Rob. You are a good lad, and true. I warrant you will be a fine lawyer one day. I can say this, as I was your first case."

"Nay," Robert shook his head, as he stroked Ophelia's

cheek. "She was my first. I saved her from a flogging. And now... now I will be as naught without... without... her."

Tris stared at Ophelia a moment, then said, "If I had not called you traitor; if I had released you sooner, you would have been able to untie her before the blast." He shook his head. "You would have both been able to jump safely down to the harbour like the rest of us."

"Nay, 'tis done now." Robert gave him a weak, watery smile. "What is done is done."

There was a small cough from beside him. Then Ophelia muttered, "Why, what is done?"

As Robert and Tris stared at her, she added, "My back hurts."

19

CHAPTER NINETEEN

It was half an hour later and Robert and Tris were seated in a small private back room in the nearest dockside tavern.

They had carried Ophelia gently inside and secured a room with a bed so she could rest and recover. A large red-faced woman who Robert discovered was called Mildred had taken it on herself to care for Ophelia, and had exclaimed in horror over the girl's raw back when she had unlaced the scorched dress. She had placed Ophelia on her side in the bed, and began smearing goose fat across her skin. "The burns are not too deep, thank the Lord. The linen gave her some small protection, for all the flames had their evil effect." Mildred paused smearing the fat and looked up at Robert. "'Tis a shame she was not wearing a heavy jerkin such as yours, lad. It would have stopped any burns for sure." She laid a thin sheet over Ophelia. "The fat will help restore the skin. Then we are in God's hands for a full recovery."

"Amen to that," Robert replied, as Tris said, "I will leave you together. Join me downstairs," and left the room.

Robert leaned over the bed and took Ophelia's hand. "Get some rest, my sweet; you need to let God do his work."

"We did it, did we not?" she whispered with a small smile. "We destroyed the ship."

"Aye," he replied.

"So the rebellion is ended?"

"The seaborne part is."

"Good." Then she frowned at him. "That man who was here just now," she said. "The one who helped you bring me in."

"Tris? What of him?"

"He has a strange hooked nose. I have seen one like that somewhere before." Her frown deepened, then her face cleared. "I know," she whispered. "It was the old fellow who stopped me in the market place after I took the bread. He also spoke up for me in court." She closed her eyes and settled her head on the bolster. "He smelled nice, too."

Robert thought back and did vaguely recall an old fellow telling how Ophelia had shaken in his arms, before the baker had pressed his case. But before he could comment, Mildred pulled him away and shooed him out of the room. "Give the girl some space!" she said. "The poor child needs rest and sleep, not having you bothering her. Get thee hence; I will care for her. Go on, get thee hence!"

Reassured that Ophelia was in safe hands, Robert had gone down to the tap room. Tris had appeared as soon as he entered and bundled him quickly into the back room.

"You have just caused The Flying Cloud to explode," he said as he locked the door. "The sailors and the men of

Kernow are all about the harbour. They would string you up and dance on your corpse if they find you."

Robert nodded. "I can see this; I would do the same if it was my ship consumed in a powder blast."

"Yes, well, for now we must keep you hidden from sight."

Robert voiced the obvious issue. "We cannot stay hidden forever."

"True." Tris observed him with a frown. "But that can be a problem for later."

Robert thought this through. Assuming the men now considered their part of the rebellion over – as surely they must – with luck they would soon disperse and start their journeys back to their homes in Cornwall. Maybe in a few hours it would be safe to make a quiet exit from their locked sanctuary. Then he frowned. "But what of Ophelia?" he asked. "Is she safe?"

"I would warrant she is." Tris answered. "I do not believe the men would see value in attacking so young a girl, particularly one guarded by the fearsome Mildred." He paused. "They are good Catholic men, and many also have daughters."

Robert leaned forward. "Even when the leader had her tied to the wheel and the men were invited to humiliate her? I cannot bear the thought of what might have happened to her."

"Few of them seemed to see the opportunity, I understand," Tris replied. "It appears she was abused with words alone."

Robert sat back. "Heaven be praised," he said. "It is bad enough that she was held just above the powder keg knowing it could blow at any moment. It was sufficient to scare the poor girl half to death." The image of Ophelia screaming in terror was not one he would readily forget.

He observed Tris a moment; this man who had thought him a traitor, yet still released him from bondage, who took pride in the thought of being Robert's first legal case. This man who had helped carry Ophelia into the tavern and was now keeping him secure in this back room. "I must give you my sincere thanks," Robert said. "You have made it your business to see me safe. That puts you at risk also."

"I know that, Rob." Tris nodded slowly. "And I am no doubt a fool for doing so." He shrugged. "But it seems the right thing to do."

Robert put his fingertips together and said, "Some two weeks ago, my friend Ophelia was attacked in a Devon forest, then arrested as a thief and vagrant in the market over a loaf of bread. There was an old fellow with a similar look to you who acted most kindly towards her in court." He raised an enquiring eyebrow. "Your father?"

Tris's mouth opened. "That was the girl?" He pointed upward in the general direction of the rooms above them. "That was her?" He nodded. "Aye, it was my pa that day." He leaned forward. "He told me he had stopped a girl, and she had been shaking like a frightened little fawn when he held her." He frowned, then his eyes suddenly widened. "Then it was you in the court who defended her? My pa told me a bright young lad who would be a lawyer presented a most inventive argument. So when you said you saved her from a flogging just now... That was you?" Robert nodded and Tris smiled. "Then I am doubly honoured that I am even your second case! I have no doubt that my words on the ship were true, and you will be a great lawyer one day as a legacy of these early cases. I shall be able to tell how you once came to my rescue!"

Robert laughed. "You do me great honour, Tris," he said, then looked more serious. "And I must thank you again for your help and support."

"Glad of it," Tris replied.

After a minute or two of companionable silence, Robert asked a question that had been in his mind for a while. "How many men were killed in the explosion?" he asked. "I wanted only to stop the rebellion, not kill any man."

Tris raised his eyebrows. "You know not?" he asked. Then he shook his head. "No, I suppose that is so." He paused. "Only two men were killed. The Captain and most of the crew of sailors had gone ashore anyway and all the others managed to flee the ship when you gave the warning, or were flung into the waters of the harbour by the blast. They were soon rescued by those at the dockside, and have since been accounted for in full."

"And the two who were killed?" Robert supposed he knew the answer, but he asked anyway.

"Our leader Tresillick and Jake."

Tresillick must have been Robin with the rasping voice. Robert could feel little pity for the man who had caused much pain to himself, and more particularly, to Ophelia. And Jake had been Bulldog, the one who had tied him up and shoved that filthy gag into his mouth. Had it been necessary to send them down to the powder room believing they had more time, so they would be killed? He could see them in his mind's eye, struggling to get the bolt free, when the blast hit. He nodded to himself. Yes, in this situation, he had served the needs of the law by executing two proven traitors – indeed perhaps he had even shown them mercy by giving them a quick death, when the law would have had them hung and drawn in agony, then quartered. He frowned. But had the law truly been served? Had he, Robert Wychwoode, taken it into his own hands and been both judge and executioner? If he was to have the career in the law he so deeply desired – and which Tris seemed so sure of – could he do so knowing he had acted in such a way? He took a deep breath. Yes, he would have to accept that it had happened. It could not be changed. But he could learn from it. Be a better lawyer as a consequence.

He looked up at Tris. "They would have faced death in any case."

Tris shrugged. "It may be so, but..."

He did not get to finish his sentence, as a loud, insistent knocking suddenly came on the door, making it visibly shake under the onslaught.

Robert and Tris looked at each other with wide eyes. Tris brought his finger to his lips to signal silence. Robert nodded.

"Wychwoode!" came a sharp barking shout from the other side of the door. "Are you there? Young Wychwoode! Open up I say!"

"Oh!" Robert whispered. "I know that voice." He stood up. Tris raised his hand as if to stop him, but Robert ignored it and opened the door.

It was Sir Francis Williams and Thomas Cromwell.

—o—

Robert might have hoped that Ophelia's father would be

thankful they had helped to thwart the rebellious plot. But sadly this did not appear to be the case.

Sir Francis seemed barely able to contain his rage.

He stood just inside the room, his face red and his hand hovering over the hilt of his sword. Robert feared he might draw it at any moment and run him through.

"What, in the name of all that is holy, were you thinking?" he exclaimed. "Getting out of a room most securely locked? Stealing away from the house in the dead of night in silence? Putting my daughter in the most mortal danger?" He moved his hand to his hip, as if he was deliberately trying to prevent himself from drawing the sword by instinct alone. "And now I see you have exploded Sir John's ship and sent it to the bottom of the harbour!" He glanced at Cromwell beside him, as if looking for the King's Secretary to endorse his position. Cromwell, however, remained impassive, his small dark eyes fixed on Robert.

"Indeed, sir," Robert replied. He kept his voice quiet, hoping this might help dampen the older man's anger. "The motive for all we did was to uncover – and ideally thwart – a new traitorous Cornish rebellion. In this we were, I am pleased to say, successful." He paused. "And Ophelia is kept sound, but for some small burning on her back as we were blown off the ship by the blast."

Sir Francis's mouth dropped open as he stared at Robert. "Small burning?" he spluttered, his face turning from red to white in a heartbeat "You were blown off the... By Heavens!" Then he seemed to gather himself. "Where exactly is my daughter?"

"She is in a room above, being cared for by a woman called Mildred," Robert said. "She sleeps."

God be praised he was not having to tell Sir Francis that Ophelia had fallen asleep for all eternity. It was not hard to think that her father would have drawn his sword for sure, and dealt the same fate to the young man he held responsible.

Robert took a small breath. But would that have been so bad? The thought of living the rest of his life without Ophelia was more than he could bear. If she had indeed died, then his own death would have been most welcome.

"I am truly sorry, sir," he said, "that Ophelia became involved in this. But I repeat, the result was that we have stopped this seaborne plot. I hope that makes some reparation for the manner in which it was achieved."

"Oh, aye. This part of their venture is ended, for sure," Sir Francis replied. "Thanks to the local magistrate and a body of militiamen, we have been able to round up all the rebels at the dockside, and have them held securely nearby."

"What will happen to them?" asked Robert, his eyes sliding over to Tris, who was listening intently to this exchange.

Sir Francis followed this movement, and although he answered Robert, he seemed to be addressing his answer directly to the Cornishman. "They are not the leaders of this venture. So they will be sent to their homes and bound to keep the peace," he said. "Apart from one by the name of Jack Ingleby, who I understand did have a position of leadership, plus a scarfaced man called Carveth. They will both be tried as traitors." He looked back at Robert. "Two other men; Tresillick, who we hear was the overall leader, and one other man we know only as Jake, have not been found – so we take it they were killed in the blast you caused. At least there you have spared the executioner his gruesome task."

"And Sir John Bowlby, who owned The Flying Cloud?" asked Robert. "Is he not the master plotter behind this whole venture? I understand his part was not just overall leadership; he was also raising a land army to march on London as The Flying Cloud was sailing up the Thames, in a twin attack."

"I have sent troops to have him arrested so he can stand trial for treason and face his crimes," Sir Francis said. "So if he is gathering a land army, then this will also be stopped." He paused. "And I am most confident we will get to him in good time. All parts of the man's venture are now ended, I can assure you. And, I may say, it pains me greatly to find him a traitor, for I thought him a friend." He stared at Robert with a look of utter distaste, as if the boy was personally to blame for Bowlby's treachery. "And now I wish to see to my daughter. You will remain here, Wychwoode. I shall return presently and we will discuss what is to happen to you for your part in this." He nodded to Cromwell and left.

There was an uneasy silence, then Cromwell spoke in his quiet, but authoritative voice.

"You, fellow," he looked at Tris. "Leave us. I would be alone with Master Wychwoode. Please wait outside, and make certain none can disturb us."

Tris got up and walked out.

"I recall when we first met," Cromwell continued once they were alone, "that I counselled you to retain the element of surprise. Given you managed to surprise every man by exploding their vessel, I take it you heeded my counsel." It did not seem to be a question, but Robert nodded. "And the two men who died in the blast – I assume it was by some trick of yours that they were in the right place at the right time to be consumed in the explosion?"

Robert nodded again. "Yes, I..." He stopped as Cromwell raised his hand for silence.

"Nay, I care not what conceit you used to ensure they were positioned in such danger. If it was as devious as... what was it Sir Francis said... escaping from a locked chamber..?" He raised an eyebrow. "Getting away in the night in complete silence? And much more besides, I warrant. If it was as devious or as secretive as these, then I applaud you."

Robert was unsure exactly where this was going, so he waited without saying anything.

After a moment, Cromwell continued. "I would like to make you a proposition, Master Wychwoode. I know you are young. I know you are preparing to study the law. But I want you to work for me at the same time as you are studying, and thereafter as well. I want you to be my intelligencer, going into situations where there may be a threat to the person of the King, or the security of the state. I want you to be my eyes and ears on such occasions, able to report back to me so I may have worthy intelligence, or even take action if that is warranted."

He paused, his dark, unblinking eyes never leaving Robert's.

"I want to make use of your cunning," he continued. "Your ability to conceive a plan and to execute it, while retaining the secrecy needed to maintain the element of surprise. I see a real talent in you, and I must admit that I am most selfish. I want that talent for my own use, and I want it to benefit my master, the King." He paused again. "It will not be easy,

I assure you. There will be difficult decisions that must be made, alone and at speed. There will be danger, maybe even mortal. But I see what Sir Francis cannot. I see that you, no doubt with the help of his daughter – for she is also a brave, clever, and may I say, rather devious young woman – have succeeded in stopping hundreds – maybe thousands – of men from mounting a rebellion. That is indeed a rare achievement, and all the more so, because you and she are barely adults. So you understand my purpose, Master Wychwoode. You have faced danger. You have made decisions alone and at speed. Good decisions. You have proved to me that you are more than capable of succeeding in the clandestine work that I want you to carry out. Will you do this, Master Wychwoode? Work for me?"

Cromwell let silence settle on the little room.

Robert shifted his weight slightly from one foot to the other, as he tried to absorb the enormity of the proposition being put to him by the foremost minister in the land.

Should he accept? Could he truly become a secret intelligencer? Yet – was this not exactly what he had been doing these past few days? Ever since he and Ophelia had overheard Robin – Tresillick – at the fair, had he not been scheming and planning to thwart the man's aims? And he had succeeded in this, had he not? Even if it had taken the destruction of a ship and deprived the law of the opportunity to deliver justice to Tresillick and Jake – he had succeeded in stopping the rebellion. For sure, he had made some errors. He should have been more careful to keep his long hair hidden from observation after they had run into the crowds at the fair. He should not have left Ophelia alone in the tavern, nor should he have let Tris take him aboard The Flying Cloud. And he should definitely have looked more carefully when he came up from the hatch after setting the fuse.

But these were the errors of a novice.

Perhaps he was not such a consummate planner as he had always supposed. Perhaps he still had a lot to learn, or he would not have made such mistakes?

In truth, he would learn from those, and become a better man as a result. A better lawyer. A better planner.

"I would have an answer, Master Wychwoode," said Cromwell. "I am offering you the chance to continue doing what you have proved able to do so well. What clearly excites you."

Robert took a sharp breath. Yes – it had been exciting. And yes, the thought of being given such a chance was not one to be missed. But should such a big decision be taken so quickly? Should there not be more thought put into such a thing? Discussions with his father? And with Ophelia, who might have concerns about him placing himself in frequent danger? How could he put her through such worry and concern once they were sharing their lives together? That would not be fair on her.

Perhaps it would be better to ask if the decision could be deferred a short while?

"Master Secretary Cromwell, I..." he began, but got no further. Suddenly the door crashed open and Ophelia's father strode in, his face redder than Robert had ever seen.

"Wychwoode!" shouted Sir Francis. "My daughter is grievously injured – and I hold you to blame!" Sir Francis marched up to Robert and took hold of his collar, then pushed him up against the wall. "She has burns to her back! Were these not dressed by some goodwife here, then they would leave her permanently scarred." He pushed his red face into Robert's. "What say you, boy?"

"I have said I am sorry, sir," Robert answered, trying to ignore the small strings of spittle in the corners of the man's mouth. "But with God's good grace and the dressings applied, the burns will heal, as you say. Then Ophelia will be whole once more." He paused. "And I will make sure she is never hurt again, believe me, sir. Never."

Sir Francis shook his head. "Nay, boy, you will not have the opportunity." He let go of Robert's collar and stood back. "If you ever had a thought of making a life with my daughter, then be very clear, that is not going to happen." His lip curled in a sneer. "Know this; I will make it my business to find her a suitable husband, and she will be wed to him as soon as she is fully healed. And he will be a man able to take proper care of her, not one to let her find mischief or get herself burned. In other words, not you, Master Wychwoode! You will never see her again, let me assure you of that."

Robert felt as if he had been punched in the belly, but he said nothing. For the first time in his life, he could think of nothing appropriate to say.

"This is your payment for your actions these past few days," continued Sir Francis. "I will take Ophelia back in a carriage this very day, to have her looked after in her own home until I find another man able to look to her care. And that is the end of the matter."

Robert found his voice. "Never to see her again?" he whispered. "May I not even say farewell?"

"Certainly not." Sir Francis snapped. He marched over to

the door, then paused with his hand on it. "After all she has suffered," he added, "she is most clear that she has no wish to see you. Not now; not ever again." He marched out and slammed the door shut.

There was a long silence after he had gone.

"It is not real," Robert muttered, sinking down into a seat with his head in his hands. "It cannot be the truth of Ophelia's feelings. I do not believe it." He looked up. "I will not give her up. I will chase after her."

Cromwell shook his head. "I would not counsel it," he said. "Leave it awhile. After time has passed, belike both father and daughter will have softened their hearts."

Robert shook his head. "But she is to be married. I will lose her for all time."

"I speak to my cousin regularly," Cromwell put a hand on Robert's shoulder. "So I will know of Ophelia's situation. I can keep you informed." He paused. "Although I would of course need to have regular contact with you..." He left it hanging a moment, before adding softly, "Which I will, naturally, if you work for me..."

Naturally...

Robert knew he was being manipulated, but if it meant he would have even the slimmest chance of winning Ophelia back, was that not fair compensation?

It was enough. Robert stood up, then held out his hand to the King's Secretary. "Yes," he said, as they shook hands. "I will work for you, Master Cromwell. When do I start?"

20

CHAPTER TWENTY

Robert thanked the servant who was holding the door open for him, and walked slowly into Cromwell's study.

It was a dark room, lit only by a small fire, a couple of candles and the weak light from a single diamond-paned window. Cromwell was at his desk, scratching slowly on a piece of paper with a feather quill, which he re-inked frequently from a silver pot.

Robert waited, standing just inside the door.

Eventually Cromwell finished writing, blotted and folded the paper, then sealed it and put it to one side. He looked up. "Come in, young Wychwoode, come in." He gestured towards a meeting table and chairs close by the fire. "Sit yourself down. Welcome to the Palace of Westminster."

Robert sat and crossed his legs, then spotted a hole in the knee of his hose, so quickly re-crossed them to hide it.

"You sent for me, Master Secretary?" he said.

Cromwell looked at him with his small, unsmiling eyes. "Indeed I did." He sat back. "But first, tell me, how you have been settling at Gray's Inn?. It has been a few weeks since the, ah, explosive events in Weymouth. The summer has passed most quickly since then."

"I am settling in well, thank you," Robert replied.

"And your studies of the law?"

"Also well. I am starting to get the grounding I seek."

"Good." Cromwell said. "Good. But your studies may need to be halted for a short while. I have a mission for you. The first, I hope, of many. And it is one for which you are notably well suited."

Robert said nothing, waiting to see where this was going.

"You recall, I assume," Cromwell began, "Sir John Bowlby; the guiding hand behind the whole Cornish rebellion?"

Robert nodded. How could he forget?

"Sadly, the man remains at large. We sent troops to arrest him, but he must have had word of our approach, and he was already many hours gone when they arrived at his house."

"I see. What of the army he was raising?" Robert asked.

"Ah, yes." The corners of Cromwell's mouth twitched, which Robert took to be the closest the man ever got to a smile. "He needed to raise a body of men, much larger than the two hundred or so he recruited locally to sail on The Flying Cloud. This needed to be on a significantly larger scale, as he intended to march with an army fifty times that number up through Devon, Somerset and on to London, where he would attack while The Flying Cloud was making her own challenge from the Thames."

"So had he managed to put such an army together?" Robert asked.

"Yes, indeed. He had issued muster letters to all his squires, telling them to call up their tenants, servants, and others under their authority as fighting men. By God's good grace when we searched his house we found the certificates from his squires, revealing that an army numbering fully ten thousand was even then mustering in their towns and villages on the route, about to march. We immediately sent orders to each of the squires to stand their men down, on pain of arrest for treason. That they did."

Robert allowed himself a small smile of satisfaction. "So the rebellion was truly finished?"

"Indeed it was." Cromwell sat back, and gave him what looked like an actual smile. "And that, my dear young Wychwoode, was almost exclusively due to your and Ophelia's exploding of the ship. Not only did you prevent the attack by sea, but you also prompted our move to stop Sir John Bowlby gathering his army."

"So what would you have me do?" Robert asked, pleased to be reminded of this man's recognition for his earlier success. "Now that the Cornish rebellion is over?"

"As I indicated, Bowlby had disappeared when we arrived to arrest him, along with his wife and children – a small girl and an infant boy." Cromwell's eyes never left Robert's.

"Do you have any idea where they might have gone?"

"Bowlby has a house in London, so I sent an intelligencer to watch it, hoping to catch sight of them, but my man stood for some days and there was no sign of the family. So we made some further enquiries, and it appears that they have gone north, almost certainly using a false name, and most likely heading for Yorkshire." Cromwell gave a small sigh. "Which is the worst thing for us."

Robert asked, "Why so?"

"Because the north has a high number of Catholic nobles who, like Bowlby, do not like the religious changes by the King following his divorce from Katherine of Aragon and marriage to Queen Anne Boleyn. Men such as Percy, Constable and Hussey. A fellow called Aske is also of interest. At present they are all quiet, but a man like Bowlby moving amongst them could be just the spark to ignite the powder of their rebellion."

Robert winced at the illusion – the memory of being blown off the ship with Ophelia was still too fresh in his mind. "And if the north rises," Cromwell continued, "it could be much worse than anything coming out of the West Country. So I want him found, and brought to justice before he can cause any more harm."

"So you want me to travel north for this purpose?" Robert asked. A thought occurred. "Will I be working alone?"

Cromwell tapped his fingers on the desk a moment, then shook his head. "Not alone. I have a man up there already, so I want you to meet up with him and work together. He can be found at this inn located in the city of York." Cromwell passed across a folded slip of paper. "Find him there and he will brief you in full on what he has found, and you can both decide how best to locate this Bowlby." Cromwell tapped his fingers again, then said softly, "My man is Jasper Williams, Ophelia's brother."

Robert nodded. He was not surprised by this news.

Ophelia had said that her brother was up north on the King's secret business, so it made some sense.

But the mention of her name brought on a more pressing question.

"Ophelia," Robert asked. "You said you would tell me of her. How does she fare?"

Cromwell sighed. "I thought you would bring up the subject of my young cousin," he said softly. "And the news I have will not please you."

Robert felt the room suddenly chill as he stared at the older man. "Tell me," he said woodenly. "I would know, whatever is your news."

Cromwell nodded slowly. "She is to be married, as you knew, but it has all happened very quickly. The wedding takes place tomorrow, here in London."

Robert asked through clenched teeth, "And the fortunate fellow is?"

"One by the name of Rufus Moreland."

"And what of him?" It was the question Robert did not really want answered, but, like picking off a scab, it had to be done.

"He is nearer my age than yours, and has already lost two wives; one in a stillbirth and one to a fever," Cromwell said, his words cutting like a sword into Robert's chest. "He is solid and reliable rather than high-born, but I suppose that is not unusual with a marriage to a youngest daughter. Anyhow, he has made it clear to Sir Francis that he will brook no nonsense from Ophelia. She will move with him to his house on Dartmoor, which I understand is, er, somewhat isolated."

"Isolated?" Robert muttered. "How isolated?"

Cromwell sucked through his teeth. "Two hours' ride to the nearest town." He gave a small grimace, then added, "Maybe more."

"By Heavens!" Robert burst out, all propriety forgotten. "She is sent to jail!"

"More that she is kept safe and out of trouble."

"I will not allow it!"

"I am sorry, Robert," Cromwell looked almost sympathetic. "But it is not within your grasp to allow it or not."

"Ophelia will escape, then," Robert replied. "She has a skill at slipping away."

"I understand her family have anticipated just this eventuality. Until she is safely taken to the church and wed, all the doors and windows of their London house are kept securely locked, and guards are even stationed outside."

"To stop a girl of sixteen years getting away?

Cromwell raised an eyebrow. "A girl who, as you say, has demonstrated an exceptional skill at escaping."

"So she is a prisoner already? At the Williams' London house?"

"I am afraid so," Cromwell said. He stood up, and indicated the door. "I bid you farewell, young Wychwoode, and I wish you success in your mission to find Bowlby."

Robert went out into the dull summer's day with Cromwell's parting words repeating in his head over and over, like a hammer hitting on an anvil. "Ophelia Williams will be married to Rufus Moreland tomorrow, and that is final."

21

CHAPTER
TWENTY-ONE

The stray dog sniffed curiously at Ophelia's feet.

It was a mangy looking terrier; its matted coat a mixture of thick fur and bald patches. It had one ear standing proud, while the other was flopped over and appeared to have a size-able piece missing, as if it had once been bitten off by some other dog.

Ophelia gave it a soft kick with her boot, not to hurt it but to make it go away. "Shoo!" she hissed. "Go on, shoo!" She glanced towards the end of the dark alley where she was hiding, in case one of her pursuers was alerted by the move-ment and noise of the dog.

After a moment the animal lost interest and trotted off to sniff at a bundle of rags piled up against the wall.

Ophelia crept as softly as she could to the end of the alley where he had come in, then crouched down and peered out, hoping that any watcher was looking higher up and would miss movement at this low level.

There were plenty of people in the City of London street; vendors selling their wares off carts; women carrying baskets of vegetables and meats from shops; merchants walking briskly along. But thankfully, no sign of the two burly men Rufus Moreland had brought with him from Dartmoor, and who had been stationed outside her father's London house to make sure that if she did somehow manage to escape through the locked doors and windows, she did not get any further.

It was clear that her father, Cressida and Moreland had thought it most likely that she would try to get away, and had set the locks and the guards accordingly.

She permitted herself a small smile. They had expected her to break out, so how could she possibly disappoint them?

And who would not seek freedom, if the alternative was to submit to this appalling marriage? To wed a man as old as her father, with a rough, red, weather-beaten face that pleased her not? A man who made it clear she was to remain in his draughty old house in the middle of nowhere for the rest of her life?

It had been an escape that had taken some planning, such as would make Robert most proud of her. And it had very nearly gone without a hitch.

Very nearly.

It had been put in motion an hour or so earlier. She had been concealed in the laundry room near the kitchens, when the scullion boy had walked past. She had suddenly reached out and pulled him inside before he could protest. Then she had stood with her back to the door so he could not get out.

Holding up a shiny shilling coin before the shocked lad, she whispered, "This is yours, if you do as I ask."

"Wassat then, mistress?" he replied, staring at the coin with eyes open so wide she was concerned they might drop out of his grubby little face.

"I want you to change clothes with me." He frowned, so she added, "I want you to pretend to be me for a while."

"Whyssat?"

"I have an urge to see what it is like to be in the kitchens," she lied. "And I will wager you would want to see what it is to be one of the fine family?"

"Not if I must dress as a girl."

"Oh come now," she smiled. "It would only be for a short time. It would be fun!" She waved the coin. "And I would give you this shilling..."

This seemed to settle his doubts. "Arright, then."

She quickly struggled out of her robe, sleeves, kirtle, stockings and hood, until she was standing in just her chemise. He pulled off his jerkin and breeches, so that he was down to a grey shift. She quickly put his things on, including the boots, which were tight but wearable, then bunched her hair up under his cap. There was no doubt she now smelled fairly rank, but should have the passable look of a scullion boy. She reached for a cloth, wet it in the washtub, then started cleaning the accumulated grime off his face. "Your name, boy?" she asked as she scrubbed.

"They calls me Tam, mistress."

"Well, Tam, I am Ophelia, if anyone asks."

"How long till we changes back?"

Ophelia gave a chuckle at the thought that she would hopefully be long gone before he was discovered. "An hour or so, no more," she said as she stood back to admire his now clean features, then used a corner of the cloth to wipe away a small bit of grime she had missed by his ear.

"Wot if I is called out afore then?"

"Then you say it was all my fault," she said. "Which it is. No one will blame you for this."

He grunted in acknowledgment, while she rubbed the cloth over his hands to clean them as well. Then she put the filthy cloth down and held up her robe. "Right. Now let us see how you look."

A few minutes of struggles, protests and 'keep still' admonishments later, Tam was standing in all her finery. With his clean face and his bare legs hidden under the gown, he looked a passable imitation of her. She nodded in satisfaction, then added the hood as the finishing touch.

She stood back again. The final result looked good enough for her purpose, so she said, "I would you go up to the first bedchamber at the top of the stairs, the one with the flower posy on the door, and sit in the seat by the window. Be sure to look out for a while, and if you see any men outside, give them a friendly wave." She held up the coin. "Now take this for your troubles."

He snatched it and nodded, then pushed open the door and scampered off.

Ophelia hoped he would do as she asked, and keep any watchers satisfied that she was still in her chamber. She chuckled again. Maybe his deception would be so good, that he would become the third Mistress Moreland on the morrow!

On that amusing thought, Ophelia used the same cloth to make her own face and hands as dirty as she could, holding her breath against the smell. Then she reached behind a chest and retrieved a package that she had previously hidden. It contained Scarhead's knife, which she had kept concealed ever since retrieving it on her return to Penryn, a bulging purse of coin and a belt. She put the belt on under her jerkin and secured the knife and purse, then slipped down the passage towards the kitchens.

—o—

At first the plan had gone surprisingly well.

Arriving in the kitchens, she had kept her head down to avoid Cook and any of his servants talking to her. Thankfully they were all too busy to comment on what appeared to be Tam the scullion boy walking though.

But for sure they would comment if Tam stood there doing nothing, so she picked up a bucket of slops and strode purposefully to the back door, then pushed it open and stepped out into the street.

She had guessed – correctly it seemed – that the back door would be left unlocked during the day, to allow for all the comings and goings by Cook and the servants. Of course if she had tried to walk out as Ophelia, the cook would have been under strict orders by Cressida to stop her. But as Tam, she had the freedom to walk out with ease.

Freedom!

It felt so good, it was worth the smell of her clothing and the dirt on her face to secure it!

She put the bucket on the cobbles and looked up and down the street. Which way to go? She patted the reassuring bulk of the purse at her belt. Once again she was having to survive alone, but at least this time it was not in a forest with derelict cottages and wild boars. This time she was in the City of London, and with money. So she could find a coaching inn or tavern with rooms and hide out in some warmth and comfort for a few days, until it was safe for her to secure some proper clothing and move on.

Ophelia looked back up at the house. It was sad to be abandoning her family and setting out alone for who knew what, but in truth she had been given no option.

She turned back to the street, and spent a final moment checking directions. She decided to go left.

A hand grabbed her shoulder. She froze.

"You, scullion boy! Those slops will not empty themselves! Were you about to walk away and leave them?"

Ophelia turned slowly, keeping her head down. Before her was the bottom of an apron, with breeches and shoes visible below. One of the shoes was tapping on the slop bucket.

"Look at me, boy!" the man snapped. "I am not talking to the top of your cap."

"Sorry," she muttered.

"Sorry – Cook!"

"Sorry, Cook."

"I said to look at me, boy!" he repeated.

Then he pulled her cap off.

Ophelia looked up, conscious that her long chestnut hair

was now flowing down her back, and there was no mistaking her true identity.

Cook's eyes were wide in his large red face, and his mouth was hanging open. "Mistress Ophelia..." he breathed. But before he could say or do anything more, she had already run off down the street.

"Stop!" she heard him shout. "It is Mistress Ophelia! She is getting away! Stop I say! Stop her!"

Then she ran round a corner and his shouts became jumbled up in the general noise of the street.

She carried on running, dodging round the people in her path; women out shopping who looked at her curiously and stepped back as she passed, sellers with carts who used their bodies to shield their produce in case she tried to steal anything, riders who had to calm their skittering horses as she pelted round them – all staring at this dirty girl in a boy's jerkin and breeches, running with her long hair flying out behind her.

Ophelia slowed enough to shoot a quick glance over her shoulder, then gave a gasp as she saw the two Dartmoor men appearing around a cart, then running towards her with determined scowls.

A fork in the road came up. Shooting a quick look left then right, she went towards the left fork, but then a man with a cart crossed her path, so at the last moment she took the narrower right fork instead. This lane then had a small right turn almost immediately. Two women were standing in the road just beyond with their backs to her, so she took the turn to avoid them, hoping that the Dartmoor men would think she had gone straight on. A few strides later she saw the entrance to the dark alley. It looked safe, so she ran in. Immediately she stopped in the shadows, trying to control her ragged breathing and stay out of sight.

She then made her way as quietly as she could along the alley, which was where the stray dog had found her.

—o—

Ophelia pulled back from the corner of the street, stood up and made her way along the alley to the deeper shadows. She leaned against the wall and let out a small sigh. By God's good grace, it looked as if she had managed to evade her pursuers. She glanced back towards the street. Give it a few minutes, then find a room for the night.

She ran her fingers through her hair. Too bad Cook had taken her cap; not only had its removal identified her as Ophelia, but being bare-headed on the streets meant she was still so obviously a girl.

There was a sharp barking sound and she looked over. The dog was still by the pile of rags, standing with his tail up. He barked again, then turned to look at her. With a small shrug, she pushed off the wall and went over to him. He looked up, then back at the rags and barked again.

Ophelia studied the pile. Now she was closer she could see it was not just a jumble, but had some sort of shape. She flicked back the top piece of sacking material.

There was a man lying against the wall.

She stepped back – both at the shock of seeing him and also the foul smell.

She held her breath and pulled the sacking a little further

back, just enough to reveal his waist and the top of his dirty breeches tied with a piece rope. At this the dog jumped up and put his paws on the man's face, then started licking it while his tail wagged frantically.

After a moment the man's eyes fluttered open, and he put a hand up to pet the dog. "Hello, old fellow," he muttered in a weak voice. "What is your name then?"

Ophelia stepped forward. "Is this your dog?" she asked.

The man squinted at her. "Nay, fellow. I know him not."

"He seems to like you." The dog wagged its tail then curled up on the man's chest and yawned. "I think he wants you to keep him."

The man patted the dog and nodded. "He will be good company, if only for my final days."

Ophelia frowned. "Your final days?"

"I am not long for this world, fellow," he replied. "My time of walking these streets is done." He coughed heavily. "God is calling me and I must go to him soon. And it will be from this place I go. I will not be moving again."

Ophelia crouched down. The man had rough skin around his thin grey beard, but something about his knowing eyes made her think he had once been a man of learning. "Can I get you anything?" she asked gently. "Something to eat?"

"You are most kind, lad," he said. "A little bread would be most welcome."

Ophelia nodded and went back to the main street. She peered out and saw a bread cart close by. She checked both ways but there was no sign of the men pursuing her, so she hurried over.

A few minutes later she was back in the alley, and handed

the man a couple of cob rolls. He broke one in two and gave half to the dog, who jumped down and took it a little way off to eat.

The man bit off some for himself. "I thank you good fellow..." Then he frowned. "But..." he peered at her. "Art in truth a girl, not a fellow? My eyes are not much good, but you have the look of a girl about you..."

"Yes I am." There seemed no point in lying to this old man.

"Why is a girl in the garb of a boy, and hiding in alleyways?" he asked.

"I am running from a marriage I do not want."

He gave a small smile. "That sounds like many a girl, I warrant. But you have a story, no doubt? And I have naught else to do but listen..." He looked slightly hopeful, so Ophelia decided there was no harm in sharing her tale – especially with this man who was so close to death.

She sat down next to him, with her back to the same wall. "What is your name?" she asked.

"I was Jeffrey in the life I had before this alleyway."

"Well Jeffrey," she said, settling herself more comfortably, "I was riding through a forest one day, on my way to Cornwall..."

—o—

Jeffrey was silent for a while, staring forward after she finished. Eventually he said, "It is quite a tale, young Mistress Ophelia, quite a tale. You have faced more perils in your sixteen years than many face in a lifetime."

"I suppose so."

"And killed a man. That gives you a different view on life, I warrant." He turned to her. "Will you take some advice from an old fellow who has seen much life – and death – in his own days?"

"Of course," Ophelia answered, wondering what she was about to get.

"First, let us consider the pendant, that meant so much to you."

Ophelia frowned. "I said it was lost in the blast on the ship," she said, unable to keep the bitterness from her voice.

"How can you be so sure? That fellow you call Robin, he took it when he first captured you at the dockside. What is to say he was still holding it when you and young Robert sent him to hell in the blast? A piece like that would have immense value. I warrant he would have instead found a safe place for it."

"Belike," she muttered. "But if the safe place was on the ship, then the result is the same. It is still at the bottom of Weymouth harbour."

"Perhaps." He was silent a moment. "How long was the ship in dock before she blew?"

"A couple of hours. Maybe more."

"More than enough time to take it ashore and hide it. Or, more likely, give it to another for safekeeping. This man Bowlby you say – could he have been given it? As the knight leading the venture, I would have thought it likely it would have found its way to him." He looked up at her. "If Bowlby had found out Robin had taken such a piece and not told him, belike he would have exacted a terrible punishment. I do not think Robin would have risked that."

Ophelia considered this. It was possible – and understandable – that if the precious pendant was not at the bottom of the harbour, then it had somehow got into the possession of Bowlby, either directly if Bowlby had been at the harbour, or indirectly if someone had been charged with taking it to him. But had Bowlby been at the harbour? If he had, would he not have had something to say when his ship was so violently destroyed? Or perhaps he would have made himself scarce as soon as the blast happened. He could hardly have come out and complained, or he would have been arrested immediately.

"At least you have given me hope that it still exists," she said. "And if, as you say, Bowlby has it, then for sure I would get it back. It means more to me than I can possibly say."

He nodded. "So that is the pendant dealt with. And now we turn to young Wychwoode, the boy who seems to have stolen your heart."

"I did not say that," Ophelia said, a little snappily.

"My dear child, you did not need to say it out loud," Jeffrey replied. "It was perfectly clear from the way you talk of him that he is most special to you."

"Oh. I am sorry."

"So," he continued with a weak smile, "you have abandoned your marriage, and sadly, with it your family. Maybe they will take you back in time – but not now. I will talk more on that shortly. Meanwhile, I say you should find this young man of yours again." He turned to her. "Was that your aim when you made the scullion lad change clothes with you and made your escape? An excellent ruse, by the way."

"I was only thinking to get away from the house," she

said. "Anyway I have no idea where Robert is or where to find him."

Jeffrey gave a small laugh that ended in another bout of heavy coughing. "Oh, no, young Ophelia," he said when he had recovered his breath. "That is the easiest task of all!"

Ophelia's heart leapt. She could find Robert? That would be more than she could hope for! But no – it was impossible. "How can you know such a thing?" she asked doubtfully.

"The clues you have shared point only to one place. Gray's Inn. He is studying to be a lawyer, you say?" She nodded, her excitement rising with his certainty. "Then it is unlikely he will be studying elsewhere."

"And it is not too far?"

"It is in the parish of Holborn on the Fleet river, not too far from this place. Less than a half hour's walk for legs as young and strong as yours."

The dog jumped back onto Jeffrey's chest, causing further coughing. But he made no move to shift the animal, and even gave it a pat. "I would have done it myself in such time, back in happier days."

"Then I must get there at once!" she exclaimed, starting to get up. Then she stopped and sat down again. "But you said you would talk more of my family. What did you mean by that?"

"Ah yes. Your father. You say he has naught but disdain for you? That he considers you a wilful daughter who causes him only anguish?"

She nodded. "That is so."

"And you say he lost his wife, your mother, some three

years since?" She nodded again. "Hmm. And he appeared as if by some coincidence at Weymouth after the ship exploded?"

"Yes." She glanced at Jeffrey, not sure how these seemingly random thoughts were going to come together. His eyes were closed, and his breath still, so for a worrying moment she thought his time had already come. Then his eyes opened and he seemed to study her closely. "And he would have had you married to a sensible, if rather dull, man who would keep you out of harm's way on Dartmoor?"

"I suppose..."

Jeffrey leaned forward. "Then do you not see?" he said, with more strength in his voice than she had heard before. "He does love you, Ophelia, after his own fashion." He lay back. "He knows you miss your mother, and that he can never replace the love you had with her. So he understands why you must rebel all the time, even though it pains him greatly. This understanding of himself causes such frustration – leading to his flashes of anger. Yet, when you were truly in danger, what did he do? He rode at speed to Weymouth to get to you and bring you home, and tended to the burns on your back. That does not speak of a father who holds his daughter in disdain, but quite the opposite."

"Oh." Ophelia did not know what more to say. How had Jeffrey been able to interpret the story she told from her own viewpoint and understand it so clearly from her father's? And yet, now she thought on it, it did make some sense. Father's anger did always seem to be centred on her own disobedience, and always when such actions led her into danger. Maybe if he did truly love her, then he would always want what was

best for her – and be frustrated if she was continually disobeying him...

Maybe she had only ever seen his actions from her own
selfish view...

"So – should I go home now?" she asked in a small voice.

"What, and pull Tam back to his life of drudgery in
the kitchens?" Jeffrey chuckled. "Nay, but in all seriousness,
I would ask you, Ophelia, what is most important to you?
Finding the pendant which is the only link to your mother's
past love, and the boy Wychwoode who has won your heart
for the future? Or is it to comply with your father and marry
Master Dull from Dartmoor?"

She stood up. "When you put it like that, I see there is no
competition."

He stared at her a moment with his old grey eyes. "Trust
your instinct, Ophelia. It has served you well thus far."

"I will."

"Go, then," he said. "Find Holborn, Gray's Inn, and your
young man. Then see if you can recover your precious jewel. I
cannot say for sure it still exists with Bowlby, but I think it a
chance well worth pursuing." He nodded. "And then, maybe
after some time has passed, return to your father and see if he
does truly love you, as I say."

"Which direction is Holborn?" she asked.

"Head west out of the city with the sunset, then ask. That
is my best advice."

She leaned down and touched his cheek. "I cannot thank
you enough, Jeffrey."

He smiled up at her. "You brought me bread, and told me
your story. Your company has been a delight, and I will die a

far happier man for meeting you." He patted the dog. "And I have a companion for my final hours, too. What more can a man ask?"

"Will you give him a name?"

"I thought 'Ophelia' if that sits well with you."

"But he's a boy," she said with a grin.

"Do I not see a boy before me?" he asked.

"True enough," she replied. "Then you have my blessing." She stood up to go. "Again, I thank you."

"Wait," he said. "There is one but one more thing." He brought out his hand from under the rags, then raised it up. "I would have you hear my dying confession. It is not the full Last Rites, but it should mean I can face God in a state of grace when my time comes. Will you do that for me?"

"But I am a woman," she answered. "And not a priest."

"Please," he said, his eyes pleading on hers. "The Protestant church says that anyone can hear a dying confession. And I have heard your story."

"Very well then. I will do the best I can."

When he had finished, she made the sign of the cross on his forehead. "God go with you, Jeffrey," she whispered.

"And with you," he replied.

"And you, little Ophelia," she said to the dog.

"Here," he said, and he felt around under the rags, before producing a brown woollen cap. "You had better hide your hair with this, so you can travel more freely as a lad. I have no further use for it." He handed it to her. "Now go! Or it will be dark soon and they will shut the gates for the curfew!"

22

CHAPTER TWENTY-TWO

Late autumn leaves were swirling around the little York-shire churchyard, collecting in small drifts against the gravestones as the fine-looking gentleman led his family along the path to the chapel.

Nodding to the pastor who was standing just inside the door, he ushered them all inside; his wife in her thick fur cloak, his small daughter equally well covered, and a young maidservant holding a sleeping baby in her arms. The infant was so heavily wrapped in blankets that only its eyes and the tip of its nose could be seen. The father ushered them all into the middle pews, waiting as they each shuffled past him; the maidservant first, then his daughter, and finally his wife. He crossed himself and took the end seat next to her.

More worshippers arrived and took their places, blowing

on their hands to try and warm themselves as they sat; their breath making small clouds in the flickering candlelight.

The bells that had been calling people to the chapel stopped pealing. The pastor checked there were no more coming in, then pushed the door shut with a loud slam. This noise seemed to cause the baby to wake up. It made a series of small snuffling and mewling noises. As the pastor and his altar servants processed to the front of the chapel, the maidservant clutched the baby closer to her body, rocking it gently and shushing softly. The gentleman shot her an angry glance, as if to blame her for waking the infant. She clutched it more tightly, and after a moment, its eyes closed and became quiet again. She breathed a silent prayer of thanks.

Then the candles all guttered as the chapel door was thrown open once more. A man in a heavy cloak entered, as if blown in by the cold wind, then pushed the door shut. The baby's eyes opened again at the disturbance. Its little nose started to redden, which the maidservant knew meant that it might be about to howl. She shushed it urgently, prompting further angry glances from both its father and mother. Thankfully, the baby seemed to change its mind, and instead gave a small gurgle and went back to sleep.

The girl glanced over her shoulder at the newcomer, who was now seated in the last pew at the back. She wanted to see who it was that had nearly caused her such anguish. But the man was leaning forward in prayer, so all she could see was the top of his cap and his heavy woollen cloak.

The sound of the pastor tapping on the lectern made her turn back. "My brothers and sisters in Christ..." he said, and the service began.

Throughout the next two hours of standing up, sitting down, prayers and sermons, the maidservant struggled to keep the baby's noises to nothing more than the occasional grizzle or whimper, ever mindful of its parents' strong disapproval of any noise it might make. As if a such a small infant could be commanded to stay silent! she thought, as she put a finger inside its blankets and stroked its cheek. And what can be more natural than the sound of an innocent child in the house of God?

Finally the service was over, and the family got up to leave. The father stood aside to let them out of the pew. As the girl walked past, he hissed, "I have made it clear, girl, that the child is to stay quiet in church."

"I did all I could, Master Faulkner," the girl replied. "He never truly cried even once."

He frowned. "Do not counter me, girl. I could scarce hear the word of God for all the sounds he was making."

"I could stay in the house with him next time?" she asked, as they started walking out of the church.

"Nay, he must hear God's word as soon as he can," he said over his shoulder. "But he must listen in silence – that is what I charge you with."

"Yes, sir," she muttered as they walked out. "I will do as best I can."

The maidservant followed the family down the path, clutching the baby tightly to her chest in an attempt to keep him warm.

As she passed under the lychgate, a hand suddenly grabbed her arm from behind. She spun round in surprise, ready to shout for help, but was instantly silent when she saw who had stopped her.

It was the man who had come late to church and sat at the back.

Only now he was standing before her, so she could see his face and his height.

"Robert!" she exclaimed. "What are you doing here?"

"Hello Ophelia," he replied with a grin. Then he became more serious. "I need to tell you as a matter of urgency, to meet me and Jasper in the coaching inn tomorrow. We have had word from Cromwell and must share this with you."

—o—

Ophelia sat back in the nursing chair and stared up at the rough plaster ceiling of the nursery where the children slept. Beside her little baby Luke lay asleep in his cot, while his sister Jane changed the robes on her doll Persephone yet again, chattering softly to herself under her breath.

Ophelia looked across at the little girl. "It will be time for sleep soon, Jane," she said. "Say your prayers to Jesus."

"Yes, Alice," said Jane, and put Persephone carefully on her pillow, then knelt by the bed with her hands clasped, her lips moving silently. A moment later she said, "G'night, Alice."

"Goodnight, Jane."

Ophelia sat back again and shifted to get more comfortable. At least her back no longer hurt. The burns from the explosion had healed completely, for all there was some small scarring left behind. No doubt that would please Robert.

Robert. Her thoughts went back to the day they had been

reunited near London; the day she had escaped and been directed to Gray's Inn by old Jeffrey.

At first, the Gray's Inn head porter had refused entry to what appeared to be a grubby street urchin 'with a message for one Robert Wychwoode'.

"Be gone, lad!" he had growled at her. "I do not take messages for any of my students from the likes of you! Master Wychwoode is not to be disturbed."

So Jeffrey had been correct that Robert was there! Ophelia had wanted to hug the porter and jump for joy at the thought she had found him!

But it seemed that the porter had a different idea. He grabbed her sleeve and started to drag her out of his lodge. "Out, lad! I will not have you in here!"

"You must tell him the message is from Ophelia Williams!" she yelled in desperation. "Master Wychwoode will be most angered if you do not!"

The porter paused a moment and frowned. "That is not the voice of a lad," he muttered, as he studied her closely. Then he whipped the cap off her head so that once again her long hair flowed down past her shoulders.

"I thought as much," he said triumphantly. "Art a girl!" He handed the cap back. "And I take it that you are this Ophelia Williams?" She nodded. "Very well, I will ask if he wishes to see you. But I will say this, it is most irregular, and I will certainly not allow you in his chambers. You can wait outside the gate while I ask."

So Ophelia had waited by the fine gates, kicking a stone around the dusty cobbles in the light of the flaming braziers fixed to the posts.

After several anxious minutes, she heard footsteps coming across the square, then the gates opened and suddenly she was in Robert's arms, and he was holding her tight and stroking her hair and she was pressing her head to his chest...

It was a moment that she savoured, breathing in the scent of him and wishing it would never end...

"By Heavens, Ophelia, I have missed you so!" he exclaimed. "It has pained me greatly that we have been apart these weeks! Your father said you wanted never to see me again."

She stood back, holding him at arm's length. "He said that?" she exclaimed. "But he said to me you would never want my company again, ever!"

They stared at each other in the flickering light. "He has told the same to both of us," Robert whispered.

"That is not a father's love," she muttered, as she buried her head into his chest again.

After a few moments, he pushed her back. "Why are you dressed as a boy; and a street rat at that?" he asked. Then his face cleared and he nodded knowingly. "I warrant this is how you have escaped, eh? How you have avoided the wedding?" He looked at her with a cheeky grin. "I said to Cromwell when I met him this morning that no lock could hold you, and I was correct! You can tell me the full tale in good time. I am sure it was a most elaborate plan, eh?"

"You saw my cousin Cromwell?" she asked. "What did he want of you?"

Robert was immediately serious. "I cannot tell you. I am sworn to secrecy."

"Oh, do not be such a goose!" Ophelia said, giving him a

small kick in the shin to emphasise her point. "You have no secrets from me!"

"Ow! That hurt!" He gave his leg a quick rub. "But I am sworn."

She put her hands on her hips and faced him. "Would you have me kick you again, Master Wychwoode?" she asked. "This time with some actual force?"

"Do you threaten me?"

"Yes, that is exactly what I do. Tell me."

His face fell and he gave a deep sigh. "I cannot believe I am doing this... And you must not admit it to your cousin." He shook his head. "Cromwell would have me go to Yorkshire, to find Sir John Bowlby. He believes that the man is gone north to escape justice, and also to try and stir up another rebellion."

"Bowlby?" she frowned. "Gone north? I also want to find him, for sure."

"You, Ophelia?" Robert asked. "Why?"

"Belike he may have taken my mother's pendant from that man we knew as Robin before we exploded the ship," she said. "I know it is only a possibility, but if there's any chance he has it, then by Heaven, I would do whatever it takes to get it back." She looked up at him in the flickering light of the braziers. "So I am coming with you."

He shook his head. "No. Absolutely not. There might be danger. I forbid it."

She raised a challenging eyebrow. He sighed deeply again.

"What on earth would I tell Cromwell?"

"You will think of something, I am sure."

23

CHAPTER TWENTY-THREE

It was the afternoon after Robert and Ophelia had met in the churchyard. The light was already beginning to fade to dusk as Ophelia pushed open the heavy door of the coaching inn and went inside.

Robert and her brother Jasper were seated by the fire, talking quietly. They both looked up as she pulled back the hood of her cape and went over.

"Hello, little sister," said Jasper, standing. "You are well met." He smiled down at her, looking every inch a younger version of their father, but with a more open, friendly face. Where Sir Francis Williams had thinning hair cut short, Jasper's was thick and dark. It flopped across his forehead, making him frequently need to push it back. He indicated the chair beside them and she sat. "Some wine?" She nodded and he poured some from their jug. "How is it in the household of Master Faulkner?" he asked.

"As well as can be expected," she answered as she accepted the goblet. "Although the man will constantly belittle me when all I try and do is take care of his babe, and look to the wellbeing of his little daughter."

"He is for sure an unpleasant-seeming man," said Robert, "I marked his face yesterday when you and he were walking out of church together, and it was twisted into such a sneer that I thought it may be permanent."

"It is that," she agreed. "He wears a frown most times."

"But to the point, Ophelia," said Jasper. "We need more evidence that this man Faulkner is in truth our fugitive, Sir John Bowlby. We need more than just a sour disposition and a sneering expression."

"He does vaguely match the description given by Cromwell," said Robert. "A fellow of average height and average build with dark hair and a dark beard." He shrugged. "Although to be sure, that could be almost any man."

"Aye, 'tis true," Jasper agreed, "and while he has arrived here only recently with a similar wife, daughter and babe to Bowlby's, that could also be a mere coincidence." He put his hand over hers and gave her a grim smile. "It is why you have been inveigled into his household to play the role of nursemaid. Cromwell is pressing us for some clear proof – he has sent word that he has troops nearby ready to make the arrest, but he needs to know for sure our investigations have revealed the right man. So we are in your hands, dear sister. What can you tell us?"

Ophelia thought back over the past few days, since their

investigations had identified this man Faulkner and his family as the most likely candidates to be the Bowlbys. The three of them had then agreed to get someone into the house to investigate further – and it had naturally been Ophelia who had put herself forward. As she had said, what could be better than a nursemaid, looking after the small children, able to move freely about the house seeking evidence?

So Jasper had arranged it that the previous nursemaid had met with an unfortunate accident, slipping mysteriously on some wet leaves. This girl had then taken to her bed, complaining of a sore back. So it was no surprise that when Ophelia had arrived offering her services as a replacement, Mistress Faulkner had been only too pleased to accept 'Alice' into her house.

At first Ophelia had been very careful not to do anything obvious, but settle herself into the household routine; bringing baby Luke to his wet nurse for feeding, putting him into his cot and watching as he slept; keeping an eye on three-year-old Jane – making sure she had dolls to play with, clean clothes to wear and food to eat.

Then, gradually, Ophelia had started searching the house, looking for any evidence of Faulkner's possible real identity. Whenever she knew that the master and mistress were otherwise occupied, such as when they were breaking their fast, dining in the evening or going out for their regular afternoon walk, she had taken the opportunity to make a quick exploration of rooms such as the parlour, the solar, and particularly, the master's study. But although she had found many official-looking documents, they were all in the name of Faulkner.

There was nothing she found that even contained the name 'Bowlby', let alone connected it to the master.

But, of course, the thing she was really looking for was the pendant. Not only because she needed to get it back so badly that it hurt, but also because to find it would prove without doubt that Faulkner was indeed Bowlby.

So she did not confine her search to papers in the master's rooms, but also went through the chests and boxes in their bed chamber, in case it was concealed there.

"I have searched in every room, and in every place I can think of looking," she said, "Sadly I have not found anything that could make the connection." She looked at them both. "I am sorry."

There was a long silence, then Robert said, "You are living in the man's house, Ophelia. You see him each day. What is your view? Do you think he really is Bowlby?"

Ophelia took a sip of wine as she thought. There was no doubt the man was deeply unpleasant, but that was not in itself proof of his identity. Could he truly be Bowlby? She wished she could ask Jeffrey what he thought – his wisdom had been remarkable. But he was back in the alley in London... she shuddered – most likely he was dead by now, as he was so sure he only had a few days left.

"Ophelia? What say you?" Jasper and Robert were looking at her expectantly, waiting for her answer. But she saw only Jeffrey's old grey eyes. "Trust your instinct, Ophelia. It has served you well thus far."

"Yes," she said, nodding slowly. "I do truly believe that he is Bowlby."

Robert rested his chin on his hand and observed Ophelia

through narrowed eyes. "There is something about the man that makes me agree with you," he observed. "But as we have said, we must find a way to be certain. Cromwell has charged us with finding Bowlby, not throwing accusations at innocent men. So we need to construct a plan; one that will make him admit it."

"I also agree that it is Bowlby," said Jasper. "But this could be dangerous." He turned to Ophelia. "If it goes wrong then we could be putting you in a difficult position, little sister."

"If it puts Bowlby on trial and returns me Mother's pendant, then I am ready," she replied. "What is in your mind, Robert?"

Robert sat back and looked across them both. "Here is my idea..." he began.

24

CHAPTER
TWENTY-FOUR

It was evening the next day and Ophelia was in the nursery at the Faulkner house.

Jane was already curled up in her bed asleep, her arm firmly round Persephone. Luke was finishing suckling from Mabel, the wet nurse who came in to feed him each day.

Ophelia took Luke carefully from Mabel and put him over her shoulder. After rubbing his back gently for a while, she was rewarded with a loud burp in her ear and the feel of a little wetness on her shoulder.

"Has he posseted?" Mabel asked, as she stood up from the nursing chair and laced her bodice. Ophelia lifted Luke off her shoulder briefly, allowing Mabel to inspect the area. "Aye, that he has," the nurse observed with some satisfaction as she wiped Ophelia's shoulder with a cloth. "As good as ever, eh,

Alice?" She put on her heavy cloak and lifted the hood over her head. "I will be back in the morning," she said. "Good e'en." Then she left.

"Good e'en," Ophelia muttered as she put Luke down into his crib and pulled the blankets over his tiny body. "And goodbye, no doubt." She looked down at the baby. "Sleep well, little one," she said as she cupped his cheek in her hand. "If all goes to plan, I may never see you again, either." She glanced briefly over at the other bed. "Or your sister Jane." The baby smiled up at her with his large blue eyes, and gurgled happily. "And if it all goes wrong, I suspect the result will be much the same." She stroked him a moment, then eased her finger under his covers and let him clutch it with his tiny hand. "So strong a grip, Luke," she said with a smile. "Maybe one day we will meet again, and I can tell you tales of your little tempers, your mighty wind, and more." She chuckled. "You will not thank me now, but belike you will thank me later for your good care."

Ophelia waited until Luke's eyes were closed and his breathing had become regular, then she stoked the fire for warmth, before checking the crib was far enough away from the fireplace. Better the child was slightly less warm than a stray spark set his blankets alight.

She made her way to the parlour, where the master and Mistress Faulkner were used to sitting after their supper. She knocked and waited to be admitted.

"Jane and the baban are asleep, Mistress," she said to the wife after she had curtsied. "Luke has a full belly and a clean bottom."

"Thank you," Mistress Faulkner replied, playing idly with

the chain at her neck, "You may go." Ophelia curtsied again and withdrew.

But instead of walking down the corridor to the other side of the house and taking the narrow back stairs up to her little room, she waited near the door, listening for what might be said inside.

Almost immediately there was a loud snort from the master. "What did that girl say?" he demanded.

"That the children are asleep?" came the voice of his wife, seeming unconcerned.

"No – what did she call Luke? What word did she use?"

"Baby?"

"No, by thunder! She called him a 'baban'. I heard her clear. You know what a 'baban' is?" There was a pause, which was presumably his wife shaking her head. "It is the Cornish for babe! Cornish, I tell you!" There was another pause, which Ophelia imagined was the mistress going white and her mouth falling open. "The girl must have let it slip! By the Lord's Wounds, Katherine, she is Cornish!"

"Nay, nay, she is local – she was most clear on that."

"Not if she uses that word! No girl would say that unless they were come out of Kernow." There was a longer silence. Then the mistress's voice.

"But what of it, John? Belike it means naught?"

"Do not be a fool, woman!" snapped her husband. "All men and women of Kernow know of Sir John and Lady Bowlby and that they are wanted for treason, so there is little chance she knows not who we really are. And if she made clear she was from another part of the country, and kept her Cornish past hidden, then it is certain why she is here. She means to spy on us!"

"Think you so, John?" asked the mistress. "But there is naught in this house to link us to Cornwall – we have made certain of that. And we have not said aught to her since she came that could make her know any different."

"Aye, but think on it, Katherine, think on it! That last girl..."

"Agnes..."

"Yes, yes, her. She slips on some leaves, and within an hour this, this..."

"Alice?"

"If that is what she calls herself. This Alice comes to the door and asks if we need a nursemaid. How convenient is that? It was all planned to get her into the house! She means to spy on us, I tell you!"

There was another silence, which Ophelia thought could well be the mistress pointing at the door; indicating that Ophelia could very well be listening right now. Quickly she slipped off her shoes and ran as quietly as she could down the corridor. Just as she turned the corner and started up the back stairs she heard the door opening from the parlour, and heavy footsteps coming out.

Reaching her room, she jumped into bed and pulled the blanket up around her neck. It was not a moment too soon, as almost immediately she heard a heavy tread on the stairs, then the door half opened and the master's head appeared.

"Alice?" he said with a frown.

"Yes, Master Faulkner?" she said, putting on her most innocent expression.

"Alice," he repeated, looking unsure what to say next. Then he seemed to gather himself. "The mistress and I have been considering your position here."

"Is there aught wrong, Master?" she asked, looking only mildly concerned. "I have been taking good care of Luke and Jane."

"I do not doubt that, but we have decided that an older woman would be better for their well-being."

"Why so, Master? I have not done or said anything that could justify this."

The master opened the door a little further and stepped into the room; stooping to get under the low doorway. Ophelia maintained her neutral expression, but now with a tinge more concern – as if she was unaware of what this man was going to do or say next. And she could see that all of a sudden, young Alice, who he had previously thought was of no consequence, had now become very inconvenient indeed.

"I do not seek your approval for my decisions, girl," he growled. "So I would you accept that you no longer have the care of my children."

"Then you would turn me out?" she asked.

She could see him thinking this through, weighing up the risks. It was not difficult to see where his best option lay. If he chose to let her go free, then she could expose him at any time. But if he kept her here, then she could be a major inconvenience, as he could not keep her a prisoner indefinitely. In which case... she saw the exact moment when the thought crossed his mind.

That she had become too dangerous to be allowed to live.

He took a step forward and closed the door carefully behind him.

"Please, Master," she said, her heart now racing. "What are you going to do?"

"Come now, Alice, if that is indeed your name," he said, his cold eyes fixed on hers. "You are not local, are you?" He took another step towards the bed. "You are of Kernow."

"Nay," she whispered. "Why do you say such a thing?"

"You said 'baban' – that is a Cornish word." He came up to the side of the bed. "So you know who I really am." He stared coldly down at her. "You have been spying on me."

"No, sir. Why would I do that?"

"I know not why a young girl like you might..." then Bowlby stopped, as his eyes widened and a look of shocked understanding appeared on his face. "By Heavens," he whispered. "There is one such young girl... The one who I was told had destroyed my ship..." He suddenly leaned down and grabbed Ophelia's arm, then used it to flip her roughly onto her stomach. Then he pulled down the neck of her servant's dress, to expose the top of her back. "Burns!" he snarled. "I knew it! You are that girl! Then there is no doubt! You must die!"

Ophelia grabbed Scarhead's knife that she had been concealing beneath her pillow. Then she turned herself quickly over, just in time to see him lean down with both arms outstretched, reaching towards her neck.

As Bowlby's hands encircled her throat and started to squeeze, she swung the knife round and into his thigh.

But he seemed not to notice and continued to throttle her, his lips drawn back from his teeth. Her vision started to blacken and she knew she would soon lose consciousness, so she pushed again with the knife, this time harder.

The choking pressure on her throat was making the blackness close in more and more, until she thought, 'Here is death... Lord Jesus, welcome me to your arms...'

She gave one last desperate push with the knife.

Suddenly the pressure on her neck was released and she was coughing and fighting for breath, as Bowlby staggered back, clutching his leg and looking down at the blood that was flowing in a bright scarlet stream from between his fingers.

"You have stabbed me, girl?" he whispered. "By Heavens, you have stabbed me!" He gave a grimace of pain, and she saw the blood drain from his face, as if it was drawn down by the flow from the wound. "I will come back for you when I have bound my leg. Then I will see you in Hell, you little harridan!"

Bowlby staggered out of the room and slammed the door behind him. She heard the key turn in the lock, then the sound of him crashing unsteadily down the stairs.

Ophelia could not move for a moment, while she coughed and struggled to get her breath back. After a few moments she managed to breathe more easily, and the pain in her throat receded enough for her to stand.

She took a few deep breaths to steady herself, tried to wipe as much of Bowlby's blood off her hand as she could, then threw on her cloak and stepped into her shoes.

She pulled the blanket off the bed and eased a corner of the thick material under the door, level with the key on the other side. Hoping it was still there and Bowlby had not thought to pocket it, she pushed the tip of the knife gently into the lock. Immediately it hit the end of the key, and with a few wiggles she managed to get the key straight so she could push it out of the lock. There was a soft thud as it landed on the blanket on the other side of the door, then she pulled the blanket gently back under the door. The black key lay there like a welcome gift.

"It worked, Robert," she whispered to herself as she unlocked the door. "Just as you said."

Then she slipped softly down the stairs and peered cautiously into the corridor. Seeing that it was empty, she padded gently to the back door, and out into the night.

25

CHAPTER TWENTY-FIVE

A clear sky and a new moon lit the town with a blue glow, as Ophelia hurried through the deeply shadowed streets towards the coaching inn. She rubbed at her neck, feeling the pain and burn from Bowlby's throttling hands where he had tried to kill her.

It hurt, it was sore, and she knew Bowlby had been frighteningly close to succeeding in his deadly purpose. Indeed, he had been so focused on strangling her that he seemed unaware that she had stuck a blade in his thigh. How deep had it gone in before he had realised? Deep enough to stop him being able to walk? Ophelia thought it unlikely; if he bound it up, then he would still be able to move. And so, he was still very dangerous.

But for all that, Ophelia smiled grimly as she kicked her

way through piles of fallen leaves. What a moment of triumph it had been, as she had stood outside the parlour hearing Sir John and Lady Bowlby confirming their real identities!

Finally, she had the proof that she sought!

But now it needed to be proved also to Robert and Jasper – which meant the next part of the plan Robert had constructed needed to be put in place.

She looked down and saw that she had reached a flat path where there were no leaves. She hurried forward until there were further piles, and she could kick her way through them also. As Jasper and Robert had agreed, the plan required her to leave a clear trail for Bowlby to follow. Ophelia even ran her hand along a white wall that glowed brightly in the moonlight, to leave a pink stain from what remained of his blood.

She arrived at the coaching inn, and walked under the archway into the courtyard. The inn was to her left, brightly lit with a couple of braziers outside and light from the candles and fire inside. But she ignored that, and headed instead for the dark doorway to the right that led into the stables.

A pair of lanterns gave some dim light as she stepped inside. There was a single passageway up the middle of the stable; its floor covered in straw and open stalls on either side. Most of these had the head and back of a horse visible, and the occasional swish of a tail. Ophelia stood a moment in the middle of the passageway and gave a series of short whistles. Immediately a dark head with long flowing hair appeared from next to the nearest horse.

"Robert!" she whispered. "I am so pleased to see you!"

"So, is it true Ophelia?" he replied. "Is he Bowlby?"

"Yes, for sure," she said with a nod. "The plan worked. I heard him say it clear to his wife." She gulped. "Then he tried to throttle me. He knew me from the scarring on my back."

"By Heavens," Robert hissed, "did you defend yourself with the knife?"

"He had it to the hilt in his thigh before he let me go," she whispered, tapping her own leg to illustrate where she had stabbed Bowlby.

"But he comes here still?" Robert asked. "He was able to follow you?"

"I think so..." she began. Then there was a shout from outside the stables and the sound of a sword being drawn.

"Girl! Are you in there?"

Robert immediately ducked back out of sight, and Ophelia turned to face the door.

Bowlby limped in, his sword in one hand, while the other was clasped to his heavily bandaged thigh.

"I know not how you escaped, but you were easy to follow by the path you made through the leaves, girl," he snarled, as he advanced on her. "And a streak of blood on a wall. My blood!"

She backed deeper into the stable, her eyes fixed on the sword in the dim light. "Your foolish mistake," he added.

"You followed me, Master Faulkner?" she asked loudly. "Or should I call you by your real name, Sir John Bowlby?"

"Call me what you will," he replied, raising the sword.

"But you are Sir John Bowlby of Cornwall, are you not?" she said, her eyes never leaving the tip of the blade.

"Since you are about to die, I do not mind admitting it. Yes, I am in truth Sir John."

"I thought as much," she said.

"How so?" he asked. "Were you listening at doors, like a treacherous little spy?"

"If I did, that does not justify you trying to kill me."

"But you would have done me the same service, you little harridan," he snapped. "I have had to bind up a hole in my leg, thanks to you."

"I was defending myself," she replied, backing further.

"Belike you were, but I care not for that."

Ophelia felt her back come up against the wall at the end of the stable, and glanced to her side to see she had just missed hitting her head on an iron manger. Bowlby gave a thin smile and took another step towards her.

"You have no further to go, girl." He raised the tip of his sword. "And I have a score to settle."

"How so?" she asked.

"You know how so." He swished his sword a couple of times. "I am told that you and a boy lit a fuse to a keg of powder on my ship. Not only did it send her to the bottom of Weymouth harbour, but it also killed two of my fellows. Robin Tresillick was a good man, and you killed him."

"His name was actually Robin? In truth?" Ophelia gasped.

"Aye. What of it?"

"Nothing." Ophelia glanced again at the manger. "Robin Tresillick was not a good man. He struck me, hooded me and left me in the dark."

Bowlby gave a hollow-sounding chuckle. "That makes him a good man to me, and I aim to finish what he started."

"What, the Cornish Rebellion?" she asked. "He was your commander for the seaborne attack, was he not?"

"Aye, he was. I charged him with the success of that part of my venture, while I myself was engaged in raising a land army. Had it not been for you and that boy destroying my ship, we would have succeeded in driving this godless king from the throne and to his timely death. It was your meddling that undid the whole operation. I had to flee my home in Kernow, letting that low-born peasant Cromwell have my army stand down." He waved his sword again. "But 'tis no matter, as I now plan to make myself known to prominent Catholics up here in Yorkshire, so that I can encourage rebellion with them instead. Then I will once again be part of a glorious movement to remove this tyrant king and restore the true faith!"

Without warning he flicked his sword back, then swept it towards Ophelia's head.

At the last second she saw it coming and dropped down. The sword passed through the air no more than an inch above her head and hit the manger, making the sound of a church bell striking and creating a bright shower of sparks.

Suddenly Robert appeared behind Bowlby and punched him hard on his bandaged thigh. Bowlby gave a pained yell and staggered back, then flicked his sword at Robert, catching him on the jerkin. Ophelia screamed as Robert fell back. There was an audible thud as his head hit the wall, then he slumped to the floor with his eyes closed.

With a triumphant shout, Bowlby pulled his sword back to run the helpless Robert through, just as Jasper appeared from one of the other stalls, drawing his own sword as he ran. Bowlby turned and made a sweep at Jasper's head. Jasper parried, then they were fighting in earnest – or at least as much as was possible in the confined space between the stalls.

Jasper used short flicks and sweeps to keep Bowlby at a distance, while Bowlby looked as if he was trying to drive him back towards the open door – where presumably he could have more space, or even the opportunity to escape.

Ophelia dropped down to Robert, and felt his chest. She breathed a gasp of relief as she felt a strong, steady heartbeat. She peered down at his jerkin; it was cut cleanly in a long slit just below his ribs. She slipped her fingers inside, but there was no blood.

The sound of clashing blades brought her back to her brother and Bowlby. She gave Robert a small kiss on the forehead, then stood up.

The fight was still continuing. Ophelia could just make out Jasper's face over Bowlby's shoulder. He was concentrating on blocking the other man's thrusts and sweeps, his hair flopping over one eye as he moved.

Bowlby made a direct thrust at Jasper's chest, which Jasper turned on his own sword, so they were locked together face to face.

Jasper took a step back, but he must have caught his heel on a raised cobblestone. He staggered, lost his balance and fell to the floor.

With another shout of triumph, Bowlby stepped forward and raised his sword over Jasper's prone body.

Ophelia saw the panic in her brother's eyes as Bowlby towered over him.

She gripped her knife and moved forward. Then she plunged it with all her strength into Bowlby's back.

Bowlby gave a small cough as his sword clattered to the cobbles. Then he dropped to his knees, almost as if he was about to pray in church. As Ophelia watched frozen in shock, Bowlby seemed to crumple like a piece of old paper. He slid down onto the cobbles and lay still with the knife standing proud from his back.

Jasper struggled to his knees, then pushed Bowlby over onto his side. Ophelia crouched down as well, and together they looked at the still face of the traitor.

"That was most timely, my brave little sister," Jasper said. "I owe you my life."

Before Ophelia could answer, there was another cough from the man on the ground, and a line of blood ran from his lips into his beard. His eyes fluttered open.

"You jezebel," he whispered, staring up at Ophelia. "You led me to a trap."

"We needed to be sure who you were," she answered. "And you told us all."

"So you could have me arrested?" She nodded. His face assumed its customary sneer. "At least you have spared me a more painful death from the executioner."

"Unfortunately, yes."

"I would have a priest for my confession." He coughed again. "I need... I need the last rites so I can meet my maker in a state of grace."

Ophelia thought back to an almost identical request from Jeffrey – a man much more deserving of God's grace than this traitor, and whose confession she had heard. A thought occurred to her.

"There is no priest here," she said, "but I did the same for a dying man not long ago. Confess to me." Jasper shot her a quizzical look, but she shook her head slightly, as if to tell him not to interrupt.

"To you?" whispered Bowlby. "I am a good Catholic. I need a priest."

"Then 'tis no matter," she said, standing up. "One is hardly likely to be found in time. So prepare to meet your maker without a dying confession."

"Wait..." he breathed. She crouched down again. "Very well."

"Good." She looked at Jasper. "Please tend to Robert. I may be some time. I fear this man has much to confess."

It was many minutes later that Ophelia stood up and walked over to Jasper and Robert. Her friend was now awake, if slightly groggy looking.

"Has he gone?" Robert asked. She nodded. "Then once again, you have killed a man, Ophelia."

"And again, just as deserving. If I had not been fortunate enough to stop Scarhead, he would have killed me. And if I had not put my blade into Bowlby just now, he would have done the same to Jasper."

"True enough," agreed Robert. "And Jasper says you heard his deathbed confession?"

"I did."

"Which you will keep a secret?" Jasper asked. "As you must before God."

She regarded them both a moment. "I will keep his confession to myself, for in truth there was nothing new I learned than we did not already know of the man's sedition. By good fortune he had not yet had a chance to start spreading it up here in Yorkshire, for all he is convinced the North will rise soon anyway."

"That is for another time. Another mission," said Jasper. "For now we must ride south and report to Cromwell on the outcome of this one."

"Wait a moment," Robert said slowly to Jasper, holding up his hand. "Wait just a moment. Your sister seems to have the excited look of one who must tell us something else." He lifted a curious eyebrow. "Go on, Ophelia."

"There was one thing I learned," she said. "In truth, it was my purpose for offering to hear his confession in the first place." She gave them a triumphant smile. "I heard that he did indeed have my mother's pendant. And now I know where to find it."

26

CHAPTER TWENTY-SIX

Ophelia eased open the back door to the Faulkner house with the key she still carried, and slipped inside, leaving the door unlocked.

She walked carefully along the corridor and paused at the foot of the stairs, listening for any sounds of movement in the dead of night. Satisfied that all was quiet, she started slowly up, treading as softly as a prowling cat. Reaching the top corridor, she made for the Bowlbys' bed chamber and stood for a moment by the door, taking some deep breaths to try and calm her thumping heart.

With a last slow breath, Ophelia was ready. The chamber door was held closed by a large ring-handled latch, seeming blue in the moonlight from a nearby window. Very slowly she pressed the arm so it would not scrape on the retainer, then turned the handle.

A loud creak echoed in the stillness.

She froze.

Had she been heard?

After a few moments of silence she let out another slow breath, then resumed lifting the latch, but even more slowly than before. It finally lifted clear without further sound, so she pushed the door a few inches.

Another creak.

"Is that you, John?" came a sleepy voice from within.

Ophelia kept still and silent, hoping that Lady Bowlby would fall back to sleep. After waiting for what felt like an age, she pushed the door again, even slower.

It moved in blessed silence.

She eased herself round it and stopped just inside the room. A large bed was just before her, its heavy-looking drapes lit by the dull orange glow of a dying fire in the grate on the other side of the room. Opposite the foot of the bed was a table, covered with a jumble of pots and brushes.

A flame flared briefly in the grate with a small hiss and a pop, and something flashed briefly on the table. Ophelia went over.

And gave a tiny gasp of pure delight.

Her precious pendant was lying on a small velvet cloth, quite eclipsing the rings and other jewels beside it.

Ophelia picked the pendant up, walked past the bed and over to the grate. She held it up, letting it turn slowly before her in the light of the fire, allowing herself the pleasure of familiarising herself once again with its beauty. Watching it spin before her eyes, flashing deep red and gold, she was no longer an intruder in a house in Yorkshire. She was once again a little girl in her mother's arms, feeling the warmth and love flowing into her, only now it was channeled through this star of garnets and pearls.

"What on earth are you doing?"

Ophelia spun round to see Mistress Faulkner – Lady Katherine Bowlby – glaring at her through parted bed curtains, her eyes burning red in the light of the fire. "Put it down you little thief," she ordered. "That is mine. I wear it every day."

"No, it is not," said Ophelia, dropping the pendant in her purse. "It belonged to my mother."

"Liar!" Lady Bowlby snapped, stepping out of the bed. "My husband told me it had been in his family for many years when he gave it to me!"

"Then he was the liar."

Lady Bowlby's mouth turned up in a sneer. "Alice, if that is your name, know this. My husband will be home soon, and he will give the truth of this." Ophelia remained silent, flicking quick glances at the door, judging the distance. But to reach it would mean getting past Lady Bowlby, who was standing by the bed with her arms crossed. An avenging angel in a night dress.

"He threw you out when you cut his leg, you little Cornish brigand," Lady Bowlby continued. "We will have you hung for grievous injury and for theft. My husband will see to it when he gets home."

Again, Ophelia said nothing. If she made a quick dash, could she get past this woman and away?

"Why do you not answer, you vile little she-devil?" Lady

Bowlby demanded. "And a vagrant now, since my husband cast you out earlier, and followed you..." She faltered to a stop, the sneer being replaced by a look of shock. "Yet it is now the middle of the night, and he is not here – you are!" Her hand flew to her mouth. "He has come to harm! You have harmed him! What have you done to him?"

Time to get out!

Ophelia made a sudden move for the door.

But Lady Bowlby reacted fast. She ran at Ophelia, knocking her into the wall with a bone-jarring thump. Ophelia screamed and felt her legs give way as she fell back, hitting her head so hard that stars started spinning before her eyes.

As she struggled to get to her feet, Lady Bowlby seized her arm and twisted it up behind her back.

"Let go of me!" Ophelia yelped.

"Nay, you hellcat!" Lady Bowlby snarled in her ear. "Tell me what you have done with my husband." She pushed the arm even higher, till Ophelia thought it would soon come out of her shoulder. With her free hand she started scrabbling at her belt, seeking her knife. But Lady Bowlby must have realised what Ophelia was doing, so she quickly reached round and snatched the knife from its holder herself.

"You come armed as well?" Lady Bowlby hissed. "Would you murder me? And should I take it you have done the same to my husband?"

"He tried to kill me," Ophelia gasped, trying not to cry out from the pain in her arm.

"No more than you deserve." Lady Bowlby marched Ophelia away from the bed so they were in the middle of the room. "And to think I ever let you have charge of my children."

"I had good care of them."

"By good fortune only, I warrant." Lady Bowlby brought the knife up to Ophelia's face. "Now tell me for sure, have you killed my John?"

Ophelia stared at the blade glittering in the firelight. "I did."

Lady Bowlby gasped, and gave a little cry. She even staggered back a pace, and Ophelia thought maybe she could use the opportunity to get free. She tried to wriggle out of the other woman's clutches, but Lady Bowlby only tightened her grip, and put the knife flat against Ophelia's neck. "Then I would do you the same service now."

"And face being hung for it?" Ophelia said, her teeth gritted against the feel of cold steel.

Lady Bowlby gave a snort of laughter. "Are you serious? You are a vagrant who admits to murder, intrudes into my house and steals my property. So I think we can agree that I will escape the hangman's noose on any one of those grounds if I kill you." She moved her grip on the knife, so the edge of the blade was now touching Ophelia's skin. "So let us be done with this, and Satan can welcome you to hell for the eternity of fire he is preparing for you."

Ophelia clenched her jaw, expecting any moment to feel the bite of the knife into her throat.

But instead there was the sound of footsteps pounding up the stairs. Then the door burst open.

Ophelia almost cried out in relief as Robert ran in. But with the knife so close to her throat she dared not even make a sound. He clattered to a stop and stared wide-eyed at the scene.

"And who are you?" Lady Bowlby asked, an ominous chill in her voice. "Art come to take my possessions as well?"

"Nay," he answered, gesturing at Ophelia. "I have come to see if my friend is well, as she has not returned by the time we agreed." He took a step forward. "And it seems I was not a moment too soon."

Lady Bowlby pulled Ophelia closer to the bed. "Come any nearer," she warned, "and you will suddenly find you are too late instead." Robert took a step back and raised his hand, as if to show he was not going to make any sudden moves. "I caught her in the act of stealing my necklace," Lady Bowlby said. Then her voice rose. "But that is the least of her crimes, for the wanton little she-devil has also confessed to killing my husband!"

"I see," Robert said. "Those are two very serious accusations you make. Very serious indeed. So I would see if they can be refuted." He grasped the edges of his cloak. "Tell me mistress, what makes you believe that either of them is correct?"

"Have you taken leave of your senses, you fool?" Lady Bowlby screeched, seeming to be enraged by his calm, measured tone. She took another step away. Ophelia had to stumble back as well, fearful that the woman would cut into her throat whether it was intended or not. "I have told you!" Lady Bowlby yelled, "I caught her in the act of thieving, and she has confessed to the murder!"

"Let us take the necklace first," said Robert, his tone remaining calm in contrast to Lady Bowlby's hysterical outburst. "Why do you say it is not hers, but yours?"

"My husband gave it to me. That is enough." Ophelia could

feel the woman's heart racing, for all her tone was becoming a little less strident.

"But is it?" Robert asked. "How can you be sure it was not already stolen when it came into his possession?"

"Because he would not accept it."

"Yet this girl says it became hers when her mother sadly passed away." Robert shook his head slightly. "For sure, you must admit it is possible that she is right, and has the prior claim on the piece? If so, then she was not stealing it – she was merely retrieving her own property."

"I suppose it may be possible." A grudging admission.

"Good," Robert's tone became softer; more conciliatory. "Now, let us turn to the distressing claim that she has killed your husband."

"There is no doubting her confession!" Lady Bowlby's heart was racing again and her voice rising. "She said yes when I asked!"

"But I take it you had your knife to her throat when she said this? And you were holding her arm in the same unnatural position that you do now?"

"What if I had? She has admitted it! She said she slayed my John!"

"But you were causing her much pain and threatening her with her own life. If I did as much to you, would you not say whatever I wanted to hear?"

"Not if it was not true!"

"Yet men are put in such pain and fear each day in the Tower, and it is well known that they will say whatever they think will make it stop. The torture you are inflicting on this girl is no different."

"I am no torturer!"

"I beg to disagree," Robert said. "I see the proof clearly before me, while your only evidence that she killed your husband is her word gained under duress."

There was a silence. "So," Lady Bowlby said, "are you saying that he still lives?"

"I do have some knowledge of that." Ophelia heard Lady Bowlby gasp, and felt her own stomach tense. Where was Robert going with this?

"But," he continued. "I will not tell you what I know while you threaten her as you do."

There was a long silence.

Ophelia looked at Robert for some indication of his plan, but his face gave nothing away.

Lady Bowlby's heart seemed to slow to a more normal pace. Eventually she said, "Very well. If I let her go, will you tell me?"

Robert nodded. "If you also give me the knife. Yes, I will."

Another long silence.

Then suddenly Lady Bowlby lowered the knife and pushed Ophelia towards Robert. She staggered across the room and fell into his arms.

"Tell me," Lady Bowlby demanded.

"The knife?"

Lady Bowlby dropped it to the floor and kicked it over. Ophelia snatched it up and put it quickly into her belt. Then she moved to Robert's side and took his hand.

Robert stepped back towards the door and opened it. He turned and said, "I am sorry, Lady Bowlby, I have to tell you that he is indeed dead."

There was a howl of anguish from the woman in the night dress.

"Was it the girl?" she whispered.

"I do not know who killed him," Robert said quickly. "But I do know this; he was soon to be arrested for his part in the treasonous Cornish Rebellion, and would have most likely faced torture, then for sure a horrible and agonising death. In truth it was a blessing to him that he met such a swift and easy end this day. He even said as much himself."

Lady Bowlby gave a loud sob and fell to her knees.

Ophelia gave a cough to clear her throat. "I would add one more thing," she said. "There will be soldiers coming soon. I suggest you take little Jane and baby Luke, and find some place of concealment now. Or belike you will also face the same traitor's fate for your complicity in the plot. Then those lovely little children will be orphaned." She gave the woman a hard stare. "For all you would have killed me this night, I would not have those innocents suffer the loss of their mother as I lost mine." Then she looked up at Robert. "I thank you. This may not be a court of law, but you have once again proved your ability to speak in my defence. Let us go now."

27

CHAPTER TWENTY-SEVEN

Ophelia thanked the servant who was holding the door open for her, and walked into Cromwell's study, followed by Robert and Jasper.

Cromwell rose from behind his desk and came round to greet them. Then he invited them to sit at the table close by the fire.

"I am pleased all three of you have come to see me so soon upon your return from Yorkshire," he said. He looked point-edly at Jasper and Robert. "For I would have your report as quickly as possible." He turned to Ophelia. "And as for you, Mistress Williams, I understand that although you were not acting under my brief, you have been highly instrumental in the final outcome?"

"Ophelia's bravery, resourcefulness and fortitude have been

critical, sir," said Jasper. "And in truth, I owe her my life. Were it not for her, I would not be here."

He reached under the table and squeezed her hand.

Cromwell nodded silently a moment. "Then I am most grateful to you for your part in this, Mistress Williams," he said. "And, may I say, pleased that you were available to play such a part, rather than being confined on Dartmoor as Mistress Ophelia Moreland."

"A thing you did say could not be changed, sir," observed Robert.

"I did, did I not?" replied Cromwell, his mouth twitching in his version of a smile. "But I recall you also asserted how good Mistress Williams is at making an escape. 'She has a skill at slipping away', I believe you said. You seemed most impressed with this."

Ophelia glanced across at Robert. "Did you say that of me?" she asked, not sure if she should be pleased that he thought so well of her, or annoyed that he was discussing her behind her back with Cromwell.

She decided to be pleased.

Cromwell leaned forward in his chair. "This is all very well, but as I mentioned, I would have your reports. And with no detail omitted."

An hour later he sat back and looked across all three of them. "So, Sir John Bowlby is dead, and by your hand Mistress Williams." He gave a small sigh. "In truth I am pleased that he is killed, although by rights it should have been a traitor's death at Tyburn." He gave a small sigh. "But the end result is, I suppose, much the same. And as you say, Master Williams, your sister's actions saved your life."

"I did what was necessary in the moment, Master Secretary," Ophelia said.

"Indeed you did," Cromwell replied. "You have shown you can face danger and make decisions at speed. That is good." Then he added, "For you, if not for Sir John Bowlby." He gave her an impassive stare and added, "Nor for one Ned Carter, I believe? A man with a badly scarred head?"

Ophelia gave a small gasp. How did Cromwell know of that? She shot Robert an accusing look. It was supposed to be their secret!

"Do not blame Master Wychwoode," Cromwell said. "It was not he who revealed this to me."

Then who was it?

"Now, back to this man Bowlby," Cromwell continued, seeming to ignore Ophelia's dismay. "His body has been transported to London?" Jasper nodded. "Good. Then it will be cut into quarters and distributed about the land as the law demands, and his head placed on a spike at London Bridge for all to see, so that they know the consequences of such treachery."

For all she had been the one to kill him, Ophelia could not help feeling sickened at the thought of this.

"Now to his wife, Lady Katherine Bowlby," continued Cromwell. "I can report to you that my men are still seeking her and her family. When they went to the house you identified as theirs, she had disappeared. I cannot think how she was alerted, so perhaps we shall put it down to her being alarmed by her husband's continued absence." He tapped his fingers on the desk and gave Ophelia a penetrating stare. "I think that is a satisfactory explanation, is it not, Mistress Williams?"

Was there anything this man did not know? Or suspect?

She smiled weakly. "Perfectly, Master Secretary."

"Good."

There was a slightly uneasy silence, so Ophelia asked the question that had been burning her so badly ever since they had left Yorkshire. "What is to become of me, Master Secretary?" she asked in a small voice. "Must I still marry this man Moreland?"

Cromwell gave her a blank stare. "That is not a question for me, but for your father, I believe."

"But surely you can talk to him?" she asked, aware she was sounding a little desperate. "He must listen to you."

"Not on matters that relate to his decisions as a father. Those are outside my remit."

"But, what if Ophelia were to work for you formally, Master Secretary?" asked Robert. "Then you would have a say in her future and her father would have to listen to you. She makes good decisions as you said, and we agree she is most accomplished at escaping – both great qualities in an intelligencer."

Cromwell pursed his lips as he appeared to think this through. Then he looked at Jasper. "You are her oldest brother, Master Williams. What say you on this?"

"I only want what is best for Ophelia, sir," Jasper answered, then made a half-smile as Ophelia gave his hand a delighted squeeze back under the table. "And I cannot deny that she has skills we can make great use of. Skills that would be lost to us if she were to be married and isolated."

"It is most irregular," said Cromwell. "And I cannot, in all conscience, undermine the authority of a father or husband." Ophelia's head dropped and she swallowed hard. Was he really going to send her home? Once again to be under the authority of Cressida and her father? Or to be wed to Moreland, and suffer his authority instead? The thought of this made her feel physically sick.

Robert glanced at Ophelia. "As a person and as an intelligencer, she could not be more highly valued. Indeed, I cannot imagine undertaking any mission without Ophelia beside me." He smiled at her, and added, "And anyhow, if you send her home, she will only escape!"

"Yes, that is a fair point." Cromwell appeared to reach a decision. "Then I will make you a formal offer, Mistress Williams. Will you work for me as my intelligencer, undertaking such missions as I require, alongside Master Wychwoode and your brother? Will you face danger and meet it with the same fortitude as you did these past weeks?"

Ophelia glanced at Robert and broke into a broad grin, then took a breath to restore herself. She had never been more certain of anything, than that this was exactly what she wanted. "Thank you, Master Secretary," she breathed. "Yes. Yes, I will!"

"Good. Then I will talk to your father, and insist he calls off this unfortunate – and I may say   doomed – marriage."

Ophelia only just managed to stop herself shouting out for joy. "Thank you, Master Secretary," she said. "Thank you!"

"I must give you a formal welcome to my group of intelligencers, Mistress Williams. I believe you will make a most excellent and valued member of our group," Cromwell said.

"For now you may stay with your brother, under his protection." He raised his eyebrows. "Or he under yours, maybe?" Then he addressed Jasper. "You have your own house here in London, I believe?"

Jasper nodded. "I do."

"Good. Then I suggest that is the best arrangement for now." He turned to Robert. "And you, Master Wychwoode. You once told me that you would always seek to defend the innocent, and strive to ensure that the guilty are justly punished. Do you feel you have lived up to that principle these past few weeks?"

Ophelia gave Robert a sideways glance. How admirable that he had such ideals. And how fortunate he had been able to use them to talk Lady Bowlby out of cutting her throat!

"I feel I have, sir," Robert said. "I made some mistakes along the way, but I believe I have learned from them."

"And while you have ambitions about not resorting to untruths – which we can all agree to be most noble and worthy – have you recognised that sometimes, justice and fairness are better served by a more practical approach?"

"That also, sir," Robert answered. "I may have been a little less idealistic and a little more practical on occasions."

"Then I am confident you will be excellent, as both a lawyer and a servant of the King," Cromwell said. "I see a very bright future for you in both fields, Master Robert Wychwoode. But," he added, "that will not happen without you applying yourself to your studies with diligence. So I would you now return to Gray's Inn and do just that."

Cromwell stood, and it was clear the meeting was concluded.

"I thank all three of you, for your constancy and application in this venture," he said. "You found the man as I asked, and he has been brought to justice, after a fashion."

They all went to the door.

"I will call on you when I next need you," he said to Robert. Then he looked at Jasper and Ophelia. "And that goes for you both as well."

Ophelia wanted to skip out of the room like a little girl, she was so happy. She was a valued member of the group! And, best of all, despite her father's attempts to prevent it, she would continue to see Robert. So who knew how that may work out?

"Oh, Mistress Williams?" Cromwell's voice brought her back to the present. "I wonder if you would wait a moment? Now you are my intelligencer, there is someone I would like you to meet. Master Williams, you may go," he said to Jasper. "I will have her brought to your house presently."

Jasper nodded, and he and Robert walked out together.

"Sit down, Ophelia," Cromwell said, indicating the same chair she had just been in. She did so, watching in uncertain anticipation as he rang a bell. Almost immediately a small man with dark hair and a wispy beard came in.

Ophelia had no idea who this might be, but assumed she would shortly find out, and why she should meet him. She smiled nervously at the man, but was blanked completely.

"Martin, would you send in the gentleman waiting in the next room, please?" asked Cromwell.

Ophelia's toes curled in her shoes at her mistake.

The next man to come in was tall and well-dressed, with a trim grey beard and kindly looking eyes.

"Hello, Ophelia" he said with a broad smile.

She frowned. He looked slightly familiar, but she could not place him. Yet he recognised her... Then suddenly she knew where she had seen those eyes! That beard! In a dirty, dark alley in London...

"JEFFREY!" she yelled. "Jeffrey! You are not dead!"

"Indeed not. Very much alive."

"And you are... you are... clean!"

Ophelia felt the room spin.

He had never been dying in that alley! She had been deceived! Deliberately!

With a feeling as if cold water had suddenly been flung over her, she realised just how greatly she had been fooled.

And how much information she had given away!

"You had me tell my full story!" She turned to Cromwell. "That is how you knew of Scarhead – Ned Carter!"

"Indeed," he said.

"Then you were testing me!" Another awful thought came to her. "And I failed! I revealed everything! You will not want me as an intelligencer now!"

"I did not say that. But I warrant you will not be so free with your information next time. A lesson learned."

Ophelia had another thought. "Then you knew all the time you would be making me an offer to work for you! You were not in truth persuaded by Robert!"

Cromwell's mouth twitched. "It was in my mind, yes. His confidence in you was the final thing I needed."

She turned to the other man. "So it was all an act?"

"Yes," Jeffrey agreed. "I apologise for the deception, but it was also necessary to learn more of your activities. And as

I said at the time, your ruse to escape was most inventive. When the man we had watching the house saw you running out in the garb of a boy, we had but a few minutes to put our plan into action before you found me in the alley."

"But why did you need to know of my activities?" she demanded. "What were they to you?"

It was Cromwell who answered. "You had been on the ship, and were instrumental in its destruction. I needed to validate what young Wychwoode had told me." Cromwell glanced at the other man. "So I had Jeffrey Pritchett here, one of my finest operatives, hear your side of the story. And incidentally, you did validate Wychwoode's version. In full. Plus I learned some new things about your exploits with Ned Carter. You are quite the killer, Mistress Williams."

"By necessity only," she said quickly, not wanting him to think her irredeemably evil.

"Sometimes it is necessary for the greater good."

"As is committing a great deception on a girl, that a man is so close to death he must make his last confession?" she asked, looking at Jeffrey, now very much alive and grinning back at her.

"Yes," said Cromwell. "And it worked. I now knew two things; one being what you and Wychwoode had done to stop the rebellion, and the other – that you are both honest with me."

Ophelia tried to take this all in; the lengths to which Cromwell had gone in order to test her and get information, and what it had meant for her.

Maybe not all bad, for it had got her and Robert back together.

She bit her lip. So that meant Cromwell had actually meant for her to join Robert and Jasper on the mission! Jeffrey had done that when he made sure she went to Gray's Inn.

Then she was already working for Cromwell – she had just not known of it when she planned her escape dressed as a boy.

Tam!

"What of the scullion boy, then?" she asked. "Do you know of him?"

"I do, as a matter of fact," said Cromwell. "He did as you told and blamed you for the deception, so was not punished at all. He even got to keep the coin you gave him."

Ophelia breathed a sigh of relief. It had weighed on her conscience that she might have got the lad in trouble when she had abandoned him in her clothes and run from the cook.

"How did you do it?" she asked Jeffrey. "You cannot have known where I would run, or left it to chance."

"A good intelligencer does not give away his secrets," Jeffrey replied with a broad smile. "Sufficient to say that every turn you made was by our will, not yours."

Ophelia gasped.

They had made quite certain she would end up in the alley!

The man with the cart who made her take the right fork...

The two women blocking the road so she had to turn into the next street...

Nothing had been real!

Then her face fell. "Oh no, Jeffrey. Your confession! That was not true either!"

"No," he replied. "But you responded with great sincerity. I thank you for that."

Ophelia shook her head in disbelief. Was all secret work

for Cromwell going to be as deceptive? Was everyone she met going to be in truth someone else?

Everyone?

"Oh!" she put her hand to her mouth. "I do have one more question."

"Yes?" asked Cromwell.

"The dog?" She looked at Cromwell and Jeffrey, her eyes wide. "Do not tell me he was one of your agents as well?"

THE END

PLEASE RATE THIS BOOK

If you have enjoyed this book, then please take a moment to rate/review it on Amazon and/or Goodreads. A rating and ideally a review mean so much to authors, and can do so much to help sell their books to other readers.

ROBERT'S STORY IS NOT YET FINISHED...

You may be interested to know that Robert Wychwoode appears as a man in his forties / fifties in all three of *The Witchfinder's Well* books, when his scheming has a great effect on the fortunes of the time-travelling heroine Justine.

You can read the first chapter of *The Witchfinder's Well* here to see how Justine's story starts.

All Jonathan's books are available on Amazon and to order through your local bookstore.

For more information and to sign up for regular news, offers and sneak previews, visit Jonathan's website at **jonathanposnerauthor.com**

THE WITCHFINDER'S WELL - CHAPTER ONE

As she surveyed the royal banquet from her high vantage point in the Minstrel's Gallery, Justine Parker twisted slightly to get more comfortable in the tight bodice of her gown.

All things considered, the banquet was going pretty well.

An army of servants had brought exotic dishes up from the kitchens into the Great Hall and presented them to the assembled ladies, gentlemen, knights and courtiers for their appreciation and amazement.

There were dishes such as the noble roast peacock with its plumage dancing in the light, guinea fowl in a deep crusty pie and legs of mutton surrounded by mountains of peas and carrots. Fine red claret was drunk copiously from silver goblets, with the servants replenishing them from silver pitchers as they weaved around the tables.

Justine leaned on the railing of the gallery and let the warm sound of conversation and laughter wash over her; the rich hubbub of noise that rose up to the furthest corners of the magnificent ornate plaster roof. Down below her, the face of every guest was bright with enjoyment, bathed in the golden glow of a thousand flickering candles.

In the middle of the high table, Her Majesty Queen Elizabeth sat bolt upright, her bright eyes dancing round the room as the courtier to her right engaged her in conversation.

Justine admired her pale beauty, set off by her striking bodice of red velvet edged with gold lace and sparkling with a thousand shimmering pearls, together with the single flashing emerald at her neck that brought out the green fire in her eyes. Then there was her red-bronze hair adorned with its simple, elegant gold crown, framed by the high pearl-edged lace ruff that flared up from her shoulders.

With a small raise of her hand, the Queen paused the conversation with the courtier beside her and looked up at the gallery. Maybe Justine's small twisting movement had caught her eye. She held Justine's gaze a moment, then gave the smallest nod of her head – so small that it could easily have been missed – as if to congratulate Justine on the success of the banquet she had organised.

With a smile Justine bowed her own head and gave a gentle curtsey. The Queen nodded again, then turned back to the courtier and resumed their conversation.

In the gallery Justine smiled again, this time to herself.

Yes, all things considered, the banquet was going pretty well.

She looked down across the room, taking in the full scene. The long high table ran along the back wall under the big windows with the Queen in the centre. On either side Justine had seated her most important courtiers, looking resplendent in their richly-coloured silk doublets with slashed sleeves and fine white ruffs. Beyond the courtiers she had seated the women, elegant in their low-cut gowns, their hair carefully parted in the centre and tucked under their French hoods – a style introduced originally by Elizabeth's mother, Anne Boleyn.

Justine's gaze moved to the table down the left side of the room. The people here were less important and their clothes reflected this – the men wore plain doublets and the women wore their hair in simple cotton coifs rather than the more elaborate French hoods of the high table. Their behaviour was no less exuberant, if anything slightly more so, and Justine smiled as they all laughed at a joke from the jester who had been moving round the tables. His brightly-coloured motley costume consisted of a tunic split into a red half and a yellow half, while his hose had one red leg and one yellow leg on the opposite sides. In his hand was a small jester head on a stick, which he was using to entertain the guests.

From behind her came the sound of the minstrels; four elderly men with lutes playing light-hearted music that was all but lost against the loud noise of the room. Their piece came to an end, and she turned to them.

"You play well, good sirs," she said with a twinkling smile. "What is next?"

"We have not yet played Greensleeves," said the eldest minstrel. "But first we need a drink." All four reached down for the tankards by their stools and drained them with great satisfaction. The oldest man then examined the bottom of his empty tankard and looked up at Justine expectantly. She laughed and reached for the large pewter jug ready by her feet, then went to each in turn, pouring more beer into their proffered tankards.

"Ahh, thank you my girl," said the oldest man, "it is always a pleasure to play at one of your banquets."

Justine curtseyed in reply. The men drank some more, then put down their tankards and launched into Greensleeves.

She turned and resumed her gaze across the Great Hall.

To her right was a smaller table seating more people, with a carving table beside it. On the wall above was a large portrait of a handsome knight in a shining breastplate standing with a white stag in the background. Her gaze stopped on this portrait, as it so often did, and she gave a small sigh as she studied the man's long blond hair and trim beard.

The jester turned from the table he'd been entertaining and looked up, catching sight of Justine as she stared across at the portrait.

His gaze took in her shoulder-length cascade of russet-coloured ringlets trying to escape from under her French hood; her small, slightly snub nose, her pale blue eyes under thick, dark eyebrows staring with a faraway look at the portrait...

He gave a little dance and waved his stick to catch her eye.

She spotted him and gave a small wave back. He raised an enquiring eyebrow, then flicked the stick up behind his back so the little jester head on the end popped up on his shoulder.

He turned to it and appeared to have a brief conversation, then pointed up at her. The little head on his shoulder nodded. He made a 'doe-eyed' face – a gross over-exaggeration of hers, with a sickly grin and fluttering eyelashes – then pointed back at her. The head nodded again, then both the jester and the head turned to look up at her, with the jester smiling broadly.

She couldn't help but laugh and he laughed back. Then he gave a low courtly bow, while she applauded.

The jester turned back to the room and started dancing sideways up towards the high table.

Still chuckling, Justine's gaze moved upwards to the large tapestries depicting heroic scenes of hunts that were hanging round the hall between the sconces. In one scene knights attacked a stag with spears and arrows in a green forest; in another a different stag was running from a pack of baying hounds, followed by nobles on horses.

Justine looked back down at the hall. The servants had cleared the main courses away and were now circulating with bowls of fruit and more wine.

'Only an hour more and we'll be cleared and finished,' she thought, as she twisted once more in the tight bodice of her gown.

Just then she became aware of an insistent beeping sound over the noise of the room. Fishing her mobile from the pocket of her gown, she swiped the screen.

"Hello, Justine Parker here."

"The taxis have started arriving," said a voice. "They're early."

"Oh, bother. I put half-eleven on the schedule." She nudged up the end of her lace sleeve with her elbow, to reveal her watch. "It's only eleven fifteen. We've just served the fruit. Would you be a sweetie and tell them they'll have to wait?"

"OK."

"And please can you tell them to turn their meters off. I

don't want one of their silly waiting charges when it's all their fault." Justine thought a moment. "It is their fault, isn't it? Oh bother and blast it, it had better be. I'll check the email I sent them. Can you be an absolute poppet and bluff it out or something?"

"Sure, no problem."

Justine tapped the email app on her phone and scrolled through to find the relevant message. There it was – 'please make sure the taxis arrive at 11:30pm'.

Tucking her mobile back into her pocket with a satisfied smile, Justine looked back down at the hall.

The Queen was dispensing her wisdom to the courtiers on either side, who were hanging on her every word and laughing sycophantically, even though Justine didn't think the Queen was actually trying to be funny.

Justine sighed deeply. For all that she liked to pretend to herself that events such as this were real, in truth this was just a modern-day re-enactment of a Tudor banquet. The setting was real enough – the magnificent Grangedean Manor genuinely dated back to the late 1400s – but now it was a National Trust property, purposefully restored to its Tudor period as a 'living museum'.

The costumes were all hired from the special fancy dress store in the old stables, and were held together with Velcro and poppers, not laced and tied as they should have been. They were a modern-day approximation of the Tudor costume; made for ease of putting on, not authenticity.

The dishes that had been served for the meal were cooked in a modern-day kitchen set up to standards demanded by the environmental health officer, and while the dishes were close enough to the Tudor recipes, the reality was that they were only interpretations for 21st century tastes. Even the peacock had really been a pheasant in disguise.

The 'courtiers' were the CEO and Board of an American corporate with offices in the UK, while the other guests were members of their teams. They had signed up for the Genuine Tudor Banquet Experience at Grangedean Manor – Complete with Her Majesty Queen Elizabeth I and as the events manager, Justine had been determined to give them their money's worth.

Looking down at the glow of the candles on the bright, happy faces, she thought she'd done OK.

She had wanted to welcome them on arrival with a full tour of the magnificent 15th century manor house and grounds, so a week before she had sought out Mrs Warburton, National Trust volunteer tour guide and retired schoolteacher, whose knowledge of Grangedean Manor was encyclopaedic and whose no-nonsense disciplined approach meant she could be relied upon to keep control of such a large party.

Justine had found Mrs. Warburton in the Master Bedroom; she was a tall, ramrod-straight woman with iron-grey hair wearing a tweed twinset that looked like it was straight out of the 1950s. She was in the middle of explaining to a family how Tudor people managed their clothing.

"Clothes were kept in wooden chests like these," she was saying, "rather than hanging in wardrobes like we do now."

"They couldn't have got much in there," said the mother, looking dubiously at the metal-bound oak chest at the end of the bed. It was about five feet long by three feet high and three feet wide.

"There may have been more than one chest in a bedroom, particularly for the nobility like Sir William de Beauvais, who owned the manor in the 1560s," explained Mrs. Warburton. "But the truth is they didn't have anywhere near as many clothes as we do now, and only really changed their underclothes to keep clean. Sometimes all they did was unlace the sleeves on their outfit and lace on new ones."

"Ugh!" exclaimed the daughter, who looked about fourteen. "Didn't they smell rank?"

"Very possibly," said Mrs. Warburton matter-of-factly, "but that would have been the same for most. Certainly the poorer people."

"So didn't they, like, have baths and stuff?" asked the girl incredulously.

"Occasionally, but only the nobility. A copper or wooden tub would be brought into the bedroom and filled with water heated on the fire. Herbs would be sprinkled on the water to make it smell good, and soap for the rich would be made with olive oil. The poor – they would wash in a stream or with a bucket of water and soap made of animal fat."

"Eww, gross," said the girl.

Justine couldn't let this go unchallenged. "No, no, no!" she interjected, her eyes shining brightly. "The Tudors were absolutely wonderful people!"

The family and Mrs. Warburton all turned to look at her in surprise.

"Sorry to butt in, Mrs. Warburton," she went on, "but I wouldn't want this young lady to think the Tudors were ghastly at all. Imagine you were in Tudor times," she said brightly. "There would be lots of dancing, great banquets that lasted for hours, riding in the park and handsome young men just itching to go out with you! It would be such fun!"

"Suppose," said the girl, not looking convinced.

"And beautiful gowns to wear and jewellery and dainty shoes..."

Just then the girl's father intervened. Casting concerned glances at Justine, he said, "Come, Shaz, time to go, I think."

The girl Shaz said, "But didn't they, like...?" then caught the expression on her father's face, and shut her mouth. The family shuffled quickly out, leaving Justine alone with Mrs. Warburton.

"You are very enthusiastic, my dear," observed the older lady drily. "Maybe just a little too much, perhaps? Although I am not sure that the girl, Shaz, wasn't starting to become just a tiny bit more interested in the Tudors."

Justine laughed. "Maybe. Maybe not. But Grangedean Manor can have that effect, can't it?"

Mrs. Warburton thought about this a moment, her hands clasped together and her lips pursed. "Yes, it can. It can certainly make you feel like the Tudors are alive, and may come through a door at any moment. But only if you're that kind of person. I am not sure that Shaz was really that kind of person." She smiled. "Anyway. Did you want me, Miss Parker?"

"Oh yes," said Justine, "Yes, yes, I did. In fact, you're absolutely the very person I wanted. I have a large party of Americans coming next Thursday for a banquet, and I would really love it if you could very kindly show them round before we get them changed into their Tudor outfits?" Justine smiled warmly. "I am sure you'll be absolutely brilliant at keeping them together and giving them a really wonderful tour.

There's no one who knows more about Grangedean Manor than you."

"I suspect you actually know at least as much as I do, Miss Parker," observed Mrs. Warburton with just a hint of amusement in her voice. "But no matter. Of course I'll show them round."

"That's great! Great! Thanks!" said Justine happily. "I'm putting the schedule together and I'll email it to you later."

"I don't really look at emails," said Mrs. Warburton. "Can you not print it out for me?"

"Yes, of course," said Justine. Then she added, "But you really should use emails – they're so easy." She held up her phone. "I get them on my PC and on this phone, so I have them wherever I go."

"I am sure that works well for you, but I prefer the old fashioned methods of communication," observed Mrs. Warburton, "such as writing," she shook her head, "and talking."

"Ahh, but this talks as well," said Justine opening up the battered cover protecting her phone.

"It is a phone, so I suppose it does. Although it is actually the other person that does the talking, is it not?"

"No, no, it's the phone," Justine insisted. She tapped to open an app and held up the screen for Mrs. Warburton to peer at vaguely. "It actually talks if you want it to! It's brilliant! You can type text into this special app, then tap on a button here and it says what you've written. You can choose what voice you want it to talk in, as well. Look..." She quickly typed and tapped the screen. The phone said, "Hello, Missus Warburton." It was slightly robotic, but reasonably clear. Justine looked at the older lady in triumph, challenging her not to be impressed.

"What will they think of next?" said Mrs. Warburton politely.

Justine closed her phone cover and dropped it back in her pocket. "Anyway, I must be getting on. Thanks, Mrs. Warburton. I'll send you the schedule for next week." She turned to leave.

"Miss Parker," Mrs Warburton stopped her. "These Americans. Is there anything particular" – she emphasised the 'tic' in the middle – "that they want to see?"

Justine considered. "No – the standard tour should be fine. The CEO told me in one of his emails, that he wants to 'absorb all your English history'."

"He sounds fascinating. I very much look forward to meeting him."

"Me too," said Justine, brightly. "Me too!"

To continue reading, please visit your local Amazon store and search *The Witchfinder's Well* – available in Paperback, Hardback, eBook and Audiobook.

READER REVIEWS

"This author is new to me so I was pleasantly surprised to find that, in many parts, I couldn't put it down. I really liked the main characters and felt like I was drawn into their trials and tribulations. The twists and turns were shocking and the narrative

ran smoothly, (I didn't have to refer back to events in order to understand what was happening), which to me, is the mark of a well-written book. Total enjoyment!"

"This is an action-packed, page-turning, time-traveling romance... Well researched with the right number of historical details. Lucky for all of us, there are two more books in the series. I listened to this book in audible, very well done. Hope the rest will be available soon."

BY THE SAME AUTHOR

The Witchfinder's Well Trilogy

PART 1 - THE WITCHFINDER'S WELL

Elizabethan England. A time-traveller. A lover condemned to die. A ruthless witchfinder.

Thrown back to the 16th century by a freak electrical storm, reluctant time-traveller Justine Parker is terrified when an accusation of witchcraft threatens her with death by fire.

Who can she turn to for help? The dashing Elizabethan Sir William de Beauvais could be her saviour – and even her lover – but his time is running out fast. A cruel twist of history says his own death is imminent.

As a 21st century girl, Justine should be able to plan an escape for them both – but Tudor England is a perilous place, the witchfinder is relentless, and her options are running out fast.

Can Justine find the courage and the ingenuity to defeat the witchfinder – and history – before it is too late?

PART 2 – ALCHEMIST'S ARMS

Lady Mary de Beauvais seems to be the perfect 16th century woman, but she hides a dark and terrible secret - she is actually a time-traveller from 2015. So when she discovers there's another traveller from her own time, she sets out across Elizabethan England to find him.

But it's a search that leads her into dreadful danger - threatening not just Mary's own future, but the life of Queen Elizabeth as well. So Mary is forced to face her fears and take control - if she wants to save herself and those she loves, in this *"gripping adventure thriller"*.

PART 3 - THE SOVEREIGN'S SECRET

Lady Mary de Beauvais's past finally catches up with her, bringing her to the attention of Queen Elizabeth's calculating spymaster, Francis Walsingham.

His daring plan then plunges her into a world of intrigue, espionage and danger. Can Mary save herself once again, and in doing so, will English history have to change?

THE BROKEN SWORD

You only discover what dangers you can overcome when you're tested to the limit...

Tudor England
When Mary Fox is ordered to marry a sadistic older man, she decides instead to strike out on her own. As a woman in a man's world, no-one expects her to survive, but Mary is determined to prove them wrong.

Challenged to return the Broken Sword talisman and so break a centuries-old curse, she soon learns how to scheme, fight and outwit those who would drag her back to a life of servitude.

And in doing so, she becomes more than a match for any man.

"Diabolically good! What makes this novel irresistibly readable is the emotional energy generated by the main character Mary Fox, her ups and downs, drawing parallels to our present times." **Gina Flyvholm**

"I would highly recommend this book for its entertainment, historical authenticity and value." **Philip Appleton**

www.ingramcontent.com/pod-product-compliance
Lightning Source LLC
Chambersburg PA
CBHW071423200726
48294CB00002B/493